RIS DABROWA

Mr. London

First edition

ISBN: 978-1-7396770-0-8

This book was professionally typeset on Reedsy.
Find out more at reedsy.com

For the writers and the dreamers.

"If you take care of your mind, you will take care of the world."

ARIANA HUFFINGTON

Contents

1

Mr. London

I'm not angry. I'm annoyed. I don't feel guilt. I feel ashamed. I have to get out. I must leave. Now.

Ten years ago, this place looked so different. I know, such a middle-aged thing to say. Well, I am. This corner of town used to be nothing and now I prefer it more than the rest. These modern buildings actually make the place desirable. I guess that's the point. They are selling you a dream. A lifestyle. It works. It's a utopian dream, but we all know that's unachievable for us. We do like to pretend.

Two minutes and you're at the river. I love it here. I love walking along it. I love looking across at the other side, watching the helicopters land and take off from the helipad. I love looking at the multi-million-pound apartments that live here. Whenever I'm here I imagine I live in those apartments.

I walk through my high-ceiling reception room with a cold alcoholic drink and join my beautiful wife on the terrace. I can't make out her face, it's a bit of a blur. We cheers, smile, and soak up the sun. I am happy. At least in that moment, I am. I must have written some good stuff to be here. I wonder how long my happiness will last? Is that woman my wife? Maybe she's a prostitute. Nothing wrong with that. Maybe I just wanted company so I could share this moment. Fuck! I own a sweet fucking apartment; I must be happy. The writing paid off, I've got security, I've got my view and I'm by the river. Then why does she get up and walk back through the apartment? Maybe her time is up. Maybe she is refilling her drink. Maybe she wants to go and walk by the river. I've heard Michael Caine has a place here.

A dog runs past me, growls, and snaps me out of it. The growl sounded like it was saying, "Wake up". That was odd. It has been an odd morning. I turn and look at the barges and boats bobbing up and down on the river. A hairy-looking man on a hippy-looking barge tends to his barbecue. I don't think they are called hippies anymore. I think they're environmentalists. His barge is covered in peace symbols, so I suppose that's why I made the connection. Funny how our brains are wired. Come to think of it, my brain is aching a bit. Maybe I need to drink some water.

The sun is shining but I'm not going to complain about how hot it is today. There are other things to complain about. We do not accept unsolicited material. This is the bane of my life. This sentence fucking infuriates me. For a long time, this has been killing me. Not softly but solidly like a hammer to my head. I don't get it. They will not read it unless it is solicited by an agent. I can't get an agent because no one will read my material because it's unsolicited. Fuck you, you're not allowed in our club.

I'm not arrogant but my shit is better than some of the shit that is represented. Fuck it. It's a lot better. The most annoying and soul-destroying realisation is getting rejected before they even know you. It's like applying for a job that you know you are more than qualified for and you send in your CV and they bin it. Rejected before the interview.

They haven't read you and they are saying no. It's the worst. No one wants to listen to you. You're being ignored. You have dug into your soul, ripped it out, and put it on the page before you and they couldn't care less. You don't exist. You are nothing. I am nothing.

Interview me, then reject me you fucks. I can live with that.

I'm standing in the middle of Battersea Bridge. I'm looking at the river again. The current is calm. It looks so sad. Depressing. I guess not being able to swim helps. I mean it will make things easier. Although I've heard it's one of the worst ways to die. How do they know this? Do they ask the victims this, just before they die?

EXT. RIVER THAMES - DAY
   [A man is standing on the bank of the river, wearing a white lab coat and holding a clipboard and pen. This is DR. DAN. The man drowning is JOHN.]
   DR. DAN: Hey mate, how are you feeling?
   JOHN: Not too good now. I'm guessing I haven't got long now.
   DR. DAN: Would you say it's one of the worst ways to die?
   [John is still flailing in the water and struggling to speak.]
   JOHN: I'd say it's pretty bad.
   DR. DAN: On a scale of one to ten, ten being bad, what would you rate it?

[John is pretty much struggling with his last breath.]
JOHN: Definitely a ten.
DR. DAN: [Dr. Dan puts his thumb up.] Thanks, mate.
JOHN: It's John.
DR. DAN: I'm sorry?
JOHN: My name's John.
[John sticks his thumb up and then drowns.]
DR. DAN: Thanks, John.
[Dr. Dan writes 'John' down on his clipboard.]

There is a phrase you may have heard, 'stop the world, I want to get off.' I think it comes from a musical of the same name.

Anyway, I feel like I got kicked off and the world carried on without me. I got left behind. It all happened so fast. Is this a mid-life crisis? I don't think so. You know what it is? I have always kept the dream going up to this point. For most of my life, I have kept hold of hope and now it has started to wither in my hands because nothing ever happened. It has turned to despair which has thrown me into the hole of misery. Fucking misery, you're such a nightmare. Why can't you be a hole of pleasure and fun? For you, Jack, that would be a woman.

"Ha." A voice laughs but I turn and see no one.

"An ounce of humour means there's an ounce of hope."

I look up and down the bridge but all I see is a blackbird standing on the railing.

"You're not going to jump, are you?" says the blackbird.

"I must be mad," I replied.

"You must be if you want to jump," says the blackbird.

The voice was warm, friendly and feminine. She looks curious as she waddles up on the railing. Her eyes blink and look like they are smiling at me. Her head twitches as she looks

4

me up and down.

"How is this happening? I mean…"

"Does it matter? It is what it is," she says.

That sentence annoys me. The same way that "things happen for a reason" does. Of course, things happen for a reason. Why else do things happen? Just saying it doesn't make you a profound philosopher, you're just stating the obvious. "It is what it is." Well yeah, of course it is. That's how it is.

"You know a mother killed two of her children here?" she says.

"Really? That's awful," I say.

"She stood where you're standing now. She calmly picked them up, one by one…" She takes a breath. "She tossed all three of them over the edge." She looks down into the river.

"I thought you said two," I said.

"Well, the seven-year-old boy and the ten-month-old girl died. The four-year-old girl was rescued." She turns and looks at me.

"Shitting hell." I look down at the river. "What makes you do something like that?"

"I'd say she had some sort of mental breakdown. Are you having a mental breakdown?"

"Erm. No. Nothing like that. I don't know. I'm not sure." I stare at the horizon.

"You know most jumpers regret it when they are halfway through their fall?" she says.

"Who says that? That's absolute rubbish. How do they possibly know that?" An image flashes of the guy in a white coat, who appears again with a clipboard and pen, gesturing this time to a guy falling past him. The image flashes away.

"That's what they say," she says ambiguously.

"Shouldn't you be heading back to the Tower of London? The place might fall down if you don't return."

"Nonsense. Absolute nonsense. By the way, that's a raven. I'm a crow, you ignoramus." She turns away.

"Sorry. I was just…"

"I suppose we all look alike, do we?" She turns back.

"No, I wasn't saying that at all."

"You know you should think before you talk. And you, a writer."

I put both my hands up. "Look, I apologise. It was ignorant and…"

"And racist," she interrupts.

"Racist? You're a raven," I exclaim.

"I'm a crow. Fuck sake." She waddles away from me. An awkward silence passes.

Finally, I speak, "I'm sorry."

"You know I'm just trying to help." She turns her head to me.

"I know. I'm just not in a good place right now. Everything is all mixed up," I say honestly.

She walks right up to me and takes a deep breath. "I know. I can help you. But you must trust me. Do you trust me?"

"Yeah," I stutter.

"That wasn't very convincing, Jack."

"I trust you," I said with conviction.

"Great. This is what I need you to do."

Walking along the Chelsea Embankment, I think about what she told me. It seems funny now, being on a mission, but I'm in a haze. Everything seems to be on auto-pilot. My feet and eyes are just doing what they do, moving at a swift pace, but they are not really taking things in. They are not checking in with the brain. Not consciously. My brain is too foggy for that. I mean, I kind of remember what she told me but I was swiftly transported to here. In a trance.

Her name is Asami. I am to deliver a message to her. I wrote it down because I didn't understand it. It is Brazilian Portuguese. That's what the crow said. I had no paper so I wrote it on a space on my arm that didn't have a tattoo. What can I say? I was curious, and the crow said she is one of the most beautiful women she has ever seen. Brazilian, Japanese. I mean, what a mix? I have to find out whether this is true. I must see her. It isn't a grand adventure but it is a task of sorts and it does fill me with a little purpose. I mean, I got time to kill. I let out a hard laugh which summons my consciousness. I look at my surroundings and I'm passing Cheyne Walk. I then walk to Albert Bridge Gardens and take the underpass to continue along the Embankment. I walk a bit more, then stop to take a breath and take in the view of Battersea Park across the river. London really is beautiful, if you stop and look sometimes. The large trees protect it from the city. They hide it like there is a secret there. A secret garden? Some may say. But if you look carefully, you can just see the thirty-three-meter-high Peace Pagoda. It is decorated with four gilded statues of the Buddha on its four sides. Why is this in a London Park you ask? It was part of Buddhist Monk Nichidatsu Fujii's advocacy of world peace and nonviolence. I really hope no one has told him how crazy happy hour can be on a Friday night. It is a beautiful park. Just looking at it now fills me with calm. Since 1985 when it was built, a monk cares for it every day. He lives in a storeroom converted into a temple in the Old English Garden. His name is Gyoro Nagase. Thank you Gyoro, it's looking good.

Just standing there I'm getting sea salt notes over sycamore and oak... with just a hint of cherry blossom. No, that's me thinking of Gyoro. Actually, maybe it's Asami. I'm getting tar and smoke now. A passing double-decker London bus will do that. It takes you away, figuratively and literally.

I'm on a double-decker bus now but I'm in no rush. The crow said I had to be at Amaterasu restaurant during dinner time. I guess that's when her shift starts. I remember her vaguely saying that Asami works there.

This really is the best way to see London. It's great being at this height. Most of the time we forget to look up, don't we? Being on the top deck is far better than the lower deck. It's three hundred and sixty-degree views up here. It feels less claustrophobic. We can breathe through our lungs and through our eyes. I cannot help but have respect for these red giants, these guardians of the city who serve their minions to keep the London machine going like clockwork. I manage a proud smile.

I get off at Sloane Square. I walk past the expensive designer shops and onto Kings Road. For a split second, I imagine myself in a designer suit and develop a swagger. A posh woman squints at me strangely and, with a puff of magic smoke, I'm me again. Before I know it, I'm at Duke of York's Square. It's food market day and this is why I'm here. It's a small market but it has great stuff. From the front, it starts with Maldon Oysters, my first stop. From there it then snakes round to the left with various stalls with cheeses, bread, chocolate, and sweets. A cacophony of flavours invading your nose and competing for supremacy. Then you hit a cul-de-sac, which changes from time to time. One time there was a French stall that specialised only in Caneles de Bordeaux. Not to be missed. Another time there was a connoisseur in fish and chips, which I recall had the best fish batter and the best ratio of crisp versus potato of any chip I've ever had. When it snakes to the right you have the world food section.

My favourite is the Brazil stall where I always stop for a Coxinha. This is shredded chicken covered with dough then battered and fried in a shape of a teardrop. It's fuckinlicious. Then I proceed to the Prosecco stall to wash things down and exit back past Maldon Oysters. Firstly, let's take delight in a plate of oysters. The best and most common ones sold here are the Maldon Rock and Maldon Pacific. Sometimes you get meaty ones, sometimes you get sleek streamlined ones. One isn't better than the other. A chewy meaty one lends perspective and deep thought to your day. A slippery sleek one disappears so quickly, making you think life is short, don't miss it. This sensory experience is heightened further if you add some whisky on top. Hello, hip flask. I mean it. Just pour a wee dram over the oyster into the shell and knock it back. My favourite is an Islay whisky. The peat and smokiness really compliment the salty flavour of the oyster.

Taste is really the one sense I do not want to lose. They say it can cause depression. I think that would finish me off. I remember hearing about a rock star who lost his taste from a head injury and he was so depressed he couldn't taste his supermodel girlfriend anymore. I understand that completely. If pleasure is taken away from me without so much as a verbal or written warning, then I'm going to lose my shit. Talking as a heterosexual man, I think the taste of a woman's fandango is one of the most delicious taste sensations of all time. The beauty of her rose garden, her foo-foo, her hoo-hoo, her lulu, her coochie, her coochie coo, her twinkle, her sprinkle, her crinkle, her fam-

fam, her flim-flam, her bam-bam, and my favourite, which is a play on the old classic pussy, her pu-say (I guess depending on its mood it tells you what it wants) is that they all taste different. I guess the whisky has kicked in as I'm talking sex now. The Prosecco on top probably doesn't help. The bubbles feed the water of life around the bloodstream quicker, giving me a hell of a buzz. Whisky for some reason is like liquid dopamine for me. It fires electricity in me and makes me very, very horny. The trick is to go with it and enjoy the ride but sometimes "Captain Jack" takes over the controls and leaves Jack behind. It's always a constant battle which I think I'll win every time we meet. He just smiles that smile and flies off on his "Charisma carpet".

Anyway, back to pussy. Obviously, I'm talking from a male gaze perspective. Don't let that fool you into thinking I'm a male chauvinist twat.

I'm not a chauvinist. In fact, I have way too much respect for women. I actually put them on a pedestal. They are the stronger sex. They are more intelligent. Naked, they are aesthetically pleasing to the eye, more so than men. Okay, maybe the gay community will disagree with that. Maybe they won't. They are emotionally stronger and more supportive. They can produce life for fucks sake, and let's not forget they can have multiple orgasms. Plus they put up with our shit.

Like the male penis, the vagina comes in different sizes and forms. Like the oyster, you have meaty and sleek ones. And let me tell you this, they all taste different and that is the joy. Obviously, diets have a hand in this and I'm sure many women will tell you horror stories of the time they swallowed and it was revolting. Well, let me tell you after she has been drinking acidic fruit juices all night, it's not a walk in the park either. That aside I suggest you never refuse to go down on a woman.

To give pleasure is highly recommended over receiving. At least to do it first anyhow. Once you give her that orgasm, she can't wait to return the favour. The trick is to give her that orgasm, so don't give up. Do you remember prawn cocktail Skips? I had one woman who tasted of this. I love prawn cocktail Skips. Every time I went down on her it was like catnip. No pun intended. I couldn't get enough. I kept going back for another lick, and another and another. Before I knew it, she was loving it.

I was just overdosing on my favourite crisps until management in the basement decided they were hungry too.

Yep, it's definitely kicked in now. You know some women get turned on by what they hear? I guess that's why charm sometimes prevails, and why sense of humour does too. These two things are irresistible. It could also explain why a lot of overweight men are with beautiful women. Either they are rich or genuinely in love or very forgiving to put up with a huge beer belly. That makes them even more special because I don't think many men would be forgiving if she had a beer belly. I fear the beer belly, so I don't drink beer. It won't happen, not on my watch. I don't want to be forgiven. I want her to desire me. I just have to find her. Now, I have a thing for foreign accents. There isn't a word for this. A glossophile is someone who is enthusiastic about language. I will subscribe to this but it's not exactly what I'm trying to explain. Accentphilia would make sense and is self-explanatory, but if I'm honest it sounds terrible and I hate it. An audiophiliac is someone who has an ardent interest in stereo or high-fidelity sound reproduction. This definition is close and I actually love it. I don't think audiophiliac should be used exclusively for stereo and high fidelity. It should be used in the context of someone who is enthusiastic only about sound. Audiophiliac will define people's obsession with sound. My obsession is people's accents. However, an accent I like for a man is not necessarily the same accent I like for a woman. I'm not going to divulge the accents I dislike as that would be unfair, plus karma will find a way to kick me in the nuts for it. Just to put the record straight, I hate my own accent.

Why have I not tried to get rid of it or refine it until I'm happy with it? Well, it shows you where I came from and you should never be embarrassed about that. It's part of who I am, so I live with it. I suppose it's like looking at your own face. We can all pick faults with it. We all think about fixing things we're not happy about but I'm not going to. I'm going to live with it. These are the cards I got dealt.

Actually, I was dealt a bad hand at thirteen. 1988 was when my hair started to turn grey. I know? What the fuck. It was gradual at first. You know how most men in their forties get flecks of grey? It was like that, only I'm getting it as a teenager. It didn't bother me at first, it was a novelty. Then the novelty became a nickname and "grandad" was what stuck for a while. A few years actually. When I got to the end of school, I would get the occasional "it's the Richard Gere look", which I didn't mind, and then in college, in my twenties, it was "George Clooney". Can't complain about that. That's when I embraced it. Those bad-boy grey locks made me awesome, like Samson's hair did for him. I felt powerful, alive, and virile. Boy did I fuck.

Then in my thirties, it wasn't so special anymore. Now the forties, the grey took over completely. I mean I still go to the gym. To be honest I would say I have the body of a thirty-year-old. However, the grey spread to the beard too so now the face looks old. So, it was dye time, and I have to say this natural organic crap really has reversed the years a bit. It will do for now. Anyway, I digressed once again. Accents. I have to say I have a few favourites. Brazilian Portuguese and Italian are right up there. They are spoken like they are singing a song. Music to my ears that is playful and friendly even if they are insulting you. This reminds me of a time when I had to tell my staff to shut up and get back to work because it sounded like insults were being thrown. It turns out she was arranging a dinner date. She was Eastern European and it sounded so harsh and aggressive that I totally misread the situation. Now when she talked in pidgin English, I have to say I found her more attractive. She sounded vulnerable but still assertive and confident. Like a femdom letting her mask slip just for a second before she raises her whip to strike you. I loved it. She hated her English but it was a damn sight better than my attempts at her language. Fuck, I did it again. Spanish is very fast and the tongue is pushed to produce many lisp sounds. In full flow, it's like a rapid machine gun of words bombarding you. English with the Spanish accent or Spanglish is an endearing fusion.

It's not so much a song but a sympathetic sound, and quite hypnotic when listening to a story. One lovely Spanish girl I worked with was so nice and kind and I still remember her talking of her ambitions to work in a museum. Japanese is such a nice language and beautiful to the ear too. You can hear the honour and grace in it as it's carefully spun in the spoken word. Everything is thought out and respectful. The intricacy and use of breath is mesmerising. The one that does it for me the most is French. I think this is because I love the language too. The way the vowels flow into the consonants makes it smooth and moreish. If my ear was a mouth, it would be drinking a delicious chocolate milkshake. I think the fusion here is franglais and it just makes me melt. It's intriguing and it tickles the ear, constantly giving audio pleasure. I can forget being angry, forget what I'm doing, and even forget who I am and why I'm here. It's just so damn sexy. Just thinking about it an image of Sophie Marceau flashes before my eyes. I would reject all the supermodels in the world for Sophie Marceau. She could be reading my shopping receipt and it would give me a throbbing erection. J'adore les francais et leurs femmes, c'est mon genre de vie.

I'm rambling. I've got to slow down, it's still early. I stand at the corner of the square and survey the scene. A woman looks at me in disgust. She's looking at my erection. I shift it to the left, drink some more whisky from my hip flask and smile back. I feel Captain Jack lurking. I decide to leave and walk off, enjoying the feeling before it subsides, and then darkness.

The beginning of *Sounds of Silence* by *Simon & Garfunkel* fades in.

It echoes and fades away. I hear a drumbeat coming in. No, wait, that's my heart. What is happening? Where am I? Who put me here? What was in that whisky? Did I pass out? A door creaks open and I see a ray of light.

Break On Through (To the Other Side) by *The Doors* kicks in.

I go through the door. The room is dark and I can just make out figures sitting at wooden tables. I hear them murmur and making bullshit conversations. It must be a bar. Probably a theme bar. It must be a rock bar as this would explain the music I just heard. However, it looks like a bar from centuries ago with low ceilings. It has wooden floors with sawdust thrown over it. Where the walls and ceiling meet it curves so it looks cave-like. I can smell barley, sweat, and whisky. I walk to the bar and sit on the one and only stool that is there. The room goes quiet and the bar illuminates with low-key lighting. I turn behind me as the space fades to black.

"Bonjour, Jack," she says smiling.

I turn back to the bar to see a slim, curvy, tattooed woman. Her head is shaved and she wears a black T-shirt and black tight shorts. Her whole body is covered in artwork of the highest order. It's amazing. She has random text, blackout mixed with symmetrical patterns, beadwork, jewels, and a couple of cute birds. She has her nipples pierced because you can see through her T-shirt and a bifurcated tongue. She even has ink on her face. She looks great. She is beautiful. The two things that shock me are the two horns sticking out of her head. They are not long curly ones but short stumpy ones. It's like she has just grown them. I've seen these in magazines but never in real life. She must be really committed to having implants.

"L'habitude?" she softly speaks.

"Oui, bien sûr," I say.

She goes to the back of the bar and pulls out a bottle hiding in a secret compartment. She pours me a large glass. Exactly how I like it. She places it in front of me and leaves the bottle on the bar. I take a sip, then a large gulp.

"Lagavulin 16," I say. I smell it, savour it, and smile.

"Bien sûr. Est-ce que tu préfères que je parle Anglais ?"

I think about this for a second and realise my head hurts.

"Yes please," I reply.

She lifts her arm so her wrist is facing her. She taps it like she would a smartphone. A hologram image pops up and she taps some more. A light flashes with an implant above her ear. I thought it was a piercing when I first looked at it. The floating image disappears and she taps her wrist again.

"It's been a while, Jack," she says in English but still with a French accent.

She must know I like this and made this alteration on her wrist phone or whatever it's called. Is this the future? Am I on a trip? What was in that whisky?

"It is good to see you, but if you're here then we got to talk." She pours herself a large Lagavulin.

"Am I in the future?" I say.

She nearly spits out the whisky but she manages to swallow it and laughs.

"Am I dead?" I say searching her face. She pours herself another glass and tops mine up.

"But I've been here before?"

"Oh yes."

"When?"

"Many moons ago," she says like an old storyteller.

Who talks like that? I thought. Is she some sort of witch? She slaps me hard across the face.

"What was that for?" I grab my stinging face.

"For calling me a witch." She downs her whisky and pours another.

"Now you listen to me, Jack. I'm here to help you."

I finish my drink and she quickly pours me another.

"If you're here, all is not lost. There is still hope."

"I don't know why I'm here."

"This is your happy place."

16

"Really?"

"Kind of. More of a backup place."

"Am I sick?"

"Don't ever say you're sick."

"You know you're a beautiful person."

"Thank you, Jack. Flattery will get you everywhere." The room around me glows with a red-pink hue.

"I mean it. You're easy on the eye too." The red-pink hue glows brighter and appears to be throbbing.

"Keep them coming, Jack. Stay with me." The hue turns red and it throbs some more, this time accompanied by a heartbeat.

"Jack?" The heartbeat drums faster.

"Jack?" Dark red spreads and erases her face, sucking it out of existence. The heart is now beating to hardcore drum and bass levels. I feel sick and everything turns black.

I open my eyes and see a grey table leg on a large white rug. A black Bic pen looks lonely and abandoned on the edge of it. I peel off a red-letter notice from the council tax that sticks to the underside of my cheek. As I stumble to get up, the room shakes and I fall down again. Darkness.

"Jack?" she says. The word reverberates and, in an instant, I'm sucked back into the bar.

"Look I'll say this fast, because I don't know how long we have got."

"What's happening?"

"Listen and remember."

"What?"

"The answer sometimes is right in front of you."

"What?"

"Just say it."

"Why?"

"The answer sometimes is right in front of you," she says and pours two drinks. "Say it," she shouts.

"The answer sometimes is right in front of you."

"Now drink." She necks hers back and stares at me. I follow suit. She pours two more.

"Again."

"The answer sometimes is right in front of you."

"Drink." We knock the drinks back. She pours two more.

"Again."

This time she says it with me. "The answer sometimes is right in front of you."

We drink the whisky and she's gone. I'm gone too.

Have you ever had that feeling when you have entered a room and you have forgotten what you came in for? They say our memories are divided into episodes and recalling earlier episodes can be tricky. When we walk through a doorway, we create a new episode so it's difficult to recall our purpose or previous memory. They say doorways have an almost magic effect on our brains. I'm now standing outside the Sovereign's Entrance of The Houses of Parliament. I've no memory of how I got here. When you stand under it and look up and see how huge it is, you almost expect a huge Gothic giant monster to emerge. It would then grab the arch and use it as leverage so it can get out and wreak havoc on the streets of London. I've often thought I could wreak havoc on London, but it's London that wreaks havoc on you. That I do remember. I also remember I must go to Amaterasu. I check my watch and see I still have plenty of time.

The Houses of Parliament is a great building and you can't help but be in awe of it. It truly is awesome. This word is highly over-used and mostly used in the wrong context. Here I've used it the right fucking way. The 87 bus that took me to work passed this every day and I never got bored looking at it. It's a masterpiece built under William the Second and then rebuilt by the architect Charles Barry, taking him twenty years to complete. That's right, thirty years. I mean credit to the builders, it's not like renovating a barn, but can you imagine the stress from Charles? I'm sure he got loads of aggro from the press.

INT. PRESS ROOM – DAY

[CHARLES stands with his foreman, MICK before a lectern in front of the PRESS.]

PRESS: So, when is this gonna be finished, Charles?

CHARLES: Well, I just spoke to the builders and they said any day now.

PRESS: Charles, it's already been twenty-nine years. You 'aving a laugh?

CHARLES: I would say I'm not having a laugh. It's actually quite stressful. I thought this was going to be completed at least twenty five years ago.

PRESS: Come off it. All those spires and extensive stonework. You couldn't get the right spires or the right stone. I bet it looked great on paper.

CHARLES: Well, actually it does. But let me say, Mick here, the leading foreman, has assured me it's not long now. Mick?

MICK: Yes, we can see the light at the end of the tunnel now.

PRESS: How long then?

MICK: I reckon. In about a year.

PRESS: You've been saying that for the last twenty-five years.

MICK: Yeah well, we didn't see the larger picture then, but

we are all good now. We just gotta put the windows in. We just need to get the right glass and the right size glass.

When people think of Gothic buildings, this is the place. I imagine myself as a 19th century masked avenger with Parliament as my backdrop while I rough up criminals and throw politicians in the Thames.

"Who are you?" the scared politician crook says.

"I'm The Guardian," I reply.

"For who?"

"For Her."

"Who?"

"For London."

The politician's face changes into a perplexed look before I let him fall to his death, crashing into the Thames.

"That's the London way," I say as I look up at Parliament and then disappear into the city smog.

I'd watch that. That could be the opening of the pilot episode.

I suppose you're wondering why I personified London as a woman? Well, that's just the image that I see when I think of London. Actually, I see two images. See, she is two types of women. The first one is elegant, glamorous, seductive and enticing. Let's call her Sweet Lonnie. Sweet Lonnie is fun but you must have the money to share the fruits she bears. It's a beautiful relationship when you share the spoils. She loves you and hugs you, and sucks you until you are left smiling till the hangover kicks in. That's when the second one arrives. I call her Lady Grey because she's snooty and brings grey clouds over all proceedings. She isn't helpful when you're down on your luck or in the gutter and she has a habit of rubbing your nose in it. She doesn't want to know you, she doesn't remember you and, frankly, she couldn't care less. It's a break-up, only you see her every day and you realise you have been used. However, you can't help but still hang around because you think one day, "She will be mine again".

This may sound a bit sad and a tad stalkerish, but I want to show her I can be great and be around longer next time. I want to show her a better me. I'm not disillusioned, I just know what she is like. I'm pretty sure she would accept me with open arms if she could see me again. For now, I got to deal with Lady Grey so I take a sip of whisky from my hip flask. That's always a good start.

When you walk around London without a sense of urgency, you feel a wonderful sense of freedom. The only thing you have to do is navigate through the chaos. Transport can be a bitch and tourists can stifle your journey as they are not up to London speed. London speed is walking five miles per hour. That's a fast walk. If you're in the way of a Londoner, they will not give a fuck about you and walk right through you. It's easy to spot the tourists as they're the ones looking up. Deliveries to businesses in London happen all day, which adds to the traffic. People on their lunch break add to the hundreds of people on the streets shop-hopping. It's tough to negotiate these elements but a Londoner reacts to them in milliseconds. It's easy to spot someone who's lost as they are on a totally different time zone and London overwhelms them. Londoners are always switched on, but today I've flicked the switch to chill. I've told urgency to fuck off and so I join the tourists and look up too.

I sit down by one of the fountains in Trafalgar Square and look up at Nelson on his column. Such a phallic monument to boast victory. The square has changed in my time. I remember when you could drive all around it. There used to be a road that would go right past the National Portrait Gallery. It's pedestrianised now and occupied by statue artists.

You still have the little roundabout in front of Nelson's Column and it does no favours to the traffic. They still haven't figured out the best way to navigate entry into the West End. Back in the day you could also jump into this fountain if you were brave enough. I remember on my eighteenth birthday I did that with a friend of mine. I managed to go one further and climb to the top because I had something to prove. Well, you do at eighteen. I achieved it but not without a few cuts and bruises. I didn't feel it of course, as I was eighteen, but mainly I was out of my fucking skull. I was ducking and diving in that fountain-like I was Flipper the dolphin. I was absolutely soaked. Funny how that doesn't bother you at that age. I drink mostly at home now. No chance of fountain diving now as they have "forbidden" signs and large security doing shifts on the Square. I guess I started a trend or something to do with health and safety. You know what else has changed? Pigeons. You won't see any more pigeons here and that's because they employed a couple of hawks. They got the heavies in to get rid of the riff-raff. Good job and all. They are nothing but flying vermin.

EXT. TRAFALGAR SQUARE - DAY

[A brown hawk, SAM lands beautifully next to a spotted hawk, DAVE.]

DAVE: Oi, oi. Morning Sam.

SAM: Morning Dave. Did I miss breakfast?

DAVE: Had a cheeky little so and so earlier, nothing major. Let him go but he knows who's boss. We won't see him again.

SAM: You let him go?

DAVE: He was a baby.

SAM: A baby. Blimey, you never see baby pigeons. Ever.

DAVE: I know, that's why I let him go. Poor thing.

SAM: Wish I saw it.

DAVE: It was a right little cutie, Sam. Nearly broke my heart when I saw him up close.

SAM: I can imagine.

DAVE: Well, you know how hard it is to stop going at our speed

SAM: Don't I just. Remember last Tuesday. My beak hasn't been the same since.

DAVE: I could have killed him, Sam. As soon as I realised, I let him go right away.

SAM: Yeah, course you did.

DAVE: The old talon nicked him though, so there was a bit of blood.

SAM: Well, it's not your fault. You were just doing your job.

DAVE: Once he flew away, I was fine. But it was touch and go there for a sec.

SAM: I can imagine. It's alright mate.

[Sam brings his wing around and taps him on the back]

SAM: I'm gonna speak to the boss today.

DAVE: Oh no, don't mention this.

SAM: No, not this. I want some compensation for the beak and I'm thinking of asking for a raise.

DAVE: You're brave.

SAM: C'mon mate, we deserve it. We've changed this place. The riff-raff is gone. Even the white shit has gone. Look how clean it is down there. I mean, even up there. Look at whatshisname. Clean as a whistle. No pigeon shit on his head anymore.

DAVE: Nelson. His name is Nelson.
SAM: What a strange name?
DAVE: I dunno, Sam.
SAM: Look, mate. If we fuck off, they are in the shit. Literally.
DAVE: True.
SAM: You in?
DAVE: I got your back. I'm in.
SAM: Let's fly.

I walk past Charing Cross Station and slide down the walkway by the side as if I'm going to the Embankment. I then nip into Gordon's Wine Bar which is neatly tucked away. As soon as you pass through the iron gates the modern world blends before your very eyes into Dickensian London. As I enter already my writer's head is bombarded with the ghosts of the 19th century.

Writers, prostitutes, robbers, thieves, actors, singers, aristocrats, and scoundrels have all been here forgetting their problems or celebrating new ones. I wonder how different their problems were from today. I'm sure they were just the same.

All of us at one point or another have thought about having a time machine to visit the past and the future. Mostly it's to see visual differences up close. The decor if you like. The different car types, the way houses and apartments were the fashion of the time and the music. When I was a teenager, I asked my Dad, "What were the sixties like? It looked so much fun."

"Yeah, it was a time of change, I'm sure Mick Jagger and Michael Caine had fun but you know for the rest of us we just had to carry on and get on with it."

I never understood this or believed it at the time, until I experienced Britpop. An unimaginative label but this was our sixties. I was in my early twenties and I remember it fondly. There was a buzz about England. Sorry, Britain (stick a pin in that as I will come back to it), and we were cool again. "Cool Britannia" is what they called it and it was good times. It was only when we weren't working or studying. Britpop was just the weekends and it lasted three, four years max. It was all done by 1997. I think the hangover lasted through to Diana's death, then we carried on and decided to fear the Millennium.

I guess certain eras have periods that are flag posted and edited by the media to popularise and glamourise the country's most successful achievements. No one wants to hear about how difficult the changes in the sixties were. Well, it turns out my Dad's generation, the "baby boomers" as they were called, did alright in the end. I think most of them pretty much own their own house. Not something you can say these days. Now that looks like a pipe dream. The banks have already started buying property and soon we will become a rental market like Germany. Anyway, I digress.

You know we all have our own time machine built within us? It's our five senses. Well, most of us have them. Each sense can transport us back in time. It's remarkable. We have all done it. If I hear a track from the Britpop era, I'm in my twenties again, getting drunk and trying to get a shag. Music is great like that. Different tracks can mean many different things to us. They can remind us of our first love, our wedding day, a funeral of a loved one. It transports us to that place again in an instant. Smell is a good one. I could be walking down the street and an aroma of mashed potato and gravy will immediately send me back to primary school dinners. Cut grass and hay will put me on my summer lunch break rushing down the steepest field ever with my little legs running faster than they can carry me and then falling at the end. The strong smell of flowers conjures up my Nan and an even stronger smell of musk will summon up my Grandad. It must have been "Old Spice" or "Brut". The eighties reeked of these aromas, not like these days where subtlety is king. I heard that as you get older you lose your sense of smell, I guess that's why my grandparents splashed more perfume on. I think it's down to the fact you get desensitised. It's the same with taste. Taste. As a child your taste buds are hypersensitive. They are brand new and tasting things for the first time. Sweet flavours are generally always welcome but sometimes, bitter and savoury don't go down well. Literally. Vegetables especially. When that broccoli goes over our taste buds, alarm bells go off and we spit it out. The flavour is super strong and we can't handle it. The only way we can is through repetition and a sweet treat promised by our mums. Good auld Mum. We may live in a "patriarchal" society but it's our mothers who really keep things together and make sure things run smoothly. As time goes on and we try new things our taste buds do desensitise. Remember when you had that curry? Which one? Exactly. Most of the time now you are probably trying to go hotter and hotter as your taste buds need more to get that spicy hit again. It's not the fact that your taste buds change as you get older it's the fact that they are fucked. This is because most of us in our adult lives tend to eat much of the same things over and over. You can actually retrain your taste buds if you can be bothered. A good start would be to get rid of beer and start drinking whisky. Far healthier.

Lips are always worthy of discussion. Especially tasting them. Thin, full, slim, voluptuous, delicate, firm, wet, dry. Brown, white, black, pale, dark. All taste beautiful and send you to heaven no matter what time zone you're in. You remember them all. The taste, the pleasure you receive from their touch. Tantalising the nerve endings on your lips. Millions of delightful pins and needles lighting up your pillow of pleasure, which then sends the blood rushing around your body to delight your obvious areas. Something so simple as a kiss can excite you that you get lost in your search for the orgasmic climax that explodes from within. There is nothing sexier than a woman's face lost in ecstasy.

It's primal, it's honest, it's freedom, it's pure pleasure, the unabridged version. When she is able to show you that, she is showing her true self. In that orgasmic moment, she has forgotten herself and given herself entirely to pleasure. Men don't do that, not in the beginning anyway. I'm not even saying that we are different because, to be honest, women fuck like men too. No qualms with that.

Most men prefer to enjoy their ecstasy privately. The main reason for that is, that they think they look ridiculous. One man said it's like they are taking a shit and someone caught them doing it. The shame is too much. That's probably why "doggy style" is so popular. It's nothing to do with connection, it's about not getting caught looking like a filthy deviant.

INT. BEDROOM – NIGHT

[A large beer-bellied man, RAY lays on top of his petite wife, BRENDA.]

BRENDA: What the hell was that, Ray?

RAY: What do you mean, Brenda?

BRENDA: That face you pulled.

RAY: That was me cumming.

BRENDA: Well, don't fucking do it again. That put me right off.

RAY: Yes, love.
BRENDA: Go and brush your teeth.
RAY: Yes, love.

Some women like men's cum faces. One loved seeing the honest and filthy deviant look. For some, it's a turn-on. Different strokes, I guess. Maybe men need to hear that more.

Release the pose guys, don't hide it. Share the glare. That sounds frightening. Just fucking cum and don't worry who sees it. Embrace the space. Fill the void. Okay, I'm done.

Touch is a difficult one. It's not one that accesses the memories as quickly as the others. The only thing that comes to mind is how soft and smooth a girlfriend's legs were. I used to love running my hands up and down these marble columns like they were works of art. My fingertips tingling on every pass, carefully trying not to tickle her. Nothing reminded me of this though. I had to search for this. I guess it would have been strange to run my hand down a table leg to remind me of said girlfriend. She wouldn't have liked that, I can tell you.

The beauty of these time travels is that the senses have made memory files so you can access them and relive them. Sometimes you can search for them and sometimes they will appear to you out of the blue and pleasantly surprise you.

Women and sex seem to plague my brain. I don't have control of it. I guess it's a happy place. Somewhere safe, away from harm. The go-to place when things are lonely and uncertain. I guess it's a comfort. I think when I'm down it releases dopamine into my bloodstream and makes me happy. The slow build-up as my imagination conjures up beautiful images and cascades down my arms and legs and then finally into my cock, fighting to get out. Release the beast.

"We are fully armed. Repeat, fully armed. Waiting for further instructions," says the Colonel.

"This is one-eyed Jack, we have no visual on a female of the species."

"What's going on?"

"Yeah Colonel, we're ready to go."

"Keep it down, men. I'm receiving Intel. Message received."

"Okay, men, we got the hand coming in."

"Whose hand?"

"Yeah, whose hand? Hers or his?"

"Hold. Wait for it. It's his."

"Oh, not again."

"We're doomed."

"Get in line, men. That doesn't mean anything." The soldiers start to jump around erratically.

"I said get in line. Wait for it. On my command."

"Colonel, he's gonna blow," says one-eyed Jack.

"We're gonna die."

"We're gonna die out in the open."

"God speed men. It's been an honour," says the Colonel.

"Oh shit, here we go."

"Fuck. Tell my family I love them."

"You have my word," says the Colonel.

Life can be funny but it can be bloody hard too. I guess this is where religion comes in. Everyone else talks about it so why can't I? I'll start by saying that I'm an atheist. I was brought up a Catholic but then I started to think for myself and realised how absurd it is. Religion. What is it good for? This is where Frankie Goes to Hollywood comes in and sings "Absolutely Nothing". I would however give a little chuckle and then say,

"Frankie, I disagree". Frankly, I would disagree.

I understand the why. People need it. It's comforting and it tells those people that they are not alone. They want to know that there is a superior being that is looking out for them. They want to know that there is something after this life. I guess they feel that there must be something, otherwise what is the point? Why are we born? Why do we die? There has to be more. It's also fear. I think people are scared that there is nothing. In case there is something, they believe, so they don't burn in hell. They want to get into the good place so they have belief and faith, hoping things will turn out well in the end. For eternity, according to the Bible. I mean, that's a huge sell considering there is no proof. Oh yes, there was a Jesus and he made a sacrifice, but for who? I guess the marketing team came up with the perfect slogan to stop the cynics arguing about God:

"You got to have faith".

It's beautiful. It stops the argument right there, doesn't it. Although it will produce a dumbfounded reaction.

"There is no God. There is no proof."

"Yeah, well, you gotta have faith."

"Really? That's the best you got?"

"You got to have faith."

"So, you putting complete confidence and trust into something you can't see or aren't sure even exists?"

"I am. Because I have faith."

"You're mental."

"Well, there is no need to be rude."

"I'm sorry. I'm out of line."

"I forgive you."

"Wow, that's very gracious of you. Well, I must be going, I

better get this last taxi."

"Goodbye."

"Excuse me. Do you mind lending me thirty pounds to pay for the taxi?"

"I don't really know you."

"I'm good, don't worry, you just gotta trust me."

"Okay. When will I get the money back?" He hands him the money.

"Soon. Very soon. You got to have faith." He waves goodbye from the taxi, never to be seen again.

Fine, it's a bit harsh, but the church has taken far more from people. Poor people at that. Getting rich off the poor because of faith. It's "The Great Big Con".

The other problem I have is getting preached at. You don't see me on the streets saying there is no God. Fine, I'm preaching now, but the time seems right for some reason. You always think about religion when you're in vulnerable or confusing circumstances. I forget where I was. Also, I am not killing in the name of God. I don't kill in anyone's name. Sure, I've thought about it, but never acted on it. I bet you a lot fewer atheists have killed a lot fewer people, than religious people. That's a tricky one to get your head around. Some people believe in their religion so much that they think it's worth killing and dying for. What the fuck? Morally that doesn't make sense, and I'm sure in their religion it doesn't either. Oh wait, you can ask for forgiveness, so it will all be okay.

The whole God thing just doesn't stack up. It has been said that "if God doesn't exist then man would invent him". This, for me, is exactly what happened. Man, let's say, men. Actually, let's say "some men" decided that we need an answer to life, the universe, and everything else. The biggest question: Why? Needed a big answer. What's bigger than God? To answer a mystery, why not solve it with a mystery. Solve it with something that is not entirely answerable. It just is. Remember when you were a child and you go through that stage of asking your parents lots of questions? Eventually, they get so pissed off and they don't know the answer, they reply "because". "But why Dad?", "Because, just because." Well, it's rather like that.

The major problem I have about the existence of God is that he doesn't do anything. Not a single fucking thing. He is a fucking lazy bastard. If I was a God, I would constantly lap up the adoration and actually turn up occasionally to receive it. Maybe even have a few drinks.

INT. GOLDEN FLEECE PUB – NIGHT
  [JIM the landlord wipes down the bar. GOD enters.]
  JIM: Well look who it is.
  GOD: Evening Jim.
  JIM: The usual?
  GOD: Yeah, go on.
  [Jim the Landlord pours a pint of Guinness and hands it to God.]
  JIM: Absolutely fucking remarkable what you did today. Forgive me. Didn't mean to curse.
  GOD: Cheers Jim. Sure, I made a few curses meself today but it all turned out good in the end.
  JIM: On me.
  GOD: Thanks very much. All the best.
  [A small disheveled man squeezes in past God and orders a pint. This is FERGAL.]
  FERGAL: Same again, Jim.

[Jim pours a lager and hands it to Fergal. Fergal gets his coins out and counts them awkwardly. He is short. He looks to God.]

FERGAL: Do you have a Euro, your holiness?

GOD: Erm. Sure.

JIM: Oh Jesus Christ, Fergal.

[God looks over at Jim.]

JIM: Sorry. God Almighty.

[God hands the Euro to Fergal. Fergal pays.]

FERGAL: Thanks a million.

GOD: No bother.

[Fergal sips his lager and stands next to God.]

FERGAL: So, what's the craic?

GOD: Not much now, Fergal. Just a minor disaster averted, millions were saved. The usual. Howse yer self and your woman?

FERGAL: I'm grand. The wife passed. Long gone. You must have known that?

GOD: Oh Jesus, sorry Fergal. Been up to my ears in it today.

FERGAL: Work has dried up. I had to sell the car and then I had to put Keano down today. I'll miss him but you know he was an awfully old dog.

GOD: Sorry to hear that. I'm sure things will look up soon.

FERGAL: Do you think so? I mean, do you know something? I mean, you could always tell me. C'mon now, we've known each other all my life.

GOD: You know, Fergal, I can't do that.

FERGAL: Why the feck not? I'm not asking much. I wouldn't ask for help if I didn't need it now.

JIM: Is he bothering you?

GOD: Not at all. He's grand.

FERGAL: Well, what do you say? C'mon.

33

GOD: I can't have favourites, Fergal. You know that.

FERGAL: Well, what about yer man? Jesus. He was a favourite.

JIM: Right, that's enough. Get out Fergal.

FERGAL: I'm only saying.

[God takes out his mobile phone.]

GOD: Right. Right so. Well, I must make tracks. Another emergency.

JIM: Okay, God Almighty. Take care.

FERGAL: Good luck.

JIM: You never leave him alone.

FERGAL: Ah c'mon. His phone didn't even ring. Feckin' bastard.

You can't see God but he sees everything you do. He's a voyeur. A stalker who doesn't act. Or. God is just not there. Why? Because.

Most religious people don't want to believe this. They want to 'go to the other side'. They want to see their loved ones that died before them. They want to go onto another life where they have no money, no problems, and most importantly – no death. I believe when you die that's it. You're done and then you're dusted. Does this fill me with gloom and doom? Absolutely not. Do I think about it a lot? Sometimes, like now.

You know we all just need to be good to each other. That's all. You don't need religion for that. Yes, we are all different. If we were all the same it would be boring, but I tell you, sometimes my blood boils. Fuck, sometimes I can't fathom how different we are. I mean sometimes, even when I'm going to the supermarket, I can't believe how some people behave. I mean there are some real twats out there. You know some people start eating the stuff before they have even paid for it? Who taught them that? The same people will also go to the supermarket dressed in their pyjamas. Even worse, tracksuits. When did tracksuits become the normal casual dress of the human race? I look around me and all I see are overweight, fully grown children parading about. Where did all the adults go? These same people will argue with each other because they jumped the queue or didn't see the queue or took the last toilet roll. Then they hurl the personal insults as they hoist up their tracksuit bottoms, all in the name of survival. Sir David Attenborough and his team would have a field day capturing these exchanges. Just produce it with great cinematography, add a Hans Zimmer composition and you have the next successful reality drama in the bag.

The major problem is, people are so judgemental. With the rise of social media, everyone has a voice and everyone wants to be heard. Yes, everyone. You can't help yourself when you feel you have to make a comment. You get an itch. If someone says that Jaws isn't the best film but The Godfather is, be prepared for a storm of criticism. What about the best Seinfeld episode? Or the best Bond? Don't even bother. It's easy to hide behind a keyboard. No one can see that big nose of yours. That bald head. Those hairy hands. You're invisible, so you say what you want. Unfortunately, what you say kind of sums you up as a person, so be careful or you will be judged very quickly. Most people won't care what they say and when it becomes racial or prejudicial, then it's harmful and detrimental. Why do people behave this way? Do they think it's funny? It doesn't sound funny. I guess I can summarise.

Some people are just cunts.

Surely there is a reason, Jack? No, they are just cunts. I don't like using this word often but it has a place. It is, after all, the worst curse word out there. Our Spanish cousins tend to use something along the lines of puta madre or "mother fucker". Americans like that too but none have more impact than cunt. I have to say, no one can deliver it better than the British. That includes all members of the United Kingdom. Their accents give it strength and power and it's probably the only time when they hit the end of the consonants. Believe me, when they hit the end of this word, it's a knockout blow that sends ripples all around the room. Be on your guard, because someone is about to transform into beast mode.

I break away from my pontificating and eat the last piece of blue Stilton and wash it down with some Chateauneuf-du-Pape. For me a great pairing, as I like the saltiness followed by full-bodied silk. Reminds me of someone but I forgot her name. I look at my watch and realise I still have time, so I leave and make my way to Simpsons on The Strand. One must pay one's respect to Alfred Hitchcock's old drinking hole.

As soon as I enter, I'm agitated as someone is sitting at Hitchcock's booth. Fuck sake, it's not even busy. I'm seated in the booth behind and I can't take my eyes off the woman seated in his spot. I bet she doesn't know anything about Hitchcock. This makes me angrier. I order an Old fashioned as it's a good test for the establishment to see if they are any good. The waiter brings it to me and waits. I sip it and give a smile and a nod. He smiles back. Maybe a knowing smile or a smile of respect. It is a good Old fashioned. The woman looks a lot like the film actress Louise Brooks. It's uncanny. Hitchcock never put Brooks in a film, only her image in the background of his film *Stage Fright*. I bet she doesn't know that. She seems so comfortable in her skin, which is so attractive. It's as if liquid mercury flows through her body, moving her limbs. Mesmerising. She turns and catches my eye. I look into my drink and take a sip.

"Would you like to join me?" she says.

I look behind me and see no one. I turn back to her.

"There is only you and me, darling. Come on, don't be shy."

I pick up my drink and I sit opposite her. Damn, I wish I was sitting in her spot.

"So, what's your favourite Hitchcock film?" she says smiling. I'm shocked.

"C'mon, it's obvious you're a fan. Your eyes have been burning into my back ever since you sat down."

I take another sip of my Old fashioned. I pause for a moment. "Rear Window."

"Wow, that was worth the wait. Most people say Psycho or Ver.. "

"Vertigo. Yeah, Vertigo is number two for me."

"Rear Window? Mmmmmmmm. You know that says a lot about you?"

"Really? How so?"

"You're something of a voyeur. You like to watch people. You like to look into people's apartments. You also have commitment issues. Also, you don't like it when things don't go your way."

I finish my drink. She summons the waiter.

"Same again. Put them on my tab." The waiter smiles and turns away.

"You know, instead of thinking about sitting in Hitchcock's place, you should think about sitting in his booth. Who sat in his booth and the fact that you are sitting opposite him."

She makes a very good point. Women generally do make

good points. They see things from different perspectives. They break free from the narrow confines that men get tied up in. Why do we tie ourselves up sometimes? It's like self-torture. Maybe subconsciously we want to be rescued. Maybe we want to be tortured.

"I love Rear Window too. Is it my favourite? It changes day to day."

"So, it's Vertigo?" I say. The waiter arrives with our drinks. I grab my Old fashioned and then curiously stare at her drink.

"It's a Martini," she says.

"I can see that but it's very cloudy," I reply.

"I ask for lots of brine. I call it a filthy Martini," she laughs and exposes her straight white teeth. They look perfect except for one front tooth that overlaps the other, ever so slightly. She sees me looking at it and licks it with her tongue.

"Vertigo is up there. I would say it's a good deconstruction of misogyny and also the contrast between an independent and submissive woman."

"So, you favour the films where his women are strong and independent?"

"Yes. Don't you?" she says as I sip my Old fashioned.

"I do." I totally didn't expect to have this conversation with this woman. I'm starting to really like her.

"Take Grace Kelly in Rear Window. While James Stewart is a photographer and voyeur, he is contemplating his own life. All those apartments he peers into are projections of himself. Miss Lonelyhearts, Miss Torso, and a composer who fears his career is going nowhere. Grace cares for him and shows him that she loves him but he is far more comfortable framing people from a distance than holding them up close in his arms. Fear of commitment but Grace is his saviour."

She nailed it. She pours the rest of her filthy Martini down her throat. She sticks up two of her fingers, then swishes them between the two of us. The waiter nods and smiles.

"Notorious," I say.

"Good shout. Bergman still keeps her self-worth intact. The whole plot would fail without her cooperation. They need her. She achieves far more with her patriotic determination and intelligence than the CIA's pencil-pushing."

"Then it has to be…"

"Psycho. Yes," she says. I finish my drink and the waiter arrives with our new ones. "Janet Leigh is the epitome of an independent woman ahead of her time. She takes initiative to steal money and build a future with a married man but at the last minute she repents, and in the famous shower scene where she is cleansing herself of her sins, she is murdered. Forty-seven minutes into the film. We have invested everything in her up to this point then she is killed. And Hitchcock becomes immortal forever because of it. So today it's Psycho. Seems fitting as you came and sat next to me," she smiles.

"You think I'm a psycho?" I say, shocked.

"No. But I might be." She raises her eyebrows.

"I have to pee. Back in a sec." She stands up and leaves.

As she walks away, I wait a couple of seconds before I turn to look at her. She turns back at the same time and catches me. She smiles back.

I had just met her in under five minutes and already I was invested, but who was she? I loved the fact she advertised she has to "pee". She doesn't care about airs and graces. She isn't out to impress. Maybe she doesn't like me, that's why. If I was attractive to her, she would have just excused herself. Maybe she just feels so comfortable with me. They say if you like someone you can tell within the first three seconds. First seven seconds to form a solid impression of someone and one-fifth of a second to fall in love. Maybe I spend too much time thinking. I loved listening to her and I have to say, she's easy on the eye. I can't believe she caught me looking at her arse but luckily, she seemed to like that I looked. Maybe she smiled because she caught me. Dammit, I'm doing it again. Just be. Just be Jack. That's another thing women are better at than men. Looking. Women can steal looks like nobody's business. Men are useless at it and I think we have given up trying. How many times have we been busted glancing at their breasts when we should be listening to what they are saying. Even when we are checking out the bottom region, they know. They look us right in the eye to show they know. Women are far more subtle. They check men out all the time but we just don't see it. I'm not just talking about our hands, chest, legs and shoulders, knees and toes. Knees and toes. Sorry, the nursery rhyme crept in there. Women check out our bottom regions too. Yes, they check out our arse and more often than not they check out our cocks. Yes, they check out that bulge. When we are sitting, walking, and even running. If we noticed how often they did it to us we would so understand objectification. As they are more refined than us, they are masters of subtlety and secret looks. They are ninja thieves, a species that has perfected the stolen glance that they only talk about at secret gatherings or hen parties.

The waiter brings our drinks. She returns and plonks herself back down in Hitchcock's seat.

"Put those on my tab please," I say.

"Merci." She sips her drink.

"You know I'm surprised you didn't sit in the seat," she says.

"I am too."

"Bet you were itching to."

"Not really."

"Really? Not even a little bit?" she smiles. "Maybe you did and you quickly sat back in your seat just before I came back."

"Is that what you would have done?"

"Totally."

"I could have but I was just thinking."

"Interesting. About what?"

"This and that. Nothing really. Usual stuff. Meaningless stuff."

"Do you think a lot?"

"I guess. Don't we all."

"Yes we do but some more than others. I'm Amelie."

I smile.

"What's so funny?"

"That may have been the longest introduction ever."

"I could say the same for you. You are?"

"Jack."

"Enchanté Jack."

"You speak French?"

"Bien sûr. I'm half French. My mother is, was French."

"Oh, I'm sorry to.."

"It's okay, she died when I was very young. So, what do you do, Jack?"

I snort as I'm not sure how to answer. I stare at my drink, then take a sip for inspiration. Fuck it. Just be honest.

"I'm a writer."

"Interesting. Who for?" she says excitedly.

"For… me?"

"Tell me more. Have I read anything of yours?"

"Not yet. Still banging them out. I mainly write screenplays.

41

TV pilots and feature films."

"Well, it only takes one, then you're on your way." She smiles back at me.

That wasn't too painful. She didn't do the sympathy eyes and sigh and she actually made me feel better.

"Of course, it has to be something special."

"Of course."

"You think you have it? Do you have it in you?" I paused for a moment, then snapped out of it.

"Yeah, I do."

"Good. All you got to do now is prove it and stick it to the bastards."

"Which bastards?"

"The critics."

I hate most of those people. They get shed-loads of money for criticising artists for their craft. Most of them seem to have gone to the A.A. Gill School of insults to increase their stock and value. It's hard to find a decent reviewer these days, most of their comments are very personal and derogatory. There is one critic who is fucking awful. She gets off on her own insults. She is a real queen bitch. The filthier the better. Her weekly shtick is her weekly kick. One can only hope this petrol head fuelled by insults will soon be canceled by a world of Tesla minds electrified with constructive criticism.

"You okay?"

"Yeah, I think too much. Sorry."

"Don't apologise. Isn't that what writers do?"

"I guess. I don't consider myself a true professional as I haven't got paid yet. So…"

"Yeah, I get that. But you can write. You're a writer."

"I know but…"

"You write. You're a writer. Listen, we need to talk about this at length but now is not the time. Damn, I think I'm out of cards. Give me your number." She hands me her phone. I pause and stare for a second.

"C'mon, darling. I have people to see."

I type my number in. She calls my phone immediately and then ends the call.

"That's me," she says. "Go on then."

The first thing I think is that she wants me to kiss her, so I stand up, but before I get close she steps aside.

"Go on. I want to see you sit in his seat."

I smile, feeling slightly embarrassed. It's like a teacher punishing me in front of the whole class. I sit down.

"Well?"

"Feels good," I say smiling. "Now what?"

"Now you get to admire the view." She bends down and kisses me softly on the lips.

"We will do this again, soon. Ciao, Jack." She walks away and I admire the view.

I look at my phone and realise time has flown by. It's time to go to Amaterasu and meet Asami. I finish my drink and leave on a mission. I stand under a bus stop shelter as the rain pelts down. I survey the surroundings and then try and look through the window of the restaurant. The neon lights from the lanterns are blurred in this weather and create a serene yet eery atmosphere. Apart from the rain, you wouldn't think you are in London. It starts to get cold so I make a dash for the entrance.

Inside you have stepped into Japan. Immediately you hear the koto being played by an elegant woman dressed in a kimono sitting in the corner of the room. Koi carp swim under a glass floor which snakes around all the tables in the restaurant. Real pink cherry blossom trees sprout from all corners and a gigantic one in the middle takes centre stage. Its presence emanates strength, love, and serenity. It's effective and affective.

It's all very cliché but it's not tacky in the slightest. The Japanese don't do tacky, they do elegance and tranquillity served with honour and respect.

The hostess greets me and bows. I bow back, caught a little off guard, and then she motions me to the bar. She offers to take my coat but I decline. I take a seat at the bar and order a Yoichi ten-year-old. The bar woman smiles at me. I'm hoping it's out of respect and recognition rather than the thirty-pound dram price. I take a sip and it's bloody gorgeous. Anything the Japanese love, they treat it with high regard and delicacy until they perfect it. Whether it be engineering or whisky. I smile as the dram trickles across my palate and down the back of my throat. The bar woman sees my pleasure and smiles back. I recognise the smile. It's a connoisseur's smile, so I smile back.

"Arigato," I say.

"Arigato." She smiles again.

"Is Asami here?" I ask.

"Asami? Yes."

"Can I see her please?"

She leaves the bar and bows again. I take in my surroundings and enjoy my whisky. I look down into the floor at the Koi carp. It's hypnotic watching them swim around the room. One fish stops and raises itself against the glass, winks at me, smiles, and swims off.

"I'm Asami." A voice appears behind me.

I turn and see a shy navel-gazing woman. When she looks up, I see her true beauty. She's breathtaking. So much so, that I can't speak.

"Konichiwa," she says.

"Hello. Konichiwa," I stutter.

I can't stop staring. It must appear very rude, as she looks back down.

"I'm sorry. I'm Jack, I'm here to deliver a message," I say more confidently.

She looks up and smiles. I smile back. I pull my sleeve up to reveal the writing on my arm. She holds my arm and turns her head. She smiles.

"You must come with me."

"What?" I say with my drink halfway to my mouth.

"You must come with me. Now."

"I just had to deliver the message." I drink some more of my Yoichi.

"Yes, but we go now."

I stared at her and realised her face was serious. I didn't imagine there would be anything more to the mission the crow gave me. I didn't know what the message meant but I could see in her eyes that she needed my help. Maybe the crow sent me to help her. Was she in trouble? I couldn't help but look at her bright green eyes. They were feline and sparkled against her coffee-coloured skin. Her cheeks were delicately pinched and her lips were only slightly plump. She was remarkable-looking. She was slim yet curvaceous. I've never seen a woman like it and now she wanted my help. How could I resist? I knocked back my drink.

"Let's go," I said.

She leads me behind the bar and the bartender snaps at Asami. Asami calmly talks to her with her hand out but the bartender snaps back and mentions Yoichi. I then realise I haven't paid for the whisky. Asami snaps back, stares at her, then calmly says.

"Sono melyo no tame ni."

The bartender bows to Asami and returns to her work. It was magical. Asami leads me out the back, grabs her coat, and an umbrella and we leave through an emergency door. Asami grabs my hand, pulls me under her umbrella and walks me to the end of the road. She looks around frantically.

"What do you need me to do?" I say over the heavy rain.

"What?" she shouts.

"What did the message say?" I say pointing to my arm.

"We need to go to my Grandmother's," she says.

She hails a taxi and it slides up to the curb. As I let Asami get in first, I am startled by the emergency door swinging open. I turn and see a dark shadow hurtling towards us.

"Get in. Quickly," she says.

"What is that?" I say, stunned.

All I can see is a dark mass which seems to be in flight for some part but then rapidly pounces puddles of water the next, heading straight for me. Asami pulls me into the taxi and slams the door shut. The taxi drives off. There is momentary relief, but then we hear a thud on the roof. The driver panics and puts his foot down. We hear another thud followed by numerous scratches and scrapes. The driver makes a sharp turn and we see the shadow fall and scramble under a street light. The driver doesn't hesitate and drives off in the opposite direction.

"What was that?" I say breathlessly.

"That was Kukan."

What mission had I got myself involved in? Things were getting weird.

"Why are we going to your Grandmother's?"

"We have to get the Securus."

"Of course we do."

Getting to her Grandmother's was a mission in itself. It was a maze of alleys, side streets and stranger's gardens. It was actually a good way of not being followed. Entering through the front door wasn't an option so we ascended the iron fire escape, then we had to side jump onto a roof and climb through an open window where an old man is watching Bake-Off on the television.

"Konichiwa Ojichan," Asami says as we walk past. The old man nods and grunts without taking his eyes off the television. We walk through his kitchen, through its window, across another roof, and through another window.

"Wait. Where are we going? Who was that?" I say with exhaustion.

"My Grandfather."

"So where is your Grandmother?"

"She lives here," she says as she pulls me up. It was a struggle as I caught my head on the washing line just outside it. Asami helped me get untangled and got me through the window. I dust myself down. Before I open my mouth, she has already poured me a glass of water. I gulp it down.

"Asami. Anatana no?" A voice shouts from the living room.

"Hai, sono watashi to yujin," Asami shouts back.

"Kare ni uisuki o age nasai. Beikuofu wa mada ondesu," her Grandmother screams back.

Asami goes to the cupboard and gets a Yoichi ten-year-old and pours two glasses. I guess her Grandmother has taste.

"She's watching Bake-Off. She said we can drink."

"Cheers. Kanpai," she says.

"Kanpai," I say back.

We clink glasses and sip our stress away. The kitchen is small and basic but it's very homely with its Japanese ornaments, figurines, tiny lanterns and pagodas and, strangely, a framed photograph of Paul Newman on the wall. Asami catches me looking at it.

"Grandmother loves him."

"Yeah? He was a good actor. Pretty cool."

I sniff and realise the room smells sweet and sugary. Not at all what I was expecting.

"Grandmother always bakes when Bake-Off is on. It makes her hungry," she says.

"Ah."

"Should be a nice treat. It's always good." She sips her whisky.

Sitting with her in the kitchen is nice. It feels great that I am helping her. I guess this is how carers feel. I'm actually glad I wasn't just delivering a message, as this is much more exciting. Although that Kukan was scary. Whatever that was.

"What was the thing we have to get?"

"What?" she says, confused.

"The thing. The seck thingy? Seck?"

"The Securus. My grandmother has it."

"What is it? Why do you need it?" I said.

"Let's wait for Grandmother," she calmly responded.

She then got up and grabbed a board with black and white stones on it. She placed it on the table with two small hand-crafted bowls that were embossed, one with a dragon and the other with a fox.

"Do you know how to play?"

"No. I've always wanted to learn."

"Good. I'll show you."

GO is one of the oldest board games. It's about four thousand years old. The object of the game is to obtain more territory than your opponent, to make you the winner. It felt like we had been playing for ages as it's a game of strategy and thought. It was taking me a while to grasp the rules as I was playing. Anyway, Asami seemed to be having fun when I laid my stones as she couldn't stop smiling at my dumb moves. This didn't deter me, it actually made me more determined, but I was no match for her. It was intriguing and I would definitely have another go, no pun intended. However, today wasn't the day as her Grandmother walked in. Bake-Off had finished.

Asami introduces me.

"Konichiwa, Jack," her Grandmother says. She bows and smiles.

Just as she says this, a loud booming voice comes from outside the window.

Grandmother goes to the window and shouts back waving her arms. She then goes to the oven and opens the door. The waft of ginger slaps us in the face, while sugar and cinnamon open their arms and hug us. I get why baking is so rewarding. Grandmother takes her biscuits out and distributes three-quarters on a plate and the rest in a brown paper bag. Asami has already cleared GO away and lets Grandmother put the biscuits down before us. She smiles and gestures for us to eat. She then attaches the brown paper bag to the washing line and uses a pulley system to transport it to her husband in the building next to her.

"Oi," Grandmother shouts.

The Grandfather appears at his window and unhooks the brown paper bag.

"Arigato," Grandfather says. He shakes the bag. He is miffed that it's light.

Grandmother looks at me and raises her eyebrows. I take a bite of the biscuit.

"Hmmm. Lovely," I say.

"Good," she says and she sits down at the table with us. She stares at me and smiles. To break the awkward silence I point to Paul Newman.

"Paul Newman," I say.

"Paul Newman." She smiles back. "You like."

"I like."

I'm confused and embarrassed at my own vernacular. I show her the tattoo on my right arm. It reads, "Sometimes nothing can be a real cool hand".

"Cool Hand Luke." She smiles some more.

"Yeah, Cool Hand Luke."

"Very good." Asami smiles with her. I think Grandmother likes me.

"The fall will kill you," she raises her voice.

"What?" I say looking to Asami. Asami looks back at me confused.

"The fall will kill you," she emphasizes with more gusto. "Probably," she adds.

"Oh. Butch Cassidy" I solve finally. "The fall will probably kill you."

"Yes. The fall will probably kill you. Very funny."

Grandmother starts laughing. I laugh with her but a little at her too. She says something to Asami, gets another glass and pours her Grandmother a whisky. Grandmother sips it and exhales in delight. Normally this would annoy me but from her, it is satisfying to watch. It reminds me of my own grandmother and how much I miss her.

She turns to Asami and they talk seriously. All I understand is 'Securus'. When I hear it, Grandmother stops and looks at me, confused. She looks at me like she is reading me then turns to talk to Asami.

"Bango," Grandmother is shocked.

"Hai," Asami casually responds.

"Bango," Grandmother is surprised.

"Hai," Asami replies with more conviction.

It seemed they were talking about me. I pretty much worked out that "bango" was "no" and "hai" was "yes". Did Grandmother not have confidence in me helping Asami? What was wrong with me? I thought we were getting on just fine. Why the sudden change?

"Okay," Grandmother says and leaves the kitchen.

"Everything okay?" I say, perplexed.

"Everything is fine. Another whisky?"

"Yes please," I say. I needed it now more than ever. Asami pours me a large one. I drink half of it immediately. She makes a fake smile.

Grandmother returns with a small box wrapped in a black silk handkerchief embroidered with Japanese writing. She delicately unwraps it, closes her eyes, speaking incantations. Asami closes her eyes too. I sip my whisky quietly. When Grandmother stops speaking, she opens her eyes, as does Asami and opens her hands theatrically like she was presenting something amazing. A small black mirrored cuboid. Small enough to keep in one hand but not small enough to put in your jeans pocket. Small enough to put in your coat pocket, no problem. Grandmother turns to me and starts reading my face again. After a long pause, she gives a big sigh, taps my shoulder twice, rubs my back and kisses me on the forehead. Just like my grandmother. She gets up, takes her whisky and returns to the living room.

"We must go," Asami says.

She puts some biscuits in the silk napkin and stuffs them into her bag. She puts the black cube in her coat pocket. I knew it would fit in there. I take a handful of biscuits too and carry on eating. I make my way to the window but Asami finds another door.

"This way. Trust me," she says.

I trust her, so I follow her. We go down a flight of creaky wooden stairs. At the bottom is a matte black wooden door. Asami tries to move it but fails.

"Here. Let me," I say chivalrously.

I barge at it with my full body but it still doesn't budge. I make an embarrassed smile but give it more force this time. Luckily it opens. I hold it open and let her go through.

"Arigato," she smiles again.

I follow after her and grab my throbbing shoulder and just smile through it.

We walk through what looks like a deserted pub. There are no tables and chairs, just an empty bar with a huge dirty mirror behind it. The floor is wooden and rotten in some places. Asami nearly trips into a hole. The space looks familiar but I suppose a lot of pubs do. As we go down some stairs, I wonder how many pubs and bars were ruined because of COVID. Asami goes to a sash window and starts to push it upwards. It needs a lot of effort so I step in to help. This was doing my shoulder no favours. Eventually, I shift it but I have to hold it while Asami squeezes through. I follow behind her or I should say, fall behind her onto the street. I hate sash windows. I quickly recover to show I'm not a complete dick.

"Let's go," she says.

I turn back and see the run-down old pub. I look at the swinging sign outside. It reads, 'Rose and Crown'.

"Where are we going now?" I say.

"Activate the Securus," Asami says.

"Activate it? How do we activate it?"

"The question. Where to activate it?" She stares into the distance.

"What do you mean?"

"A place where they wouldn't be."

"They?"

"Him."

"Him. Who's him?"

"Kukan," she says.

"That thing that was chasing after us? What is he?

"He's a demon fox," she says.

"A demon fox. Why is there a demon fox after us?"

"He wants the Securus."

"Right. Can we not just give it to him? Why do we have this Securus?"

"We must not give it away. This Securus is earned and it will solve everything in the end. It is our mission."

"What is our mission?"

"First we must activate it."

"Fine. So where are we going?"

"I was thinking. One Tree Hill, Honor Oak?" She pauses and looks at me.

"Bit far isn't it."

"Exactly, so?" She stares at me again. "Hampstead Heath?"

"You asking or telling?"

"Now I'm thinking Sky Garden."

"Okay."

"Maybe, Rooftop Bar Cinema Club?" she finally says, her eyes fixed on me.

"Ooooooooo," I said like an excited owl.

"Yes, the Cinema Club," she says with certainty.

As we walk to the station, I can't help but think: Does she actually need me? Does she even find me attractive? Come to think of it, do I find her attractive? Sure, she's beautiful, but in the last couple of hours, we haven't flirted or caught each other's eye. Now I'm starting to feel useless around her. The crow said to trust her, so I guess I'll stick around for the time being.

I'm sure this was the crow's way of setting me up for love or some kind of adventure. One will have to see how this all unfolds. It's certainly intriguing but intriguingly uncertain.

London's tube really is a marvel. It's the oldest underground railway system in the world since 1863 when it started with the Metropolitan line. Since then, it has expanded to eleven lines, handles five million passengers a day, and serves 272 stations with 250 miles of track. The longer I live here the more I seem to know. I guess we are strengthening our connection.

The first tunnels were built by the cut and cover method. They would dig a trench and then roof it over with an overhead support system. Later they built smaller, roughly circular tunnels which were dug through at a deeper level. The interesting thing here is that actually, only forty-five percent of the system is underground, the rest is on the surface.

It's been a long time since I have been on the tube. Glad I have my mask with me. It amazes me now that half of the people still don't wear them. I mean venues and public transport are the worst areas to get viruses. You know that if you can smell someone's breath then you are likely to be exposed to their germs and viruses. If someone sneezes in a carriage or even on a bus their germs or viruses can be airborne up to twenty-metres. Some people are sick and some people are pricks. Some are both. Asami wears a black silk mask. I have a standard medical-looking one which has probably got two more wears left in it. The pricks opposite us don't have any masks on and one is chewing gum thinking he's a tough guy from Grease The Musical. The guy next to me wears a mask that has a photo of big smiling teeth surrounded by big red lips on it. I guess he thinks it's funny but, although I respect him for wearing a mask, he still looks like a prick.

It's a little bit noisier this time of evening. It's not like rush hour, where people keep to themselves and don't talk. Now the alcohol is flowing, people care less about who is listening to them. To be honest, with the number of people, it's just a vacuum of murmurs and mumbling.

Thankfully people can't get signals on their mobile phones down here. I hate it when people talk so loud that you can even work out what the other person on the other end of the phone is saying. I don't give a fuck, I'm trying to read my book so please shut the fuck up. Why can't you get a signal in the tube? Security of course. If there was a phone or internet signal, it would be easy for a terrorist to activate his bomb. With London having had its fair share of attacks, it comes as no surprise that it also has the strictest surveillance system of public spaces in the world. I guess "Lady Grey" is looking after herself or she's quite the voyeur.

I have to say the tube is quick and reliable but it can be claustrophobic. I couldn't wait to get out and resurface and get some of that good old fresh London air again. I notice passengers eyeing up Asami. Men and women. She doesn't take notice or she chooses to ignore it. I imagine it's what friends or partners of famous people feel like. Invisible. It feels strange watching this around me. I'm there but I'm not there. Asami nudges me as the train arrives at Peckham Rye station. As we exit through the doors all the passengers try and get a last look at her. I catch one passenger checking her out whose expression changes to "what the fuck" when she sees I'm with her.

The Rooftop Cinema Club was exactly what it said on the tin. There were about a hundred stripy deck chairs and most importantly a bar. Lights would illuminate all along the roof edge leading to the big screen at the other end. Tonight they were playing *Cinema Paradiso*. This was one of my all-time top ten films. I can see why they are playing it, as there is one scene where Alfredo the projectionist projects the film out onto the wall of the village square. It's a beautiful moment that will be heightened for the audience watching it on the roof tonight. I stand, admiring the poster, getting misty-eyed.

"Can we..."

"No. We are not watching film," Asami interrupts. "You must activate the Securus." She takes it out of her coat pocket and hands it to me.

"What do I do?"

"You must hold it out to get best view. Like a photo. The view must be honest and true for you."

"Wait. Why am I doing this?"

"I'm keeping look. Hurry."

"But I can look and you can..."

"I like popcorn. I'm getting popcorn," she interrupts again.

"Fine," I say and walk away.

I try and get a good view for the photo. Thankfully most people are at the bar because I kind of look like a fool holding a black cube stretching out like a selfie stick. I try and get the poster and the skyline but I don't have the cinema screen in shot. I then move around some deckchairs, eyeing up angles. A man from behind the bar stares at me but Asami intercepts him and says something. Finally, I'm semi-happy with my view. I hold the Securus out and wait. Nothing. Asami is next to me, snacking on her popcorn.

"Well?"

"What's meant to happen?" I say dumbfounded.

"Activate."

"Well I don't think it's working."

"You happy?"

"Yeah," I say hesitantly.

"We must go. Not the right place."

"I mean yeah, I'm happy," I say, more confident and assertive.

"Hurry."

As I follow her, she stops dead in her tracks. I follow her eye line to the top of the bar roof. There, in an attack pose, is an animal staring at us with his illuminated blue eyes.

"Kukan. Run."

As we scarper away the demon fox launches himself from the roof. He then scrambles over some deckchairs and onto the roof ledge where he intercepts Asami. He eyes her up, so I start waving at him with the Securus. It works like a charm because he instantly gives chase.

"Run, Jack," Asami shouts.

I run around the cinema screen and take on an assault course of trestle tables, beer kegs and boxes of soft drinks until I come to the end of the roof. There are only two options of escape. Down or jump across. If I was playing a virtual game now, I would totally jump across but, standing here, adrenaline pumped, you still realise you don't get another life.

Down is risky too. Let's just say it's very precarious, as I lower myself down slowly on a cable screwed into the side of the building. Between each support section there is just enough space to get my hand behind it. What cable? I can only assume some sort of TV cable or even aerial. Whatever it is, I'm impressed by the workmanship of said cable as it is taking my weight.

I can't look down so I look up and see Kukan looking back at me. The good news is he's not following me, so I'm happy about that result. I guess his stupid paws can't grab cable. I take a sneaky peek down and realise I'm halfway to the ground. I look back up and smile at Kukan but he has gone. I continue my descent and, just as I was feeling good about myself, the cable starts to come away from the wall. Mum always said not to get full of yourself. I clench so hard that I clench my hands too.

I am now hanging forty-five degrees from the building, hoping the rest of the cable doesn't detach. I look like Harold Lloyd when he was hanging from that clock, only this time I'm not laughing. Just when I thought things couldn't get any worse, I see Kukan propel himself over to the next building. He lands on a balcony on a lower level. Quite impressive. He then backs up as far as he can go, then makes an almighty jump to a balcony on the building near me.

"Fuck," I say aloud.

I look at the building he just left and then to my building and realise that he is zigzagging all the way down. Clever bastard. I quicken my descent and this in return breaks the support brackets of my life-saving cable.

As I slide down, they snap faster and faster until my fall to the ground is as graceful as a sumo gymnast. Before I can moan about the pain, I'm on my feet. I check my pocket for the Securus and run.

I'm quite fit for my age. A doctor told me once I have the body of someone twenty years younger. I asked him 'What about my face?' He just grinned and said nothing. As I'm running down the alley I am feeling my age. I want my legs to go faster but they're at full capacity. I turn and see Kukan enter the alley and jump from wall to wall, then finally cutting off the path in front of me.

We stare at each other. I break the stare to look behind me and decide it's not worth it to run back. I look at him.

"Listen to me very carefully," he smiled. It was unsettling.

I did not expect him to speak. Okay, I spoke to a crow this morning, but I wasn't expecting a talking demon fox too. He was scary enough and now he was terrifying with his voice. It was creepy, slightly feminine and husky. I mean, now I'm not even sure he's a he. Maybe it's a she-demon. Maybe it's neither. Maybe it's a non-gender demon fox. Do demon foxes have a gender? Should I call this a non-binary fox?

"I am a Kukan. You can call me Nogitsune."

"Why do you want the Securus?"

Nogitsune smirks at me. I'm not sure how to take that reaction.

"Let's just say, it calls to me. I must obey and be loyal."

"Really. I'm not sure I believe that. How can it call you when it hasn't been activated yet?"

Nogitsune's expression changes. His attack stance relaxes. We then find ourselves circling each other and as I look to exit the alley, Nogitsune has disappeared.

I make my way back to the tube station and Asami is on the

59

platform waiting for me.

"Kukan realised it wasn't activated?" she says.

"Yeah. I told him, her. I wish I knew that before I nearly fell off the side of the building."

"Don't worry, Kukan won't be far behind. In fact, Kukan will be waiting for us. We must never give up the Securus. Remember this Jack."

"Sure. Where are we going now?"

"The Sky Bar."

They call it 'the walkie-talkie building.' You know when you were kids, one would hide and the other would try and find you and you would give clues if they were close, or maybe you would lie to amuse yourself. Hand-held radios that didn't have much range but enough to amuse you for at least an hour. Well, the building looks like those radios. The building kind of leans forward and you can easily pick it from London's skyline. At the top of this building is the Sky Bar.

It looks like something from a science fiction movie. A utopian bar blended with a dining area spaced evenly where the elitists talk shit and look down on the other classes of the city through the large floor-to-ceiling windows. In contrast to this, you have The Sky Garden happily residing next door to give the sterility some ambience. It actually works. Pair this with the stunning London skyline and you are seduced into the dream it sells. As I look out through the glass my mind wonders and, for a while, it seems at peace until…

"We sit," Asami says.

It wasn't a question and she immediately walks to a table right by the glass. She chooses a great table and I rush to pull her chair out for her.

"Arigato."

"This view is amazing," I say.

"Yes." She stares at me for a moment. I stare back waiting, as I'm sure she is trying to say something, but she then looks down at the menu. Maybe she was trying to read me. Trying to work me out. Sometimes I can't read the signs of women. I guess we are both hard to read. If we are both trying to read each other then maybe there is something. I look down at the menu and see the extortionate prices. I guess we are paying for the view. A waiter comes over.

"What can I get you guys?" he says.

Before I can decide, or rather, have more time to browse, Asami speaks.

"This, this, this and this," she says pointing to the items on the menu.

"And sir?"

"He will have, this, this, and this. And two of these."

"And to drink?"

"Red wine?" Asami says to me.

"Sure. Why not?"

"Two glasses. This." She points again to the menu.

"As you wish," says the waiter. He takes our menus and leaves. Asami looks at me curiously. I smile back nervously.

"You like it here?"

"Yes. I actually do. I feel…"

"What do you feel?" she says excitedly.

"I'm not sure." I turn my gaze away from her and ponder the horizon, looking for words.

"Jack? Mission is both of us. It's life. It's our dreams. We work together. We must do this."

"Okay?"

"No, Jack. Listen. Important. Very important. Concentrate."

"I'm trying."

"Here. Here realises your dream. Dream makes you alive. Be alive."

Two waiters arrive at our table and place the food down. Our table can't take it all so they place a makeshift table next to us and put the rest on it.

"Thank you."

"Enjoy." The waiters smile and leave.

There is a cheese board, a charcuterie board, vegetarian board, olives, wild mushrooms in breadcrumbs and mozzarella, wasabi nuts, tomato and basil bites and Japanese nuts. It's not quite the king's feast but it will do for now.

I attack the cheese board first as I'm cutting down on meat. I actually feel better for it, not just morally speaking, but healthier and not so lethargic anymore. Asami wasn't to know this but, hey, it's more meat for her.

She goes straight for the mushrooms in breadcrumbs. The way she bites into it is so erotic I can't help but stare. They are steaming hot but this doesn't deter her from carrying on with her food seduction show.

"Good," she mumbles.

I avoid the wasabi nuts as anything too hot disagrees with me, so I go for the Japanese nuts instead. As I bite into them, I wonder why I don't have these more often. I grab a larger handful.

"Jack. I like you."

I stop crunching the Japanese nuts in my mouth.

"You know this. Yes?"

"Uhuh."

I finish eating the nuts. I pick at the vegetarian board so she can speak again.

"You like me. Yes?"

"Uhuh."

"Together. We do this. Yes?"

"Sure. Yes." I wasn't sure what she was talking about. Are we going to fuck? Or is she still on about the mission?

"Trust. Everything is trust. Yes?"

"Absolutely. Yes."

"Tell me Jack. What you want?"

I adjust my position on the seat. Fuck, does she want to fuck me?

"Look, Jack. Look at this." Asami uses her hand to gesture through the window. "You feel something? You see your dream? Can you feel it?"

Shit. She doesn't want to fuck me.

"Asami. What is this mission about? I'm very confused. I don't seem to be helping at all."

"Jack. Don't say this."

"I feel like I'm just a bodyguard of sorts."

"Yes. You. My bodyguard."

"Right," I say, dejected.

"And more. Much more," she leans in and kisses me.

Okay, so it's more than just the mission. Maybe that crazy crow had this planned all along. She knew something might happen. We are going to fuck.

"First."

"Yes," I say eagerly.

"I go to ladies. You must think more, Jack. You must activate the Securus. You must. Think what I said. This is your time, Jack. Be alive." Asami smiles at me and leaves.

I sip my red wine and look out through the glass and let her words sink in. The Sky Bar is a lot busier now. It seems to

63

have come alive at this time in the evening. The view seems to be better, if that's possible. The lit-up skyline looks like a Christmas card. A cool Christmas card that doesn't have any snow in it. Okay, it just looks like a cool London skyline picture. At night. It's pretty cool.

It reminds me of two posters I had on my wall as a teenager. They were of the New York skyline at day and at night. They were quite big and took up at least one wall each. I loved them. They were very aspirational for me. It presented America as a dream. You know, when America was really great. I'm talking about the America of the eighties.

I think America was always appealing thanks to Hollywood, but it blossomed and shone in the 1984 Los Angeles Olympics. From then on, the whole world wanted to be American or live the American dream. When nations host an Olympics, it really does great things for the economy and the country as a whole. Most importantly, a sense of camaraderie, patriotism and positivity. America had it in spades after the '84 Olympics. It was a steroid injection of positivity that created huge successes, from Carl Lewis to Spielberg, Michael Jackson to Eddie Murphy, Sylvester Stallone, Tom Cruise, Michael Jordan, Whoopi Goldberg, Sigourney Weaver, Whitney Houston. I wanted to be these people or just be with these people. So much creativity and talent from one place at one time. What was not to like? I have visited New York a couple of times. The last time I was there, I stayed there for three months. It didn't let me down. As a cinephile, I was in my element. Every time I walked down a New York Street it felt like I was in a movie. I was Robert fucking de Nero walking down those streets. Pretty sure they filmed in most of the streets I walked on and some of the bars I frequented. Initially it was meant to be work experience but that was not to be and it turned into a three-month holiday. A lot happened and it will stay with me forever, but I'll save that for another time. I remember being upset when I had to leave and return to normal life again. The dream had ended but it did make me realise what I was missing. I think it took me a month to restore my balance and reboot my Englishness and remember my roots. For that I am grateful.

The younger version of me was sold a dream and I wanted to live it and be it. Slowly over the years as I grew older and maybe a bit more cynical, America lost its shine for me, but it's nice to visit and rub shoulders with her occasionally.

It's remarkable over the years since I've known London, how the city and skyline have changed. Thirty years ago, it was quite flat and unremarkable. Check out the 1980 film *The Long Good Friday* and you will see how much London has changed. Bob Hoskin's gangster character back then predicted the changes to London and Canary Wharf. Now look at it. Now it's worthy as a poster to adorn someone's wall. Maybe someone's wall in America.

I think since London's 2012 Olympics a much-needed injection was given to the British. I think every so often we need a booster to make us feel great again. Make us get rid of those pessimistic blues. Maybe take a positivity vaccine. I guess it makes us more resilient and come back harder.

It's funny when you're this high you tend to feel superior in a way. As I look out and beyond you can't help but wonder at the glories of this city. Tower Bridge, The Tower of London, The Shard, The Mayor's Building and Old Father Thames. Old and new fused together. I feel like a king looking over his kingdom. I know I don't have much money or, for that matter, a job that fulfils me but sitting here in this moment makes me feel that London can be my kingdom and it is just waiting for me. I feel like a young boy admiring the cakes through the shop window. London is putting on a stunning display and it's teasing me, begging me to come and have a taste if it thinks I'm hard enough. It's showing me that dreams are possible. That my dream is possible.

I feel a movement in my jeans and it wasn't my cock this time. The Securus was vibrating. I take it out and put it on the table. Suddenly it jumps up and two opposite sides, open in mid-air. Everything slows down.

I'm aware everyone around me has stopped. The barman's cocktail has decided to wait in the air instead of arriving in the glass. A waiter's tray of glasses is in mid-flight. A bird outside the window has stopped flying. A beam of light from outside shoots through the Securus, illuminating it and blinding me in the eyes. The Securus spins a million miles an hour anticlockwise but the beam doesn't move. As I go to grab it, my hand feels as if it's moving against a strong current. As I get a fingertip to it, everything returns to normal and the Securus falls onto the table.

The waiter's tray makes a loud crashing noise and everyone turns to look at him. I pick the Securus up and stare at it.

"I did it," I say, looking pleased with myself.

I take a sip of wine, lean back on my chair and survey the area. They have no idea what just happened. The barman carries on with his cocktail, the waiter goes to tidy up his mess and Amelie nods at me from the bar. Wait. What?

I look back and there is Amelie raising a glass at me and gesturing me to come over. This is no coincidence.

I put the Securus back in my pocket. I manoeuvre carefully to avoid knocking the food over, pick up my glass of wine and join Amelie at the bar.

"What a coincidence." She hugs me and kisses me on both cheeks.

It takes me by surprise and I realise I'm smiling.

"Yeah, isn't it. What are you doing here?"

"Work thing."

"Wow. You're pretty busy."

"Well, if you don't put the work in, you get stuck in a rut."

"I suppose. You must get to all the London hotspots at this rate?"

"Pretty much. Can't complain. There are a lot of perks." She raises her glass. "Although if I drank all the time I'd look about fifty."

"Well yeah, so what's your secret?"

"See that plant over there?"

I look to a large plant residing in the corner. It looks like a pineapple but its leaves aren't upright. Instead, they are hanging down around itself like a teenage boy's hair would if he just got out of bed with a hangover.

"Yes."

"Well let's just say, that has seen many a good night because of me."

"Right. I'm not sure that's the best way to hydrate it."

"Hey, relax. We're buddies, me and that plant. We help each other out. Ain't that right Piney."

"Piney?"

"Yeah, Piney. You like that?"

"Why not?"

She laughs. I like it when she laughs. Doesn't everyone look better when they laugh? I laugh with her. I look at her eyes and her mouth and, in that millisecond, I realise I haven't laughed in a while. It feels good. I like being around her and she's not as hard work as Asami.

Asami. I almost forgot. I look around the room frantically.

"Anything wrong?"

"Erm. I'm actually here with a friend. I'm helping her."

"That's very chivalrous."

I clock Asami walking back to the table.

"I better go."

"Me too. Another bar, another job. Hey, you going to be out late tonight?"

"Er. Maybe, I don't know yet?"

"Well call me, I'm probably still about. It will be nice to unwind with you."

She gives me two kisses again but the last one seems to linger. She smiles at me, pours the rest of the drink into Piney and leaves.

I hustle back to the table and meet Asami there.

"Where you go?"

"Oh, my glass had a crack in it."

I sit back down and continue eating. Asami stares at me. I look back at her while chomping through the last breaded mushroom.

"Sorry, did you want this?"

"Jack. The Securus?"

"Oh." I wipe my mouth with my napkin, lean back and sip my wine.

"I did it."

"Good."

"Good? It was amazing. It opened up. It got really blue and this big beam of light shone through it. It was stunning and everything slowed down."

"I'm happy, Jack."

"Actually, it was quite euphoric."

"Good."

Asami had been on my case about activating the Securus and now when I've done it she seems somewhat underwhelmed. I mean, she's not that emotive anyway, but c'mon.

"So, now what?"

"Now we must go to Hatton Garden."

"Why? You need some jewellery?"

"No, Jack. We must see the Gem Master."

"Of course. Makes sense."

"The Gem Master must value the Securus."

"Why does the Securus need to be valued?"

"What it means? What it means, means everything."

"Right."

I give up trying to understand her, it just ties me up in knots. Going with the flow seems to help me in situations like this but I can't help but think of Amelie now. She seems so much fun and less hard work and I'm wondering what I have got myself into. She pays the bill and we are on the move once again. I turn back to have one last look at the place. Stunning but they need to change the menu.

"Jack. You trust me?"

"Well, so far I have."

"What?"

"Yes. I trust you."

Asami exits with urgency and I'm close behind her, but doubt has crept in. Again, we sit on a train, this time going eastbound. Again, we sit in silence, but I can't resist more questions.

"Are we close to completing the mission? What happens after we get it valued?"

"First, the Gem Master. After, we meet the Driver. Then finally the Starmaker."

"And what about the butcher, the baker, and the candlestick maker?"

"What?"

"Nothing, just a joke. What is my name? Do I have a name?"

"Jack?"

Asami's sense of humour wasn't great, perhaps non-existent. Maybe my jokes weren't great, but just to acknowledge that it wasn't great would have created some rapport or even banter. I really think banter is so important. It's so English and yet affectionate to some extent. It can even create sparks between people. Sadly, no sparks here, but I'll hang on in there.

"I mean. Do you have a name for me? Like. The bodyguard. The protector."

Asami laughs. I'm not sure I liked her reaction. It was a little late and she laughed in the wrong place.

"I will think."

"Thanks," I turn away and roll my eyes.

"So, what do you think the Gem Master will say?"

"The Securus will tell him."

"It speaks?" I fired another joke shot.

"No Jack. It does not speak." My shot missed.

"Colour," she says obviously.

"It did change colour when I activated it."

"Show me the Securus."

I feel my jeans pocket. Nothing. I feel the other pocket. Nothing. I check all around. Nothing. Asami's eyes widen.

"Jack?"

"It's gone. Fuck, it's gone."

The train stops and we get off and stand on the platform. I

stand embarrassed. I had one job. Asami looks mad and I'm ready for her to let rip.

"Bad. Very bad Jack."

"I'm sorry. It must have fallen out of my pocket."

Asami looks at the ground. Her eyes wonder for a few seconds then she looks up at me.

"Where were you, Jack?"

"The Sky Bar."

"When I was in the bathroom. What were you doing?"

"I was getting a new glass. It had a crack in it."

"Not true."

"What?"

"Not true. Why you leave the table?"

I look past her for a moment and think there is no problem coming clean. I just thought the mere mention of Amelie might create friction or jealously.

"I saw a friend. So, I chatted to her."

"Her?"

"Yes. Amelie. I met her earlier tonight. She happened to be in the area. A coincidence."

"That is when you lost it."

There was no question mark here but it's hard to tell when Asami speaks sometimes. Was she asking a question or stating a fact?

"No. I don't know. No. Absolutely not."

"How you know Jack?"

This was definitely a question.

"I know, okay."

"How you know this woman?"

"I told you. I met her earlier this evening. She's very nice. She has nothing to do with the Securus going missing. Why would she want it?"

"Because she's Kukan."

"What?" I burst out laughing. "That's ridiculous."

"Kukan is a shape-shifter. Not ridiculous."

"Well it's not her. Why would it be her? If I didn't mention her it would not have entered your mind."

"There is no other explanation."

"Of course there is. I dropped it. I left it at the table. Someone at the bar took it off me."

"She took it off you."

"You're crazy. If Kukan is a shape-shifter it could be the waiter, the barman, it could be anyone in the Sky Bar."

"When you left table to meet her, where you put Securus?"

"In my pocket."

"Then what? Show me."

I'm holding my arms out on a train platform looking ridiculous, but at the same time I'm feeling exposed as Asami's deductions could reveal that she is right. I hug Asami and give her two kisses like Amelie did to me. I break away from the hug and look at her.

"She has the Securus, Jack."

"No. It's not true. We need to go back to the Sky Bar."

"You have her number?" Asami was annoying me now.

I knew I shouldn't have mentioned Amelie. Maybe she was jealous or felt threatened and it seemed to be clouding her judgement. All I had to do was prove her right and find the Securus.

"Fine. Yes, I do have her number."

I'm not feeling great. Losing the Securus has made me feel worse but I'm trying to fight it. When things pile up it's harder to see through the shit. Moments ago, I felt great. Your mood can really change in an instant. I've been hanging in there for a long time and I've been so resilient. You always hear stories from famous actors or writers 'I had nothing for a long time but I never gave up'. It's been a long time for me. When will it happen for me? My head hurts and I'm tired.

"Fine."

Asami is annoying me again. Hands up it was my fault about the Securus, but it's her attitude. She has not told me what this is all about. It's always on a need-to-know basis. She doesn't even seem grateful for my presence. I mean I'm doing her a favour and not once has she thanked me. Even a small thank you feels like a big hug sometimes. Now I have to redeem myself.

After five rings Amelie answers.

"Hi. It's me, Jack. Hey. You know I was thinking. That erm, we should meet up. Okay. So, when are you free? Right. Yeah. Next hour or so? Hour and a half?" Asami nods at me.

"Yeah, I can do that. I got a couple of things to do but that sounds great. So, where are you? The Andaz Hotel. Where's? Liverpool Street. Great. See you there." I hang up.

I smile back at Asami. "We're good."

"Kukan will want sex."

"What?"

"Yes. This is her plan."

"Why is this her plan?"

"She wants your secrets."

"What secrets? I don't have any secrets."

"Everyone has secrets Jack. She wants your dreams and your secrets."

"Okay."

"Not okay. You don't tell her."

"Okay. What shall I tell her?"

"Something. Anything."

"Anything?"

"Yes."

"Fine."

"Good."

"What if I did tell her?"

"Bad. Very bad. The Securus will be hers forever."

"If she asks these questions, it doesn't mean she has the Securus. We need to find the Securus."

"Yes, Jack. We will find it."

I wasn't convinced. In fact, I was thinking more about the sex part with Amelie, not the demon fox that Asami assumed. I mean, how did she arrive at this assumption?

Women's intuition and gut instincts are more on point than men's so maybe I was going to get fucked tonight. Hopefully literally and not figuratively. I do like Amelie. She's fun, she likes a drink and she loves Hitchcock. Why wasn't she the mission? I mean I won't bail on Asami but Amelie and I could work long-term I think. I'm thinking too much about this, better to just fester in the pornographic thoughts a little while longer. It's safe there for now.

"Jack," Asami raises her voice.

"Yes," I snap out of my illicit narrative.

"You have drinks. You talk. You look for Securus."

"Yes."

"I look too. I will be very near."

"Okay."

"You go here. I go here. You go there. I go there. Yes?"

"Got it."

I still wasn't sure how she was going to achieve this but we both had our roles. My role just happens to be the honey trap by the sound of things. I didn't mind that one little bit."

"No more trains. We take cab."

While I was all for a cab, my finances weren't. I check my pockets to see if a miraculous fifty-pound note lurked in there. Alas nothing to report. I think the gesture was to alert Asami of my circumstances without actually telling her, but she wasn't looking as she already hailed a cab and held the door for me to get in. I smiled at her and nervously took my seat.

I couldn't help but wonder what Asami must think of me. I feel my status in this relationship is lower than hers. It shouldn't bother me but it does. I like the fact I'm helping her and being her chivalrous protector but I feel she is the one calling the shots here. It's like I'm a "just in case". If she gets hurt, Jack is here "just in case". If she can't carry on with the mission, Jack's here "just in case". I'm a B-movie action star. If The Rock is busy, it's fine because you can call Justin Case.

I mean, you can't help wondering what people think of you. When people say it doesn't matter, it kind of does. It firmly places you in your position. If you don't care, you're either too rich and powerful to bother about people or you're just the local idiot who no one wants to be around. Once you know your position in life, you know what you can work with. You can either stay in said position or do what you can to get out of it. I am not happy in my position and a sense of dread has crept in, which has a familiar ring to it.

The way I'm talking about myself seems so narcissistic. They do say talking about it helps. Whoever they are. I mean, sometimes it's nice to be alone with your thoughts. I'm sure Empaths would agree.

EXT. HAMPSTEAD HEATH – DAY

[EMPATH sits next to his friend NARCISSIST on a bench]

NARCISSIST: Are you saying "I think" too much?

EMPATH: Maybe a little.

NARCISSIST: Well, I can think all I want. "I think, therefore I am."

EMPATH: Maybe, you're a little sensitive.

NARCISSIST: Says you? You cheeky so and so.

EMPATH: I'm just trying to help.

NARCISSIST: You're always trying to help. You need to get yourself a life.

EMPATH: That's a bit harsh.

NARCISSIST: Don't start crying, babycakes.

EMPATH: I'm not. I've got something in my eye. You never ask stuff about me. You know maybe I can relate to you. That's all.

NARCISSIST: Fine. So, what do you think?

EMPATH: About what?

NARCISSIST: What do you think about me?

EMPATH: That's it, I'm off.

One thing I constantly think about are ideas for new screenplays. Sometimes I just imagine scenes and if I like them, they just loop over and over in my head. One scene will sometimes be the chrysalis for a movie or television pilot.

Other times I'll have an ending of a movie and the beginning, then it will fester for days while I try and fill in the middle. I'll listen to music tracks while I'm on the move and I'll use them as needle drops for my own scenes. Everything played in my head in my tiny cinema screen directed by yours truly. Sometimes, only sometimes, a smidgen of doubt creeps in and the screen changes to something shitty like, "Directed by Justin Case". That's when I wake up and that's when it's El Crapo.

"Jack. You, okay?" Asami looks at me, concerned.

"Sorry, what?"

"You are far away."

"Yes. I suppose."

"You feel bad?"

"Yes, I do actually. I'm not feeling good. I feel shit. I'm not helping. I'm making things worse. I lost the Securus. I had one job."

"Jack."

"I'm useless. I'm a hindrance. I can't do anything. There's no point..."

"Stop, Jack."

I was getting misty and I could see the cab driver looking in the mirror at me. I look at my boots.

"Don't say these things, Jack. This is not true."

"I'm trying. I really am, but things aren't going right. They never seem to go right for me. I don't understand. What am I not getting?"

"This is just... how you say? A hitch?"

I nod, still looking at my boots.

"Don't think like this Jack. It will destroy you. You hear me?"

I start counting the holes of my boots where the laces go through.

"Jack. Do you listen to me?" Asami says louder.

"Yes," I look up at her.

"I need you. I can't do this without you."

"Really?"

"Yes really. We will get Securus back. Okay. Everything will be fine. You trust me?"

I nod.

"You trust me?"

"I trust you."

"Good," she leans in and kisses me slowly on the lips.

It catches me by surprise and her soft delicate touch has made my fears and anxieties disappear like magic. It was a wonderful kiss and I sit there with my mouth still open, trying to taste it all over again. I open my eyes and the cab has stopped.

"Careful, you might catch flies," the cab driver laughs.

Asami pays and we exit the cab.

I look around and see we are in an urban area. I follow closely behind Asami as we walk past some council flats. I'm a bit wary as it's not well-lit.

"Where are we going?"

"Not far. I must never bring cab to this place. It's a secret."

"Okay."

"They would not like it. They are very private people."

"Who are?"

"The Mecklesteins."

You would think I would be used to Asami's surprises but I'm not. I mean, that kiss came out of nowhere too. I still can't stop thinking about it. I mean, it was more than a sympathy kiss, right? It felt like it was. When you kiss like that it means something. Maybe she sees something in me that I can't. Although I don't know what that is. It is nice to know someone around you is supporting you. In the beginning, I felt I was supporting Asami, but now it seems she is my metaphorical crutch.

As we turn down a road, we have gone from council blocks to luxury living in seconds. Asami stops outside a house that dominates most of the street. It's a huge black cuboid house finished off with sharp edges. It looks futuristic, dystopian and totally out of place for this area. I'm not sure if we are standing at the front, back or side of the house. Asami holds her phone against the black structure and a small camera screen panel appears at head height. At first glance it looks like two spiders are crawling across the screen, but then I realise that they are a pair of eyes.

"Who would bother us at such an hour?" the eyes proclaim.

"Sorry Maestro. Forgive me. I bring gift," Asami claims.

"A gift? Where is this gift?" The eyes widen.

Asami looks at me and I look back confused. She nods for me to come over.

"We don't have a gift," I whisper.

Asami pushes me forward. The eyes come closer to the screen and examines me.

"This is the gift?"

"He is writer."

"Interesting." The eyes narrow.

"We meet the Starmaker," Asami quickly adds.

The camera screen disappears and we are left staring at a black void. I look to Asami.

"What was that about?"

Before Asami can answer, a series of bolts start to unlock consecutively. An enormous heavy door appears from the dark matter and slowly slides open. I've never seen anything more grand or ostentatious.

"It's okay, I do talking Jack."

She looked nervous but I trusted her. I mean, I have up until this point. Maybe this is where it goes horribly wrong. Maybe this is where I die. I mean it's all part of the plan, isn't it?

As we walk through the entrance of the place it is as dark as the exterior, but the more we venture in tiny spotlights on the floor illuminate one by one to guide us. It was quite friendly the way it did that.

My worries of being murdered by a serial killer quickly disappeared but returned again when I heard the faint noise of *Cliff Richard's Mistletoe and Wine*. As we moved through the darkness, we could see light flickering from a room in the distance. We entered the room and saw a lithe figure leaning against a massive fire place drinking from a flute. Cliff was bellowing the chorus once again. After coming in from the cold the roaring fire made it very warm and welcoming. The lithe figure turns and looks me up and down. He then turns to Asami and walks over and kisses her on both cheeks.

"Darling. It's been too long," he says and looks her up and down too. "You were right to come. You can't look like this for the Starmaker."

I lean in for kisses too as I didn't want to be prudish or, for that matter, be left out. The lithe gentleman's spidery eyes widen. I now notice he has a metal splint on his nose. He smiles at the corner of his mouth, waits two seconds, then kisses me carefully on both cheeks.

"Falak."

"Jack."

"Jakob. I'm starting to like him, Asami." Asami smiles back.

"Will you turn that zevel off. We don't do Christmas," says a stout-looking man with a Viking-looking beard.

He hands Asami and me a flute each. I sip it and my brain smiles for the Prosecco reward hit.

"I'm Levi," the stout man says.

I lean in for the kisses but he steps back in surprise. Falak laughs.

"He's not a kisser, darling. He's very physical but only in the bedroom," Falak laughs again and sips his Prosecco.

Levi raises his hand like a small wave. I mirror him but his eyes stay on me.

"Oh, sorry. I'm Jack."

"Maestro," Asami whispers to me.

"Maestro."

Levi smiles with approval. Now they are closer I am able to look at them more carefully, even if it's only in fire-light. Falak has obviously had a nose job and Levi, on closer inspection, clearly has had a lot more. A nudge from Asami confirms I am right or I should stop staring. This now makes me stare at Falak some more. Asami nudges me again.

"Okay, follow me. Let's get a better look at you in our studio. Come, come Jakob."

Falak presses a button under the fireplace and a huge wall slowly slides away. We follow him down the vast corridor like ducks in a row. Blue neon lights appear on the wall as we meander through a maze of passages.

"It's Jack," Levi says with assertiveness. "I'm sorry, he always does this. Forgive him."

"Don't apologise for me. Jakob is cute. He likes it, don't you?"

"Er. Yeah, it's fine."

Asami does angry eyes at me.

"Maestro. It's fine. Maestro."

"See. He worries too much. He's a big ball of stress that one."

"I'm not. You stress me out. And Jack is just being polite."

"Okay my love," Falak takes me to the side and whispers, "I'll de-stress him later."

"I heard that. I'll distress you."

"Promises, promises," he pulls me to the side again. "It's just foreplay Jakob. We can't help ourselves."

I turn to Asami and give her an awkward smile. She gives a cheeky smile back. Finally, we stop and the studio opens before us.

"Welcome to Xanadu, Jakob," Falak proudly announces.

"Please," Levi gestures with his hand to enter.

The room is powerfully lit but not too offensive. Not surgical lighting but enough to compliment you, and amazing fabric adorns the entire room. The studio must be the size of a football field, which is impossible because from the outside, the house looked half the size of that.

I couldn't work it out but the sheer scale of different coloured fabrics, suits, dresses, shirts, blouses, skirts, trousers made me lose myself as I was drawn to touch these beautiful designs one by one. There just wasn't enough time to see them all.

"I love these moments. It's like he's taking his first baby steps," says Falak excitedly.

Levi laughs.

Asami whispers in my ear. "The Mecklesteins. Master designers of the rich and famous. Design on request only. Falak is the best with men."

"I'm sure he is."

"For suits. He will make you suit."

"What do I need a suit for?" I smile through gritted teeth so the Mecklesteins can't see my distress.

"Tonight, Jack. For the Starmaker," Asami replies through gritted teeth.

"Do we have the respectable funds?" Levi smiles.

Asami produces a small credit card wallet and removes a shiny silver, metal card. It must have been heavy because when she dropped it, it made quite a noise and quite a dent in the black floor. Asami picks it up and bows as she hands it to Levi.

"So sorry, Maestro."

Levi takes the card and examines it. Falak looks on curiously.

"Asami. You work for The Company now?"

"Yes, Maestro."

"Why didn't you say?"

"Sorry, Maestro."

Levi takes out his phone and enters in the numbers he reads from the card. He enters them in and waits until the screen loads up.

"All good my love."

Levi raises his eyebrows.

"Very good. Extremely good."

"Excellent," Falak continues rummaging through the clothes and eyeing me up at the same time.

"So, what does one require, my dear?"

"A suit for Jakob."

Falak laughs at this.

"And special dress for me."

"Wonderful. Follow me, Asami."

"Remember to call him Maestro," Asami whispers to me as she leaves with Levi.

"You work out, Jacob?"

"A little. I mean, yes Maestro." Falak smiles

"When I'm finished with you, you will look like a Hollywood star with billionaire swagger."

It was very orchestral the way he moved from fabric to fabric, then was measuring me and choosing an item here and there. He was the conductor and fabric and clothes were playing to his tune. In truth he was a master in the way he put things together, matching them to my body type and skin tone. I never forgot to call him Maestro again.

Prosecco continued to flow which seemed to enhance his immersion. He really enjoyed what he was doing. This was not a job for him. This was his passion and his love. Happiness poured from him and it was infectious and we laughed so much together. I wish I could get paid for doing what I love, instead I'm struggling for what I love. Watching Falak in his element was inspiring. I want that. More than ever. After what seemed like minutes but was actually an hour and a half, the piece was complete. I stood in front of the mirror with Falak proudly standing behind. I was speechless. He was speechless.

"It's... beautiful."

"I know. You look fucking beautiful Jakob. It might be my best piece this year," he says trying to hold back tears. "It's awesome. I've never owned something so amazing."

Falak comes closer and brushes my shoulders with his hands and straightens the jacket.

"This, Jakob, is midnight ocean blue. It's the loveliest of the blues. Not many can wear it. This one is special. The fabric changes under the light, like it's reacting to the mood of the room. It has personality. It's alive, Jakob. You and the piece must be symbiotic so you will be strong together and thrive." I started to tear up too.

"Thank you, Maestro," then I hugged and kissed him.

As Falak composes himself, Levi enters.

"Oh my. Is that midnight..." Levi stops himself and admires his husband's work.

"This is your finest, my love."

Falak is properly crying now and Levi brings him into his arms.

"How does it feel, Jack?"

"It feels… it feels like a second skin that I once lost but now it has found me."

"And you must never part again," Levi adds.

"Exactly," I confirm.

"You so handsome Jack," Asami enters.

"Allow me to introduce the tsunami that is Asami."

Asami was wearing an emerald green dress that clung to her curves and yet it swung and flowed when she moved across the room. It too seemed to express symbiosis and it was mesmerising. I couldn't take my eyes off her.

"Jack?"

"He's stunned, my darling. You're beautiful," says Falak.

"Very beautiful," I say.

"I always said emerald green. Didn't I?"

"You did, my love. I love it. Now, both of you stand together so I can take a photo," Falak says ushering us together.

As we stood there, I couldn't help but inhale her perfume.

"You smell great."

"Levi made me a perfume. 'Cherry blossom', he called it."

It smelled very floral and there were notes of jasmine, sandalwood, pears and juniper. I'm sure there were others but I couldn't detect them all. It was very subtle and light and it was a definite head-turner. It complimented Asami's pheromones and they instantly started working on me.

"Beautiful. More drinks."

"We must go, Maestros."

"One for the road, Asami. One more won't kill you. Don't take our babies just yet." Asami looks at me and I frown back.

"Okay."

We make our way back to the roaring fire. Falak pours more Prosecco. To avoid spillage, I knock shoulders with Levi. In that moment I am instantly reminded of a story and I could feel myself in my element when I had to tell them about Wolf McLean.

"Who was Wolf McLean?"

"Wolf McLean was a raconteur. In fact, he was the raconteur. And he wasn't that clean, despite the name. A puddle of mud would have made a glorious bath. Dirt lived under his nails so long that creatures were paying him rent. He was a big man. Six foot ten and some left over. He had thick black hair down to his shoulders, where it would curl up at the ends. His beard was so full and dirty it had knots in it and his big blue eyes were hypnotic. Sometimes we wouldn't see him for months, even years, for he would travel, exploring the world. One stormy night he comes crashing into the pub. I was a child at the time, drinking a coke, and everyone stopped talking and turned to look at Wolf McLean. Wolf McLean throws his bag onto the floor, gets himself a pint of Guinness and a large whisky and sits by the fire.

He lights himself a cigarette and doesn't utter a single word. The longest minute goes past and finally the landlord says."

"You okay Wolf?"

Wolf McLean says nothing and drinks half of his Guinness and then a sip of whisky.

"I have something to tell you all. And you not going to like it," he says finally.

With this announcement, we all moved closer and surrounded him by the fire. I managed to quickly grab a tiny stool next to him. I could smell the alcohol, tobacco, dirt and his big leather boots. The turf from the fire smothered us as if it was hugging us from the cold storm that was outside. We were strapped in and ready to listen.

86

"I have travelled far and wide and I can tell you what I'm about to reveal is one of the hardest things I'm ever going to do."

We were all open-mouthed. We could see fear in his eyes. What could this big man be scared of? If he's scared there is no chance for any of us. What could be bigger or mightier than Wolf McLean? Everyone took a drink for their dry mouths. I sipped my coke and looked up at this scared giant.

Wolf McLean finishes his Guinness and knocks back his whisky. Before he puts the glass down, the landlord fills it again. Wolf McLean takes a large sip.

"Many years I have travelled. You all know this. Yes, it was to discover the world. Sometimes to see if there were others like me. Sometimes to see if there were other women like me."

Wolf McLean looks at me.

"Yes, there are."

My eyes widen in disbelief.

"Sometimes to see something different. But I have realised over these years that I have really been running away from myself. Running away from my secret."

The whole pub started muttering which quickly increased to a deafening noise. Fear had infected everyone.

"Quiet," shouts the landlord.

Wolf McLean necks his whisky. The Landlord eagerly fills it to the top.

"Thank you, John." Wolf McLean smokes from his cigarette. "None of you met my real family. As you know, I was brought up by your good folks around this village. For that I am very thankful."

The people in the pub murmur in agreement.

"But my past has caught up with me and there is no escape."

Wolf McLean looks out through the window.

"Out there in those mountains is where it all began. 150 years ago, to this day. Now when I say my great, great, great, great grandfather was a werewolf you're going to think I'm mad."

"You fecking bollocks," a brave man shouts out.

Wolf McLean gets up and drinks his whisky straight down and puts the glass on the mantlepiece.

He walks over to the brave man and stands over him like a big oak tree about to crush him.

"I wasn't finished. You ever heard of lupus rash?"

The brave man, who wasn't looking so brave now, was shaking with fear.

"No."

"I have. It's a rash you get over your cheeks," another man yells out.

"Exactly. You get it on your nose too. Lupus is Latin for wolf."

Wolf McLean, despite appearances, was very well read and could outsmart anyone. At least I didn't see what happened to them if they did. Wolf McLean walks away from the man, gets his glass and holds it out for the landlord to refill.

"This lupus rash got very extreme. To disguise it, he would grow his beard and his hair. I mean long. Very long. But even then, it was still obvious. Now his features were wolflike. He was ostracised from the village and he was forced to live off the land. To get by he would eat the villagers' sheep. It's all he could do. The villagers were angry so they put traps up in the mountain but it wasn't enough, so they decided to keep the sheep in the village so they could starve him out. This only brought him down from the mountain. When he found the sheep, he was ravenous. The villagers caught up with him after finding him sleeping in the field after his big feed, and that's when they formed a lynch mob."

"Then what happened?" a man pipes up.

Wolf McLean gets up and stands by the fire and he becomes very animated. "They wrapped a rope around his neck and tied his hands. They threw the rope around that tree over there," he points to the tree swaying outside in the storm. "As they were hoisting him up, he starts to struggle like a crazy beast fighting for his life. Then suddenly. He pops his left shoulder bone. CRACK! The right shoulder bone. CRACK! The rope loosens around his body. He falls to the ground and launches himself. BY HIS HANDS. He had super human strength, something he learned when trying to survive. The traps laid for him in the mountain made him adapt and transform into an exceptional, cunning, predatory beast. He launches himself at the first man and rips into his neck. He bites the ear off another man and then he disappears back into the mountains. Never seen again."

Wolf Mclean sits back down and stares into the fire, sipping his whisky.

"That's how the legend began. He became a horror story of sorts. Shepherds would pass this story on. 'Make sure the sheep are safe, we don't know WHERE the wolf may be.' WHERE the wolf was all the shepherds thought about. As time went on it was 'Werewolf'. Something to scare the children if they were naughty. But he was real." Wolf McLean looks to me and nods.

"As he hid in the mountains over the years he settled and had a family. All of them had his transforming capabilities and much more. They were bigger and better and smarter. They moved down the other side of the mountain and hid in the town as normal people keeping their secret."

Wolf McLean drinks a big gulp of whisky.

"What they didn't know is that, at some times of the month,

their transformation was uncontrollable."

"When there was a full moon?" someone shouts.

"That's just shite. It was different every month but it was always at the end of the day, and they would hike up the mountain so no one would see them." Wolf McLean finishes his liquor. The landlord refills it again.

"Anyway, many years passed and one day I'm taking a shortcut and I see this auld fella come out of a field. It was my twenty-first birthday, John."

"Ah Jesus, I remember, you drank a truckload," said the landlord.

"Ai. I did but I soon sobered up when I saw him. His face was covered in blood and he hopped over the fence like he was a wee whipper snapper. He ran at such a speed I had no time to think. He stops right in front of me and starts sniffing."

Wolf McLean leans his head down to me and starts sniffing at me. I recoil. He leans back in his chair and continues.

"I am as stiff as a board, then suddenly he takes his arm and rubs the back of my shoulder. He smiles and runs off. I did not know what that meant until the months that followed. And I have the proof for all of you tonight."

Everyone in the pub gasped and waited with bated breath. Wolf McLean looked down at me and then got up. He moved to the fireplace, drank some whisky and put it on the mantlepiece. He went over to the not-so-brave man and Wolf McLean pulled down his jumper to expose his shoulder.

"You see that bone?" "Yes," he quivered.

"That's the bone that got passed down from generation to generation. It's the one bone that no other human has. It's the only biological proof that I am part of this werewolf family. Touch it."

The not-so-brave man is reluctant.

"C'mon, touch it."

Everyone in the bar leans forward. I scramble closer to get a look. The not-so-brave man extends his finger, slowly reaching to make contact with the bone. The whole bar is breathless with anticipation.

Finally, he touches it.

"Arrrrrrrrrrrrrgghhhhhhhhhhh," Wolf Mclean lets out an almighty roar, causing not-so-brave man to drop his pint glass.

Everyone in the bar jumps back and I pass wind. I'm pretty sure I wasn't the only one.

Wolf McLean starts to laugh so loud, the rest of the bar follow his cue. It was classic Wolf McLean. The cherry on top was when not-so-brave man said, "I felt the bone. It's real."

"Oh, it's real. Every eejut has one, you bollocks."

The whole bar roared with laughter. Everyone had fun when Wolf McLean was around.

Falak and Levi loved the story, especially when I re-enacted it and made them touch my shoulder bone to make it a more immersive experience. Asami beamed with delight and I could see that her pupils had dilated. Levi disappeared for a moment and Falak put the music up. We all danced and laughed together for another hour. Levi slipped a tiny bottle into my pocket and we said our goodbyes with hugs and tears and with good memories in our hearts.

Before we enter The Andaz hotel, Asami pulls me to the side, "Give phone, Jack."

She puts her number in and makes a drop call to her phone. "You ready?"

"Are you sure about this? I mean. Do I have to do this? If you have changed your mind and you don't want me too. That's fine."

Asami looks me dead in the eyes. The main reason I said this is because I think something was happening between us. After the drinks with the Mecklesteins and all the dancing, Asami really opened up and we got quite close. Now she was back to mission mode and flicked the cold Asami switch back on. Did she feel anything for me? Sometimes I think the Securus is more important than me.

"Jack. Don't worry."

"Okay."

"Don't think Jack. Go with flow."

"Go with the flow?"

"Yes."

It wasn't what I wanted to hear. "No Jack, don't do it. You don't have to." That is what I wanted her to say. She was talking to me like a pimp does to his prostitute. Calm, nice and gentle, protecting his investment. In her case, the Securus. I'd like to know what she was getting out of this. I guess I'll find out at the end of the mission. Let's hope things don't get violent.

I gave her a fake smile and turned away.

"Jack. A Kukan will transform when it deceives, when it's vulnerable and when they fight."

I roll my eyes.

"Remember Jack, this. Don't reveal much of yourself. Let her do revealing. Have fun. Have lots of drinks. Good luck, Jack. You won't see me. I disappear."

"Great," I said and entered The Andaz.

The hotel is over 137 years old. It was originally named The Great Eastern and was one of the original London railway hotels. It's a beautiful red brick Victorian building but inside it has fused contemporary with traditional seamlessly, bringing it into the 21st century.

Once you walk through the revolving door, you walk through a massive red curtain that has been tied up for you to make your entrance. Very theatrical. It also alerts the staff to your arrival. From twenty metres away I am acknowledged with a smile and it puts me in a good mood straight away. Fuck Asami I thought, I'm going to have a good night. Let's get it on.

As you walk past reception there is a huge seating area with chairs, stools, couches, love seats, all splashed with colour. Not Pollock-style but subtle blues, reds and orange velvet that help give it a chilled-out vibe. Although it's very inviting, I don't see anybody sitting there, I expect they are either dining or drinking.

I smile back at reception and continue past and decide to follow the noise. This place had six restaurants and bars and fifteen private dining spaces. It was going to be tricky to find Amelie but I didn't want to call her as I wanted to arrive unannounced. Also, I was a little late but I was going to use this as part of my nonchalant swagger. I didn't want to appear eager. The Prosecco had more than kicked in so that helped but my hand did feel empty without a drink. I tap my pocket and realise I have the bottle Levi gave me. I remove it and read the label, 'Raconteur'. I open it and smell it.

"Wow. He did it."

I smelt leather, tobacco, whisky, sandalwood, smoke. It was Eau de Wolf McLean. I splashed some on and put the bottle back in my pocket. I was ready. I was the personification of awesome. I was liquid awesome. Every step I made, I was dripping awesomeness.

The further I walked I couldn't help but look up when I arrived in a clearing and saw the marble columns and zodiac ceiling. The conversations of people echoed around the room like crows squawking at each other. I couldn't hear what they were saying but I could recognise the upper-class tone as they tried to talk over each other. As I tried to fight my way through to the bar, there was Amelie at the end draped against it like a beautiful swan dressed in a short black dress. She looked the business. She looked disinterested as she arched her neck back, drinking her wine as a guy hopelessly tried to flirt with her. As I moved in closer, she clocked me and headed straight for me.

"You took your time," she said and grabbed my head and kissed me. She pulls away but remains close to me. My neck hairs stand on end as I feel and hear her inhale me. "You smell gorgeous. You look amazing."

"So do you."

"Is that a Mecklestein?"

"Yes, it is actually."

"So fucking hot on you. How did you…"

"A friend," I quickly interject.

"Wow. Some friend."

"She's okay."

"A she? Should I be worried?"

I pull her close and kiss her gently. I pull away and watch her eyes open.

"No," I say confidently.

"C'mon, let's go and sit down."

She takes my hand and leads me to a curtained-off private seating area. As we sit down, a couple leaves and we are left alone. It's very snug with velvet seating once again, this time adorned with many cushions. Four tables in the middle separate the identical seating on the other side of the room. The tea-light candles compliment the low lighting and ourselves.

A waitress enters the room and smiles at Amelie.

"Hey, Katarina."

Katarina is a slim Eastern European woman with feline eyes. They looked familiar but I couldn't place them. I guess she reminded me of someone I used to know. She had long dark hair, curvy attribute and cool finger tattoos. She smiles at Amelie as old lovers do.

"Can we get two Old fashioneds? Thank you, sweetie."

Katarina picks up the empty glasses from the other table and smiles back. She gives me a wink. At least I think she did, and exits.

Amelie rests her head on the palm of her hand and just stares at me. Her eyes dilate as she stares at me. I feel nervous but, at the same time, I like it.

"So, how was work?"

"Busy as usual. But you got to put the work in if you want to succeed. It's tough working for yourself but it's worth it."

"Where did you work before?

"I used to work for a company but I decided, 'Why put my heart and soul into it and line someone else's pockets?' I wasn't valued. I wasn't appreciated. When I work for myself, I get so much more out of it."

"What do you do?"

"I invest in people. I help nurture them so they shine. I connect them to other people to help achieve success. When they are happy, I'm happy. Everyone's happy."

"You charge them obviously."

"I take a commission. A percentage. I got to make a living."

"So… is it to do with film?"

"Sometimes. I'm involved in television and books too."

"That's great. Do you do screenplays?"

"Yes, I do."

"Right."

Katarina arrives with our Old fashioneds. She places them on black paper coasters on the table.

"Thank you, honey," smiles Amelie.

Katarina nods to me and exits. What was that about? There was definitely a look there. Weird.

"So, you write screenplays?"

"Yes, I do."

"TV and Film?"

"Yes."

"Which do you prefer?"

"I like both."

"TV is just as good as film now."

"I know right? How could I choose? Both are great mediums to tell a story."

"What's the feature about? Is it Hitchcockian?"

"No. I would never attempt to be like the master."

"What's it about then? You definitely have me in suspense," she laughs and sips her drink.

I didn't want to say. Asami pops in my head, reminding me not to say too much. I wasn't comfortable yet so I changed the subject.

"Have you ever played Spoof?"

"No, but it sounds interesting."

"It's normally played with more people and it's usually for a round of drinks. You have three coins. You decide whether to hold nothing, one, two or three coins in one hand for one game."

"Okay."

"You then have to guess what the other person is holding and add it to what you are holding, without giving away what you're holding."

"Right."

"Whoever gets it right. Wins. Which means, the loser pays."

"Erm. Two things."

"Go on."

"One. I don't have coins."

"Me neither."

"Who does nowadays. Two, I'm running a tab, so I'm paying anyway."

"Right. So…"

"But what about we still play and the loser has to reveal a secret?"

"Erm."

"Or they have to do a dare or forfeit?"

I don't know why I was thinking too much about this because I had played Spoof for years. It was an old pub game that had been coined (pun very much intended) in the late fifties. The beauty of Spoof was, if you won you got a free drink. In my student days this was a godsend. I have to say, it was probably my idea most of the time to play. If I was broke but wanted to get pissed it saved many a dull Friday or Saturday night. The reason it's so appealing is the amount of chances you have at winning. If you have six people playing, you have at least five chances, which is five games to try and get out and win by calling the exact number of coins in everybody's hands. If no one calls the right number, you all get to go again, so that's another chance. If you call the right number of coins, you win and you are out. The others then play until it's a one-on-one final. The loser pays. The flip side was, if you lost, it could be disastrous. One round could be hefty to the pockets. Depending how many were playing, it could clear you out and it would be game over. It was risky but I loved it and to be honest, I was really great at it. The difference here was that we were playing finals. Also, Amelie had never played before.

"You're on."

"Does it have to be coins?"

"Well, they are small and easy to hide in the hand."

Amelie picks up three pebbles she found under the tea-light candles. She shows them to me in the palm of her hand.

"Perfect," I say as I pick up three pebbles too.

"Right then." Amelie puts both her hands around her back. I can hear the pebbles crash against each other as she switches hands.

"Remember. You can hold nothing. One, two or three."

"Got it," Amelie smiles.

I put my hands behind my back and shuffle the pebbles. I pull out my fist in front of me and look at Amelie. She smiles back and takes out her fist too. We smile at each other, nervous with excitement.

"Who goes first?" I say.

"Er. You go first."

"Okay."

"No wait. Me."

"Okay."

"No. You." Amelie's excitement is tense. "Oh man it's so stressful," she nervously giggles.

"I'll go."

"Okay. Fine… three."

Three was a safe option. To call it first in the final doesn't expose you too much. The maximum number can only be six. The minimum number can only be nothing. Three was in the middle. Amelie thinks for a moment.

"Mmm. Two."

Two was good call. If she has two pebbles in her hand, she has won. I open my hand first because I called first.

"Nothing."

Amelie opens her hand, "Nothing."

I smile and she giggles.

"What does that mean?"

"When we both hold nothing, it's called 'Spoof'. If you think the total is nothing, you can call 'Spoof'. Now we have to go again because no one got it right."

"Okay. It's so tense. I love it."

"It's even better when you win."

Now the game becomes psychological warfare. It's all about trying to read your opponent and trying to deceive them. Because we both held nothing, it's quite likely we will now hold something or we could try and double bluff each other and hold the same hand again. This is too risky because it's her call first this time. If she calls Spoof on her call she tells me her hand and then I just call my hand because I'm holding something and win. It's a bold move that may be played at a later stage but not this early in the game. She pulls out her fist. I pull out mine.

"Your call."

"Right. I'm going to go… four."

I have one in my hand. However, it's about what she thinks I have in my hand. I'm thinking she thinks I have two, which means she has two. Her two plus my one makes three.

"Three," I finally say.

She opens her hand and I open mine. She has two pebbles and I have one. The game is mine.

"Oh man. I thought you had two."

"I know."

"Okay then. I'm getting this now." She peers through the curtain and catches Katarina's eye. She holds up two fingers, then pumps them twice.

"What does that mean?" I say curiously.

"Doubles. Me and Katarina have our own language."

"Do you now?"

"Yes we do," she says with a cheeky smile.

"Let's go again."

"Hang on. You need to reveal a secret."

"Oh, so I do. Let me think."

"Wow. How many do you have?"

"Many. Don't you?"

"I wouldn't say many."

"Well, we shall see, won't we."

"I guess we shall, but I'm still waiting for your first one. Your first of many." Amelie laughed. I loved her laugh it was cheeky and sexy at the same time. It was mischievous and her whole face lit up with excitement. It drew you in.

"Okay. I slept with Katarina."

"I knew it. I could see something between you too."

"It's nothing serious. We just like to fuck each other sometimes."

"Oh, so more than once?"

"Many times."

"Many?"

"Yeah. Whenever. Whatever."

"So, you're a…"

"What? Lesbian? Don't be so ignorant, Jack."

"I was just curious."

"So was I." She knocks back her drink and does her sexy laugh again.

"Sorry. I was just…"

"Being a twat?"

"Yeah. Anyway, it wasn't much of a secret, I kind of had an inkling."

"Whoa, whoa, whoa sweet child of mine. An inkling is an inkling. I revealed the truth. Actually, a secret. Plus, it's the first one. I got to build up to the juicy ones. I got to drip-feed before I administer the full dosage. Let's go again," she says as she pulls her fist out.

"Okay. Don't be upset if you lose again."

Banter was integral to the game of Spoof. This was basic banter but the night was young. Banter added another level. It wound your opponent up and it was a laugh. If there was an Olympic sport for banter, Great Britain would be gold medal champions. It is a part of who we are. We are not boasters like some nations, we tend to be a bit more reserved. We hold back a little. When it comes to banter, we do not hold back.

Many times, when I was young, I had many eventful and drunken Saturday nights. Some were so embarrassing you were scared to show your face the following day. The reason was the piss-taking or banter you would get from your friends. Friends know you very well, so they would bring everything to their arsenal. For the first hour it was relentless and then for the rest of the day there would still be remnants. By next week your antics were forgotten and by then it was someone else's turn. What did you learn from this? One. Don't be a twat on a Saturday night. Two. Despite your friends ripping into you, you amuse them and they really love you. Three. If you can survive banter from your friends, you can survive it from anyone. Four. This is a bonus lesson, which only the Brits do well, and that is self-deprecation. Sometimes when the banter gets so bad, you join in yourself.

They will not see it coming and when you add your own banter to your own misfortunes, it dissipates the banter and gets laughs and sometimes it will stop it altogether.

Now my last comment was to wind Amelie up and, also, to mess with her head.

"Loser calls," the wind-up merchant says.

"Two," she says confidently.

She thinks I have nothing. She doesn't know I'm holding one again which means she has two. Add that to mine, that's three. However, she may have one and got the right call. Going on the fact that she's a newbie, I stick with my original thought.

"Three."

She opens her hand and reveals two pebbles. I open mine and reveal one.

"Fuck," she says.

Katarina arrives with our drinks. I smile at her knowingly.

"Thanks, sweetie."

"Thank you," I say.

"Enjoy," Katarina smiles and leaves.

"Fuck sake, Jack. Could you have made it more obvious?"

"Sorry, my brain got distracted."

"I bet it did. Okay. Another one."

"Whoa, whoa. You lost. You need to reveal a secret."

"You know, now I'm thinking we should reveal secrets after someone gets to three games."

"You can't change the rules after a loss."

"Well Jack, we are going to have plenty more games so I think it's only fair. Plus, I am actually paying for said drinks here."

"That is a fair argument and I acquiesce."

"Good."

"My call."

"Who's Michael?"

She rolls her eyes and pumps her fist.

"Three."

Safe call. Damn.

"Two."

She opens her hand and reveals three pebbles. I open my empty hand.

"Yes."

"Shit. Well I guess, beginner's luck."

"I wouldn't say beginner's luck," she gulps her drink. "I would say this is just the beginning."

She won the next two games, which meant I had to reveal something. I told her, "I used to take disco dancing lessons". She cracked up immediately.

"You're joking. How many?" she says laughing.

"Probably about five or six."

"Why disco?"

"Technically it was just modern pop stuff. That's what they called it in the eighties."

"Don't you mean the seventies?"

"I guess they called it disco to make it more appealing. I dunno?"

"Were there many of you?"

"Well. Enough for a class. I'd say about twenty."

"How many were guys?"

"About two."

"Two?"

"Me and my mate. Rob Rodriguez."

"Rob Rodriguez?" she laughs louder now.

"Why are you laughing?"

"He just sounds like a porn star."

"No. Just a regular guy. He was half English, half Spanish. He had crossed eyes."

"You're making this up."

"Absolutely true. He was a great dancer but when he was partnered up with someone they got confused because they never knew where he was looking." Amelie laughs some more.

"Stop. He was my best mate. He had to wear an eye patch to correct it. They called him Pirate Rob then. Kids are so cruel." Amelie lets out a huge snort.

"Sorry, poor Rob Rodriguez. So, what did you wear when you were dancing?"

"Yeah well, the outfits were even worse."

"Oh, please tell."

"Well, we wore these grey tracksuits and these bright luminous T-shirts."

"Oh my god."

"With matching leg warmers."

Amelie starts to roar with laughter now. After she gets her breath back she sips her drink and rests her head on her hand smiling at me.

"Please tell me you did some shows?"

"No. Eventually and obviously, Rob Rodriguez dropped out."

"Oh my god, so you were the only guy left."

"Only boy left." I take a huge gulp of my drink. "I wanted to go too but my Mum insisted I stick at it to make sure it was what I really wanted to do."

"And was it? Did you really want to quit?"

"Of course I did. I was the only boy and I was terrible."

"So how many more did you have to do?"

"About three. Longest three weeks of my life. Now thinking on it, Mum probably paid them in advance so that's why I had to go."

"That is too funny. I wish I could see photos."

"Sadly, they do not exist."

Amelie starts laughing again but this time it has developed a hiss, like a bicycle tire losing air rapidly.

"Right," I pull my fist out.

"Loser calls," Amelie pulls out hers too.

Everything becomes a blur or a montage. That is what I would write in my screenplay at this stage. The drinks flow, the games get intense and more secrets are revealed. I find out that Amelie's mother died when she was a teenager. In Monaco, she stole a billionaire's car and crashed it. She saved a bag of cats from drowning and helped fire fighters put out a house fire. I told her I can't swim and when I drink far too much, I get depressed the next day. Not as interesting as her stuff but for me, it was still revealing. When Amelie loses again, she decides not to reveal and chooses a forfeit instead.

"I forgot about that option."

"Yeah, well I'm calling it in now. You know quite a few secrets from me, I have to have some mystery."

"That's fur," I slur.

"Sorry, what was that?"

"That's fair," I over emphasise the articulation.

"So, what's it going to be?"

"Erm. Tricky."

"Hurry up, I need the toilet."

"Okay then. When you go to the toilet…"

"Yes?"

"You have to go to the men's toilets."

"Fuck. Okay, I'll do it."

Amelie grabs her bag and rushes off. Her long bushy tail follows after her. I double blink and she is gone.

That was weird. I guess I'm drunker than I thought. Asami's ideas seem to be mixing with the alcohol. She will be so disappointed when we don't get the Securus. Amelie is great. She is fun, we have a lot in common, we have the same sense of humour and she can hold her drink. Fuck, she's even got the hang of Spoof.

It's nice being in this private area. I'm actually very fussy when it comes to seating in bars or restaurants. I like to be away from everybody. I don't want to be too close where I can hear their conversation or they hear mine. I don't mind window seats as long as it's not near the entrance. Nothing worse than getting fanned by the door, wafting us with the cool night air every fucking minute. This rule applies to the kitchen as well. I don't want to get knocked by waiters coming and going constantly. Finally, seating must be absofuckinglutely nowhere near the toilets. I don't want to smell urine with my meal. Just then Amelie slips through the curtain.

"How was it?"

"I didn't realise the impact of that dare till I sat in a cubicle."

"Life-changing?"

"Well I'd say, a near-death experience just from the stench alone."

"Was anybody in there?"

"Hard to say. Not sure if someone died in there or something died in them and they just left it there."

"Oh shit."

"It was awful. You men should be disgusted with yourselves."

"Don't include me in that group."

"I nearly threw up twice and this was while I was hovering. My calves got a hell of a workout."

I'm disgusted but I'm laughing that my dare put her through this. Why do we laugh at some people's misfortunes?

"Seriously."

"Sorry. It's kind of funny. I don't know why it wasn't cleaned. Usually, they have a cleaning rota."

"Well, I didn't stick around to look. I got out of there as quick as I could."

"Luckily you didn't bump into anyone."

"That didn't bother me."

"No, the shit was bad enough. Although I think me going into the ladies could be a problem."

"Yep. Someone would report you, you pervert. I guess you better not lose then."

Amelie holds her fist out. Katarina comes in with two more drinks and leaves quickly.

"How did she know?"

"I caught her, before I went to the cesspit of hell." Amelie opens her fist and picks up her drink.

"Oh, I see. Going to bluff me, were you?" Amelie realises what she did.

"Whoopsy."

"Whoopsy? Who says that?"

"I do. Got a problem?"

"Not at all. I didn't realise I was drinking with a children's TV presenter."

"Whatever." She slides up closer to me. "You know you have nice eyes."

"Thank you."

She squints at me, "It looks like you have eyeliner on."

"I don't have eyeliner on."

"I said it looks like you do. So funny. It's just your eyelashes," she carefully touches my eyelashes. It feels so delicate and intimate. It reminded me of my optician when she checks my eyes but this feels quite erotic. I can smell the whisky on her breath too. I can't help but gaze in her eyes trying to read her thoughts, but it's difficult as she, like me, is a little drunk.

"What do you want, Jack?"

"What do you mean?" I was being careful here, as all I was thinking at this point was, wanting to sleep with her.

"Don't you have a dream? Everybody has a dream."

"Oh. Of course."

"What's your dream?" She sips her drink and leans back. Her eyes are wide.

I paused and thought. Quite a sobering question or a typical drunk question.

"I guess to be happy, doing something I love and earn a good living from it."

"And what would that be for you?"

"My writing," I said in a heartbeat.

She smiled. I smiled too. I couldn't believe I said that out loud and so quickly. I guess I felt really comfortable with Amelie. It felt good. I felt good.

"Then you must keep writing and be the best that you can be."

She kisses me and I kiss her back. My bottom lip curls her top lip and we taste each other slowly and delicately as we tease each other with just a little tongue. We then break.

"Right Mister. One for the road." She shuffles her hand behind her back.

"Then what?"

"Let's see who wins firsts" She pulls her fist out.

I shuffle my hand and pull my fist out too.

"My call?"

"Who's Michael?"

I roll my eyes but I'm also chuffed to bits she threw my own joke back at me. "Right. Erm.."

"Hold on a sec."

"What?"

"Loser calls. I lost, remember. I did the shitty men's toilet. I'll never forget that. It's me to call."

"Right you are. Apologies."

"Okay. You ready?"

"Ready."

She looks right into my eyes and I give her a cheeky smile. She responds with a cheeky smile and pumps her fist.

"Spoof."

My face drops and my eyes widen. It's a brave call to call that first. It leaves one open and exposed to a crushing defeat. However, sometimes people make this call and it can be epic.

"I've got it. I've fucking got it."

Her hand is open to reveal nothing. I smile and open my hand slowly, finger by finger. I have nothing too. My smile is the face of defeat. She got it.

"Great call."

"Yes," Amelie jumps up.

"Unbelievable. How did you do that?"

"Because I'm fucking awesome."

Amelie is dancing and jumping all over the velvet seating. I didn't even see her take her shoes off. She has gorgeous toned legs and cute feet with purple painted toe nails.

"What now?"

"I claim my prize."

"Which is?"

"You," she takes my hand and we leave the private area.

The suite is a decent size. A king-size bed, thick white duvet with two big white pillows. My head will love that. There is a lamp feature which looks like a reel of cotton balancing on two knitting needles. Interesting idea but not sure I get the reference. A cosy lounge area and the usual amenities, coffee machine, surprisingly huge TV, mini bar and a bottle of 16-year-old Lagavulin.

How did she know this was my favourite whisky? Did she plan all this? I don't remember telling her or drinking it in front of her.

"Help yourself to a drink. There's some whisky on the side," she calls from the bathroom.

"Oh yeah? Great. Thanks."

"And pour me one."

"Of course," I shout back.

I sip the beautiful nectar. For me the perfect balance of peat and smoke. It's divine. I close my eyes and savour it. For a moment I transport myself to an old Scottish tavern sitting by a fire watching it snow outside.

"I'll be out in a sec."

I open my eyes, "Take your time."

I peruse the room and notice her overnight bag splayed out on a chair in the lounge area. I don't disturb it but I hover over it looking for the Securus. Nothing, just clothes and some bathroom accessories she had stolen. It's the only thing of hers in the room. Everything else in the room remains untouched or spoiled. She's obviously not staying long. I wonder how

110

often she does this in her job? Maybe this is an exception. I gulp down the rest of the whisky, then take a seat to remove my shoes. I refill my glass then plonk myself on the king-size bed. I reach for the remote control.

"Would you mind bringing me a bottle of water?" she shouts.

"Sure," I say and slide off the bed and reach for the minibar.

"There's none left."

"There should be, in my bag."

I go to her bag and have a good rummage. A perfect opportunity to check thoroughly for the Securus. No Securus here, just a fresh unopened bottle of Fiji mineral water. It felt good to have a look with her permission, so to speak, to confirm her innocence. I felt relieved. I liked being right. Sorry Asami, but I told you so.

I double tap on the bathroom door. Amelie opens it just enough to take the bottle.

"Cheers."

I sneak a peek in the mirror and I see a bushy tail again. I double-take and Amelie has closed the door. I hear things being knocked over. I hear Amelie gasping and groaning.

"Everything all right in there?"

"Can't a woman freshen up?"

"Sorry."

"I'm fine. Put some music on, will you?"

"On it," I return to the TV.

As I scrolled through various music channels, I realised I was a bit out of touch. How and when does this happen? I used to be down with the kids. Hell, I used to be one of those kids.

THE EARS: Hang on. I just need to turn it up a bit. There. You getting it?

THE BRAIN: Yeah.

THE EARS: So. What do you think?

THE BRAIN: Okay. Different.

THE EARS: Do you like it?

THE BRAIN: Mmmm.

THE EARS: That sounds like a bad Mmmm.

THE BRAIN: It is. Not feeling it.

THE EARS: That's okay. Let's try another.

THE BRAIN: Sorry.

THE EARS: Listen, it's okay.

THE BRAIN: I'm trying. I'm really trying.

THE EARS: We know you are. Don't beat yourself up about it. Just relax.

THE BRAIN: Okay.

THE EARS: Should be coming through now.

THE BRAIN: Okay. Interesting. Mmmmmm.

THE EARS: That sounds like a good Mmmmmm.

THE BRAIN: It is.

THE EARS: Can you describe it?

THE BRAIN: Ssshhh.

THE EARS: If we shush you won't hear anything. We talked about this before.

THE BRAIN: Yeah. Sorry. It's pretty good. Love the melody. Wait. Hang on a second. What the fuck? What's happening?

THE EARS: Yeah, this is nouvo pop. Pretty out there. This is the biggest song downloaded at the moment.

THE BRAIN: My God, it's awful. Just horrendous.

THE EARS: Right.

THE BRAIN: I mean it started off well, then it totally lost it.

Went way left field.

THE EARS: Nothing wrong with left field. Bowie was left field.

THE BRAIN: Bowie invented left field.

THE EARS: Yeah well, there is new stuff now. You can't keep listening to Bowie.

THE BRAIN: I'll listen to Bowie whenever I want and so will you.

THE EARS: I didn't mean that. I mean you got to listen to newer stuff. Come on, we discussed this in the last meeting.

THE BRAIN: I listened to those guys. The Weeknd guys. They're fairly recent?

THE EARS: Guy.

THE BRAIN: What?

THE EARS: He's a guy. The Weeknd is a guy.

THE BRAIN: Well, I like him.

THE EARS: You like one song.

THE BRAIN: The blinding song.

THE EARS: Blinding Lights.

THE BRAIN: Yeah. Love it. Wouldn't dance to it though.

THE EARS: Yeah, I don't think that's going to be enough.

THE BRAIN: Right. It's just most of the new stuff isn't doing it for me. You understand right?

THE EARS: I guess so. Lately, we have been hurting a bit.

THE BRAIN: So, you understand?

THE EARS: Yeah, we kind of do.

THE BRAINS: So, are we good?

THE EARS: Well, we are going to have to set up a meeting with the legs and feet. You know, to iron things out.

THE BRAIN: How do you mean?

THE EARS: Well, we have to convince them now to refrain

and hold back.

THE BRAIN: Right. Do what you have to do.

THE EARS: It's not going to be easy. We might have to do some hard negotiations.

THE BRAIN: Meaning?

THE EARS: We might have to give them weddings and special occasions.

THE BRAIN: Fuck. Really?

THE EARS: I can't see any other way. I mean they will have help.

THE BRAINS: What do you mean? Who?

THE EARS: Al.

THE BRAIN: Al who?

THE EARS: AL Cohol.

THE BRAINS: Oh right. Of course. Well then, we have a deal. Make it happen.

THE EARS: We will get right on it. It's a damn shame but I guess it's the best for everyone.

THE BRAIN: Take care down there.

THE EARS: Will do. You too.

I settled for some classical music. I tend to listen to a lot lately. I even listen to some when I'm reading as it's not intrusive. It's wonderfully emotive and powerful and I'm particularly fond of the string section. Vivaldi does it for me. As I get comfy on the king size, *Carl Orff's O Fortuna* comes on. The choir screams out the title followed by booming bass drums as Amelie emerges in matching black lingerie. My bass drum starts to boom too.

"What is this?"

"Carl Orff."

"Well, he can fuck Orff."

She takes the remote control and quickly puts on *Blinding Lights by the Weeknd*. The mood changes instantly and she climbs onto the bed and, with a feline pounce, I am hers.

She smelt amazing. I think she sprayed a bit more perfume on herself. Everywhere in fact. It was Jean Paul Gaultier. I can recognise that as if I were blind, much like I can recognise whisky blind. Underneath that was her own scent and it was intoxicating. Everyone has their own smell and hers reminded me of a full-bodied velvety red wine. I would say something like a Chateauneuf. The more I smelt it my body would react involuntarily with kisses and touches. I wanted to devour her. As she pulled off my clothes I couldn't hold back anymore and I removed her underwear and lifted her onto my head.

The surprise gasp was soon melted by a relieved moan. She got comfortable by putting her hands on the headboard and proceeded to ride my face. My tongue was inside her tasting her exquisite juices, slurping on her sweet addictive nectar. I then turned my attention to her queen of pleasure and I bowed and pledged my allegiance and reacted to her commands. I sucked her crown as a royal subject should and I didn't stop until she shook off her troubles. She was mine.

When she grabbed it, she looked at it, inhaled, and licked it. She held it loosely because she liked to see it react to her. She liked seeing it throb, move, and dance to her tune. She was in control and she could do whatever she wanted with it. I had no problem allowing her. Teasing was the game and it was unbearable. I kept looking down, breathless and eager, and she kept smiling back at me, calm and collective. When she knew she had me, her fangs appeared and her mouth widened. I gasp and that's when she engulfed me. My fear of decapitation was quickly replaced and now I could feel the whole of her wet, hot mouth around the shaft and body. It couldn't help but throb inside of her. The power she has. I am hers.

She removes it from her mouth and smiles at me. She then tugs it towards her, manoeuvres on top, and puts it inside her. She starts grinding with her tight pussy clenching my hard cock with every stroke. I feel her bushy tail tickle my balls. I double blink. I lift my head but she slaps it down and thrusts hard. We fit so well that our bodies start melting into each other. Acting and reacting. Pushing and pulling. Grinding and riding. Sucking and Kissing. Sweating and sliding. We lose ourselves in the fucking and become one passionate filthy beast.

If it was a battle, it would have been a battle of pleasure. Both trying to outfox one another and surprise each other with an orgasmic attack. The fact that we were both heavily committed to giving pleasure, and receiving it happened naturally and tenfold. We lay there tired and exhausted. We were sweaty and stinky and our bodies were drained. We didn't care, we fucked for hours and revealed our true dirty selves. It was our worst and our best and how far we would go for pleasure and for each other. It also showed that we didn't give a fuck.

I scramble around looking for some water.

"What's the matter?"

"I'm thirsty. Where's the water?"

"In the bathroom."

"Oh yeah."

I get to my feet and then I stumble over her handbag which has been knocked all over the floor. I vaguely remember that happening during the acrobatic section. As I enter the bathroom I immediately walk over Amelie's dress. I pick it up and hang it behind the door next to her bathrobe.

As hotel bathrooms go, it's not bad. Retro seventies, white

tiles. The kind they used to use in public baths. Fixtures are finished in black and silver, including the exterior of the bath. There is also a walk-in shower. The only accessories I see are a small shampoo bottle in the walk-in and her Jean Paul Gaultier perfume on the sink. On the shelf are at least four bath towels. On the window ledge is the water bottle.

For all the noise I heard when she was freshening up, there is no mess at all. I can only put it down to paranoia and too much to drink. I gulp down lots of water but before I decide to finish it, I stop and bring it to Amelie. I throw myself down onto the bed next to her. She is face-down hugging her pillow.

"Hey. Easy."

"Sorry. Here, drink this."

"My hero," she gulps until there's a little left. "Here you go," she presents the bottle to me.

"I'm good. Finish it."

"Cool." She drinks it immediately without hesitation.

"Are you hungry?"

"I ordered room service while you were in the bathroom."

"Really? I wasn't in there that long."

"Well, long enough for me to order."

"Fair enough. What did you order?"

"Everything. Eggs, avocado on toast, croissants, yogurt, everything."

"Great."

As I said that word, it lingered inside my head as I looked at her naked body. There she was, completely fucked, not a care in the world. She was great.

As I sat opposite Amelie eating breakfast, I felt happy. Watching her munch it down like a woman possessed made me smile even more. Even with bits of her hair stuck to her face she looked sexy. How does she do that? Must be a gift.

"Howse the eggs?"

"Good. You done with your croissant?"

"Please. All yours."

She takes my half-eaten croissant and scoops the rest of the eggs out of the bowl with it.

I liked her a lot. She was genuine and I loved being around her. A little bit of doom did creep in however. Asami.

There was going to be a bit of satisfaction on my part to tell her, "No Securus". I mean, all the evidence points to it not being here. Although I'm glad I went through with her plan, otherwise Amelie and I would never have happened. Still, it doesn't solve the problem of the Securus. It was my fault after all, but what do we do now? This mission was becoming a nightmare. Also, where do I find Asami? Magically, she did disappear last night. What's my exit plan? Shit.

"Shit."

"What? What's the matter?" Amelie says with her mouth full.

"Nothing. Just having a panic attack."

"About what?"

"I'm meant to be helping my friend."

"What time?"

"Er. Soon."

"Well, I'm sure they will call you when they need you. Wait, are you trying to fuck and duck?"

"What? What's fuck and duck?"

"Exactly what it says on the tin. You fuck, then you duck out as quickly as you can."

I laugh awkwardly, "Er, no."

"Then get your sweet ass back here and finish breakfast with me."

I sit back down and drink some water. Amelie necks her orange juice down and leads me back to the bed and engulfs me. I was hers.

Lying next to her, staring at the ceiling, I was happy. It's these moments that you try to hold onto. You want to stay in bliss for as long as you can. It's these moments that make you think, it's just you and this person around. No one else on earth. This is our world for now, so let's just enjoy it before it comes to an end. The sad thing is, you know it's going to end.

While Amelie is getting ready in the bathroom, I look at my phone. I have a text from Asami, which reads:

C U IN THE LOBBY.

NO SECURUS. DOWN IN FIVE. I text back.

Amelie returns from the bathroom like she's had a rejuvenating spa day. She looks immaculate and casual. Tight black jeans, greyish blue T-shirt and a navy-blue three quarter length jacket. She's got Parisian chic style to a tee.

"Wow, you look great."

"Yeah, a good shower and 'hair of the dog' will do that." She hands me the bottle of Lagavulin.

"I should take a shower first."

"Take a wee dram first," she says in her best Scottish accent. "Trust me, it will sort you out."

I knock the whisky back and then I frown and look at my suit.

"What's the matter?"

"Well, it's a shame I've got to wear the same thing again today."

"You never had a Mecklestein before, have you?"

"No. Why?"

"Get in the shower and I'll show you after." She slaps my arse and I quickly escape into the bathroom.

In the hotel lobby, I stand confidently with Amelie. I feel rich and carefree. The Mecklestein suit is a wonder and it has really come alive this morning. In the room Amelie showed with a turn and a flick how the suit makes subtle changes and enhancements. As the morning light hits it, it has turned into a much lighter blue that shimmers through movement. It's a totally different suit and I feel great. The shower and the hair of the dog helped too.

A porter knocks past me. He doesn't apologise but stares at me instead, then he goes to check out Amelie. Something very familiar about him. I look around for Asami but she is nowhere to be seen. I walk to the entrance and see that it's pissing down out there. Most people hate the rain but today it soothes me hearing the traffic drive through it like waves of an ocean.

"Hey, you," Amelie kisses me.

"Thanks for an exhausting night," I kiss her back.

"Thanks for coming," she says cheekily.

"It was a pleasure."

"The pleasure was all mine."

"It was all mine too."

"Oh shit, I left a bag behind. I have something for you." She pulls out a ticket from her pocket and starts walking to reception. Before she gets there the same porter intercepts her.

"I can get that for you, madam," he says chillingly.

"Oh, great. Thanks."

Amelie links arms with me and we walk out while another porter opens the door for us. He gives us a huge umbrella while he opens a cab for an old lady and her little dog.

"Want to meet up tonight?" I say.

"Getting a bit clingy aren't we?"

"I was just…"

"I'm kidding."

The porter waves us to the cab and we walk over to him. As we get closer the dog starts yapping ferociously at Amelie. Amelie is startled and she leaps back causing the umbrella holder to fall. I grab her hand tight and for a weird moment it feels velvety and cold. She pulls herself up to me. The old lady pulls on her dog's lead and enters the hotel.

"You okay?"

"Yeah. I'm not good with dogs."

"So, I see."

"One bit me as a kid and I've feared them ever since."

"You okay now?"

"Yeah, I'm good. Thanks, Jack."

"No probs. I can go and beat the shit out of him if you like?" I say smirking.

"I'm good honestly. Hey, give me a call, I've got a lot on but I'll try and squeeze you in."

"I bet you will."

The creepy porter appears and gives Amelie her bag. He bows with a smile and slithers behind me.

"Thank you," she says flustered, and puts the bag in behind her.

"All good?" I say for reassurance once again.

"I'm fine. You sure you don't want to share?"

"No, I'll get the next one."

The cab drives off and I wave goodbye. I feel the creepy porter waving too so I turn around. In his place is Asami and she is waving. In her other hand is the Securus. Another cab arrives and she shoves me in it.

"Where did you come from?"

"Hatton Garden," she says to the cabbie. "Mission complete," she smiles at me.

"Amelie didn't have it, where did you get it?"

"Her bag."

"Wait, what? How?"

"Ask right questions and I'll tell you right lies."

That didn't sound right at all but this was typical trying to decipher Asami.

"The bag that the porter brought back to her?"

"Yes."

"The creepy porter?"

"What is, creepy?"

I tried to sneer and narrow my eyes but this confused her even more so I stopped. Plus, my performance was making the cabbie and I for that matter uncomfortable.

"Wait. She said she had something for me. She probably meant the Securus."

"She is Kukan, Jack."

"No, it doesn't mean that at all."

"Even dog knows."

"What?"

"Dogs can smell Kukan."

"What?"

"Even umbrella stand."

"What?"

"Umbrella stand. Long way from Kukan."

"Yes."

"So, how it fall?"

"I think the little bastard dog, scared the porter and he knocked it over."

"No. It was Kukan's tail."

"You're crazy. You weren't even there."

"I saw everything."

"You were nowhere near."

"Jack. Securus is ours. No excuses. No thinking."

That was the problem. I couldn't stop thinking now. I was thinking Asami is one crazy woman but I was also wondering why the Securus was in Amelie's bag. Either she picked it up at the Sky Bar and was returning it to me or she stole it. Stealing it didn't make sense, so I decided to rest with the former.

Hatton Garden is the mecca for jewellery in London. Situated in Farringdon and more recently famous for the big Hatton Garden Heist. In April 2015, six elderly men burgled a safe deposit facility worth an estimated sixteen million pounds. Only a third was recovered.

When I first heard of this news, it was shocking and impressive. I mean, no one got hurt and it was quite an achievement. Their ages ranged from forty-eight up to seventy-six years old. That's ballsy. Also, I thought, fuck! I walked past that building on the very night of the heist. I was dying to get home and have a drink. Did I hear any drills or banging at that time of night? In London, your ears are immune to it after a while as there are always roadworks and building work going on. If I'm honest, I really didn't hear anything.

"Here. It's fine," Asami says to the cabbie.

We stand still on the pavement and Asami waits for the cab to disappear into the distance. She takes me through Bleeding Heart Yard, which is covered in cobbled stones. We walk past the Bleeding Heart Restaurant and through a wooden door leading to Ely Place. Ely Place is a cul-de-sac and I have been here before, as I recognise St. Etheldreda church tucked away up ahead. It was here where Henry the Eighth and Catherine of Aragon enjoyed a five-day feast hosted by the Bishop of Ely. Apparently, Catherine and Henry dined in separate rooms as it was the first indication that Henry was thinking of taking a new wife as Catherine hadn't provided a son.

Asami rings on the doorbell of a house to our right and returns and waits next to me. Before my very eyes, the house shifts apart from its neighbour and reveals a secret alleyway. We slowly walk through it until it becomes completely dark. Asami grabs my hand. The sound of our footsteps echo around us leaving me even more disorientated. I squeeze Asami's hand tighter and just as I'm feeling faint a big, bright light blinds us to the core.

The first thing I hear are delicate sounds, like a microwave timer going off and someone hitting a triangle. Next, all I can make out are rainbow colours on the sides of the wall. When I finally adjust my eyes, I see we are in some sort of workshop. Then, to my horror, which I would put in the bizarre box or fear zone, I see trained rats pulling tiny carts of gems. What the fuck? A dozen of them scurry along in a line and empty their carts into a pile examined by moles with massive loupes over their eyes. Have I gone mad?

"Can I help you?" a low dulcet tone asks.

I look down to where the voice came from and there, waist-high, is a giant rat.

"Jesus, fuck," I fall backward and everyone stops working and looks at me.

"We must meet Gem Master," Asami quickly says.

"What do you have?"

"A Securus." She pulls it out and shows it to the giant rat. The giant rat's eyes widen and he sniffs at the Securus and tries to get a better look. Asami pulls it back. The giant rat smiles and puts his hands together.

"Follow me."

I dust myself off and reluctantly follow. As we walk through the workshop all the beady eyes follow me, so I quicken my pace at a safe distance. We follow the giant rat up some stairs and across a catwalk. Normally this would make me chuckle but I cannot stand rats. They freak me out. They are just riddled with disease and they are everywhere. In London, they say you are no more than fifty feet away from them. I try not to think about that too much otherwise I would be a wreck. I mean, I'm usually scared of their normal size but this giant fuck is terrorising me. I can feel it every time he turns to look at me, sniffing and wheezing. What kind of hell is this?

Finally, we arrive at an office door with Hebrew writing on it. The giant rat welcomes us in. Inside is a large desk with a huge painting of a forest hanging over it and two Japanese screens on either side. One wall is completely filled with books and the other is covered with photographs of wildlife. The floor is wooden and it's divided into squares. The different shades of wood make it look like a chess board. King rat stands in the centre of the room and Asami and I flank behind him.

"Master, we have clients."

"I'm busy," the voice comes from behind the screen.

"They have a Securus, Master."

"Do they? Have you taken payment?"

"Not yet, Master."

"Then do it."

"Of course, Master." King rat opens both his palms.

Asami hands over her company card again. The rat's eyes widen and he taps it against a machine built into the wall. It beeps a strange tune.

125

"They are from the Company?" the voice sounds shocked.

"Yes, Master. Payment received, Master."

"Good. That is all. Return to the floor."

"As you wish, Master."

King rat shuts the door behind him and the Gem Master emerges from the left screen, red, bushy tail first. She waddles backward and wiggles into her chair and fixes her beady eyes onto both of us.

"Asami? Is that you?"

"Shalom aleichem."

"Aleichem shalom," the giant red squirrel replies then looks at me.

Asami gives me a look.

"Shalom aleichem," I muster.

"Aleichem shalom."

"Show me what you have."

Asami walks over and places the Securus on the desk then steps away. The giant red squirrel picks it up with both paws and brings it close to her beady eyes. She examines it thoroughly and then removes a loupe from her fur and places it over her left eye. Her teeth and lips tick and click as she continues her assessment.

"This is happening right?" I whisper to Asami.

"Ssshh."

"That's a rare red giant squirrel?"

"You need be quiet."

The red giant squirrel stops and stares at us then looks to our feet. She puts the Securus and her loupe down on the desk, jumps over it and onto the floor in front of us, and rests on her hind legs. Her head moves quickly left and right and then she scurries on all fours left and right. Finally, she stops and lifts up one square panel from the floor. She rummages inside, but retrieves nothing so she replaces the panel. She repeats this six more times until she finds a gem and then compares it with the Securus. She compares it with three other gems and then comes back to the original one again.

Squirrels always fascinated me. They have amazing eyesight, they can rotate their hind feet and they have an incredible sense of touch. Their tail is spectacular. It keeps rain and wind off. To cool off when they are hot, they pump more blood through their tail. It can act as a counterbalance when jumping and act as a parachute. They also use it to signal with. They are quite intelligent as they can work out obstacle courses to try and get to their food. We know this as Sir David Attenborough conducted this experiment and Carlsberg famously used it in one of their adverts. With all these amazing statistics why can they never remember where they buried their nuts or treasures.

"This is remarkable." The red squirrel casts her eyes over to me, then back to the Securus. "Come."

Asami and I walk closer. She brings Asami in further.

"Look here. Look at the pavilion facets." Asami looks confused.

"Here," she points. "Now look here, deep inside," she turns it, aiming it into Asami's eye.

"Beautiful."

"Look, since activation. Look how much brighter it is."

"It's getting brighter."

"Yes, it's remarkable, and it will continue to get brighter. I haven't seen anything like this in over twenty-five years."

"What you think is potential?"

"High. Very high."

I have no idea what they are talking about but it sounds good.

"You will get a good driver for this Asami."

"Who you think?"

"Schumacher. Easy."

The red squirrel hands the Securus to Asami and jumps across her desk and gets on her landline. I'm not sure what she says as she reverts to more high-pitched clicking and ticking noises.

"What's happening?"

"She get us driver. The best. Schumacher."

"Great," I nod, feigning enthusiasm.

"This is super news."

The red squirrel slams her phone down.

"It is done. You will meet her at Smithfield Market." The red squirrel rummages in all of the drawers in her desk. I watch curiously and roll my eyes. She finally retrieves a small pen-like object and throws it at Asami.

"Here. You know what to do. You have ten minutes, so you better go."

"Thank you, Master. Shalom."

"Shalom aleichem."

"Shalom," I nod.

"Shalom aleichem." The red squirrel stares at me for a moment as I edge out of her office and then finally, she nods back.

London Central Market is the largest wholesale meat market in the United Kingdom and one of the largest in Europe. To Londoners it is known as Smithfield Market and it dates back to the tenth century. There used to be jousting here, livestock grazing, and the odd execution. The most famous execution was William Wallace.

As we walk down the street, we pass Fabric nightclub then cut right across the market, which is covered by a huge canopy.

At this time of day, the traders and packers are long gone but you can still smell the meat in the air. It wafts and buries itself in your nose and gets in your throat. Very unpleasant. Once we arrive at the other side, we welcome the change of air and Asami makes us wait outside The Butchers Hook and Cleaver pub. I have fond memories of this pub, back in the day it used to be open at five in the morning. It was really for the meat traders, but for those who liked all-day and all-night sessions, this was a treasure of a find. London is notorious for closing its pubs at eleven in the evening. Nightclubs can be open until three in the morning but then what? This was London's biggest pub secret and I literally stumbled upon it. Alas, I think those days are over and it has conformed like the rest. Shame.

"Asami? Why are we doing all this? What's it all for?"

"We make Securus activate."

"I thought it was activated."

"Activate more." She closes her fist and then opens it. She repeats the action.

"We need to open it?"

"Open. Yes."

"I thought we did this."

"Yes, but open…big." She closes her fist and then opens it again.

"Like an explosion?"

"Explosion. Yes."

Again, I was confused. Why did we need to explode it now? I'm sure she was agreeing to whatever I said just to shut me up. Why the cloak and dagger? I was thinking of Amelie now, and why I'd rather be in her company. At least I know where I am when I'm with her. I decide to pursue a few more questions.

"What happens when it opens again? When it explodes?"

"Truth will reveal."

"Right," I turn my head so she couldn't see me roll my eyes. "Do you really need me for this?" I turn back to her.

"Of course. It cannot work without you."

Yeah, I'm sure, I thought. What was her angle?

"I cannot do this without you. Stop this, Jack. Stop thinking bad thoughts. I need you."

"Really? Because I think you are okay now." I look at the floor.

"Not okay now. We very close now. You must stay. Look at me. Soon, it over. Don't give up Jack."

Those words echoed inside of me. I have lived with those words for years. Recently they dropped and disappeared by the wayside but when she said it to me, they crept back up and attached themselves again. This time they had glue and they stuck to me with a hope of permanence.

"Okay," I smiled back reassuringly. "Now what do we do?"

Asami holds out her little pen and presses it to form a long red laser beam shooting out into the sky.

"We wait."

"Seriously."

I scanned the sky looking for a helicopter. I looked at where we were standing and thought there is not enough room. How the hell would it land here? I hope we don't have to climb a ladder.

Suddenly I heard a roar so I jumped off the road as I heard a vehicle was close. Then I look up. There, hovering twenty feet above is a black four-by-four SUV. It slowly lowers itself down next to us. A small blonde woman in racing glasses leans out of her window.

"Show it to me, baby," her husky voice demands.

Asami shows her the Securus. The small woman leans out and takes a closer look.

"Beautiful. Get in," she kisses Asami. "Still gorgeous baby."

Asami opens the back passenger door and enters. Before I can follow, the blonde woman interrupts.

"Not you, handsome. You ride in front with me."

I get in the front passenger seat and can't help but look at the contraption that she is strapped into. The accelerator, brake and clutch are centimetres under the steering wheel and her legs and feet fit snugly into it. She must be at least three and a half feet tall.

"I'm Schumacher."

"I'm Jack."

"Strap yourself in, Jack. We are going crazy, baby."

I strap myself in. I look behind and see Asami has strapped herself into what looks like some kind of bodice. My eyes widen and I look for some sort of gadget. Instead, I find a button and I'm strapped in by what looks like a bin liner-slash-life jacket that envelopes my torso. As Schumacher revs the engine, I find strap two. As the revs get louder I panic, looking for strap three, and just as the revs reach the crescendo, I find it. The vehicle roars and takes off at what I can only describe as nine Gs of fuck me.

My body is pinned to the seat and unable to move. I try to turn my head to see Asami but I can only muster ninety degrees, which gives me a view of Schumacher smiling through gritted teeth. She's enjoying this whereas I'm trying my best not to shit myself. I can just about make out her screaming.

"Wahoo, baby. Give it to me, baby," she turns and smiles a devilish grin.

I try and smile back but the G-force makes my lips flap like a wizard's sleeve in a hurricane. Schumacher sees this and laughs even more. I turn my head face-on to save further embarrassment and to see where we are heading. As I look through the windscreen the speed dramatically reduces and I can suddenly feel less pressure on my body and face. Normality resumes and I admire the view from London that only high flying birds experience.

"London's beautiful right?" Schumacher puts the car in neutral.

"She's gorgeous," I say in awe.

Schumacher laughs, "Yes, she is. You like, Asami?"

"I like," she says looking out her window.

"I love these moments. Time slows down up here. It's peaceful. You know it's good for your head health."

"I'm sorry?"

"Good for your head health?"

"Oh, mental health."

"Genau. Mental health. Well-being."

I didn't understand German but I knew she meant "exactly" as the syntax made sense. Her English was amazing so she must have been here a long time. You could still detect the accent and she still searched for the odd word. I didn't mean to point out her use of language, I was merely making sure I understood. She didn't take it the wrong way, thank goodness, and she welcomed the correction as it made her English better. I hate when English people do that to foreigners, you know when they have an air of superiority about them and laugh and happily correct them. It's so crass. I detest those people who expect everyone to speak English. At least have a go at another language. It shows respect and humility.

"Genau," I smile at Schumacher. She smiles back.

"Isn't it inspiring?"

"Very."

"From here, it's as if we can stroke it. Stroke it?" She looks to me and strokes the view from right to left.

"Yes. Genau." My eyes follow Schumacher's hand and then they adjust back to the city view.

"It gives you a funny feeling inside?"

"Yes."

"Like a little fire. Burning?"

"Yes."

"Let's feed that fire, Jackie baby." Schumacher pulls it out of neutral and into first gear. "Let's go, baby."

Schumacher puts her foot down and we take off again. This time our direction is down. As the speed increases, so do her gear changes. When she gets into top gear, she grips the steering wheel with both hands and her demonic grin appears once again. Even though I'm strapped in securely my fingernails dig into the sides of my seat clawing for dear life.

At the angle of descension I thought the ground coming closer would be the last image I see. I also thought the pathologists performing my autopsy would have their work cut out for them, wiping the ton of shit expelled from my arsehole. Thankfully I would be dead because the embarrassment would kill me.

Just then Schumacher pulls up and we are back on the road. I guess to blend in. I unclench my buttocks and realise I still have my dignity. We zoom down Fleet Street and through what used to be "the ring of steel". The checkpoints are old remnants when they were used to combat IRA terrorism. I remember even in the nineties a car full of my friends and I were stopped and questioned on a lunch excursion. Quite frightening as we had no idea what was happening.

This road is notorious for slowing down traffic. I have been down this road many times and if ever you use public transport, I advise you to alight and walk as it's far quicker. This does not, however, deter Schumacher. As soon as she sees traffic, the car shifts and elevates, and goes faster. The near-crashes and deaths made me avert my vision to the sights whizzing past on my left and right which gave me other thoughts and distractions. First was Ye Olde Cock Tavern famous for being one of Oliver Reed's watering holes. Next was The Old Bank of England, even during the day they had the gas flames on outside. It has a beautiful interior and it's a converted... well, the name is self-explanatory. Up on the left was Twinnings' Tea House. Amazing place with amazing different flavours of tea in a building that looks like it's squeezed by its neighbouring buildings. Then you have The Royal Courts of Justice. Many famous cases have been held here, most recently Johnny Depp's libel case. While awaiting the verdict he nipped across the road into The George and had a tipple. It's here that Schumacher swerves the vehicle and then proceeds through a red light straight past a Greggs and then takes a hard left past Pret a Manger onto Waterloo Bridge.

"Are we there yet?" I hastily ask.

"Not far now, baby."

Just then a blue four-by-four cuts in front of Schumacher. She violently presses her loud horn and in response we see the driver give her the finger.

"Oh, no you didn't, baby."

Schumacher increases her speed and manages to get alongside her tormenter. She slams into the side of his car and this enrages him more. Neither one wants to give up, steel crashes against steel and the battle is relentless.

"You want to play, baby?"

Schumacher flicks a switch and her vehicle lowers. Her assailant looks down at us in disbelief. Schumacher's SUV slams into the blue four-by-four, this time getting under his wheels. Time slows down. The blue vehicle turns ninety degrees and knocks onto Schumacher's car causing it to flip. Schumacher then drives further into it and pushes her button to raise her vehicle again. The blue four-by-four flips into the air, falling over the bridge into the Thames. Schumacher manoeuvres the vehicle so we perform a high dive into the river instead.

"Shit," I shout.

"Yeah, baby." Schumacher flicks another switch and the vehicle seems to inhale and all its body features close itself air-tight.

As we enter the water I inhale too. The vehicle enters nose-first. Time slows down again, everything goes murky as the Thames surrounds us but it doesn't penetrate the vehicle. Schumacher flicks another switch, she changes gear, and then like a trained dolphin we emerge nose-first. Normal time resumes and Schumacher puts her foot down and we glide through the Thames as any other boat would. "Fastest way around London."

Generally, I thought it was by bicycle or motorcycle but I wasn't going to argue as I just got my breath back. I look back, concerned for the other driver. Schumacher's road rage was quite brutal.

"What about the other guy? We should see if he is okay?"

"He's fine. That was Hamilton. He's another driver. We are always playing and having fun. I got him good this time, baby." I look to Asami.

"Hamilton's fine," Asami smiles reassuringly.

"You look stressed, baby. You okay?"

"Just a little hot and bothered."

"Try this," Schumacher presses a button.

I turn and see my window going down which then allows the Thames to spray all its muddy glory into my face. Schumacher laughs manically and I struggle to find a button to put the window up.

"Better?"

"Better," I manage to say through mouthfuls of shit.

"Good." Schumacher then puts the window back up. I don't know what's worse, being cooled down by the murkiest river ever or drinking it. Schumacher seems to have got a good laugh from it and I feel disputing the fact would be futile. Thankfully my suit was saved.

We drive under the Hungerford and Golden Jubilee bridges then she slows down and parks between the Tattershall Castle and Victoria Embankment.

"Here we are, baby." Schumacher pushes the steering wheel away from her and it locks itself away.

I push a button and I am released from my seat. I turn and see Schumacher getting fitted with robotic legs that make her the size of myself. If she wasn't intimidating before she definitely was now. Behold the Schumachnator. Don't fuck with the Schumachtron. Of course, I didn't say this out loud.

"Ready babies?"

"Yes," Asami quickly says.

I look confused, thinking, ready for what? Schumacher presses another button and the roof opens up and detaches itself. It hovers ever so slightly from the vehicle with a blue neon light underneath it. Schumacher slides onto it, Starsky and Hutch-style.

"What the fuck?" I say, thinking there is no way I'm doing that.

Schumacher brings the hover roof down to a level where Asami and I can get onto it easier. With a little awkwardness, we manage it and we hold on to the grip handles that appear for safety.

Schumacher stands tall and proud and guides the roof over to dry land. The hover roof lands at street level and we alight.

"We walk from here, babies."

The roof hovers back and returns to its home and the vehicle locks itself with a recording of Schumacher's voice, "Yeah baby." Schumacher sees my surprise.

"I know. Great isn't it, baby."

I nod and fake my appreciation.

We walk to the end of Horse Guards Avenue and arrive at the Horse Guards Parade on Whitehall. On the corner on the left is a large banqueting house where even the security are dressed in tuxedos. Even though I was in a Mecklestein I felt under-dressed.

Schumacher wasn't dressed right either especially in her Robocop outfit. Schumacher takes us both to the side.

"Okay, babies. This event is packed tonight. It's going to take time to work the room. Time is not on our side. I suggest we go for the biggest fish or the hungriest fish. Yes?"

"Yes," Asami agrees.

"Erm. For what?" I add.

"Is he drunk?"

"He fine."

"Good. This is the plan. You stand at the bar and look handsome."

"I can help. I can do something."

"Ah. He's so cute," Schumacher pinches my cheeks.

"I'm here to help."

"You will be standing at the bar, baby. Everyone will see you on display. Your looks will deter people to not fuck with us. They won't disrespect us. They will show respect baby."

"Oh, right. Got it."

I had to agree. In my younger days, I was quite the catch but as I got older, I got more rough looking.

It's something you notice gradually. Little lines there, some extra wrinkles, and less hair. Then finally they add themselves altogether and you're a new you. Happens to all of us. You remember when you were young walking down the street and getting wolf whistles.

It does eventually stop but no one tells us when it's the last time, which is really unfair and cruel. I wish we could have had one last whistle to see us on our way. "You had a good run, take care now." Obviously, I didn't get wolf whistles, chance would have been a fine thing but I'm trying to illustrate a point. I'm just saying it was nice to get checked out sometimes. However, everything happens for a reason. Now at middle age I get looks like I'm about to start a fight or steal a handbag. The beauty of this is that people don't bother me anymore, which is all the better for me. I like being left alone. So, if my looks help deter people not to fuck with me, I welcome it with open arms.

"Just one thing. I don't think we are dressed appropriately."

"This is a Mecklestein, no?"

"No. I mean yes."

Schumacher pulls the collars of my suit and tugs at the back behind my neck. My suit turns very dark and a bow tie emerges and ties itself.

"One Mecklestein tuxedo at your service."

"Wow."

"It's your first one, huh baby?"

"Yes," I say brushing down the suit and adjusting my tie like I am James Bond.

"A Mecklestein is a suit for life."

Schumacher flicks a switch on her legs and her Robocop outfit transforms into a Robotux.

"How'd you like me now, baby?"

"Perfect," Asami chimes in quickly.

I was stunned and to be honest I didn't know what to say. I was still wondering whether security would let us in with this crazy Roboracer. I guess we would find out.

Schumacher links arms with Asami and I trail behind. All worries disappeared immediately when they greeted Schumacher by her name. I followed close behind as we all walked down the corridor greeted by waiters handing out glasses of Champagne.

I didn't realise until I sipped it and so I returned it to the next waiter further down the corridor. Once we got to the end it opened up into a massive room at least three floors high, floor to ceiling. The floor was polished oak and the ceiling was adorned with paintings from The Renaissance period. The lighting helped highlight the gold trimmings and made the room scream opulent. Everyone in the room was scattered in circular groups and would cast a discerning eye on the new people who entered. At that precise moment, it was me. I quickly ignored their glances and made my way to the other side of the room to the bar.

The bar was V-shaped but inverted and took up the width of the room. Behind it, hanging from the next floor was a giant bouquet of flowers. Well, it looked like that to me.

Anyway, it was rather ostentatious. The staff were appearing and disappearing through it like worker bees gathering honey. Enough was enough, it was time for me to get some nectar to numb this pretentious vibe and put my resting bastard face on display.

The barman tries to hand me another Champagne.

"Whisky?"

"We only have Johnny Walker, sir."

"What kind?"

"Er," the barman fumbles behind the bar.

"If it's red or green, you can drop it to the floor. If it's blue or black then give me some more."

I didn't mean to rhyme, I meant exactly what I said, but the barman laughed all the same.

"It's black."

"Fine. A large one please. Actually, make it a very large one."

"Of course, sir. Ice?"

"Three cubes if they are large, if not four to five."

"Absolutely sir." He hands me my drink.

"Will there be anything else?"

"Just don't forget about me."

"Impossible sir."

"Cheers." I raise my glass to him and sip the beautiful, extra-large blend.

"That's the stuff," I exhale and lean against the bar.

It's probably the first time I actually feel important to the mission. Schumacher maybe a crazy, mad, road rager but she made me feel worthy. Asami at times has made me feel like a third wheel, but Schumacher right away saw my strength and is capitalising on it. All I had to do was just be me. I look around for both of them but they have melted into the crowd or the crowd has melted into them.

This crowd. This Champagne crowd with their laughter and bodies hunched over their flutes. I can't help but mirror their disdain for me when I entered their room. I mean, the room. See, I instantly felt I was entering their room. I wish I wasn't prejudiced towards them but there is no getting away from class. It's in my working-class programming to dislike them. Besides, they dislike me. I mean, what is to like about them? These silver spooners, these hoorah henrys, these polo pricks.

"It's all about breeding, darling." That's what the female of their species say. They say it without opening their mouth. They say it through gritted teeth. I bet oral sex with them is impossible or a myth. They know nothing of breeding, like they know nothing about mortgages and bills. Have you ever watched them flirting? Their mating game is so bad.

INT. CHELSEA BAR - NIGHT

[A slim blonde woman stands at the bar. This is VERITY. A tall floppy-haired gentleman arrives next to her. This is GILES.]

VERITY: Giles?

GILES: Verity? You look well.

VERITY: Thank you. You look well. Too.

GILES: So, you er, still with Will?

VERITY: No. Turned out he was sleeping with my sister's friend's cousin's nanny.

GILES: Oh god, so sorry.

VERITY: It's fine. She's an absolute pig and peasant. I actually feel sorry for him.

GILES: Shame.

VERITY: And how is Constance, your fiancé?

GILES: Alas, she is my fiancé no more.

VERITY: Oh, no. What on earth happened?

GILES: She ran off with her second cousin. An Earl.

VERITY: Seems to be a thing. My cousin did the same thing.

GILES: Oh really?

VERITY: Yes. And he's an Earl too.

GILES: Earl of?

VERITY Mulgrave?

GILES: Mulgrave yes. Ah right.

VERITY: Shame. Shall we have a drink?

INT. VERITY'S BEDROOM – NIGHT

[Two hours later.]

VERITY: So, erm, I will take this off then? [Verity starts to undress.]

GILES: Erm, allow me.

VERITY: Well, if you insist.

[Giles helps and Verity's dress falls to the floor.]

GILES: There.

VERITY: You want me to, er?

GILES: No, no it's fine. I can take this off.

[Giles removes his trousers. Verity raises her eyebrows and looks at him wearing his shirt. Giles reads her face, removes his shirt and throws it on the floor. Giles is still wearing his socks.]

GILES: Shall we adjourn to the bed?

VERITY: Actually, I was thinking against my vanity desk. You know, be a bit adventurous.

GILES: Right. Jolly good.

VERITY: It's an antique. Been in the family for a while.

GILES: Right. My mother has something similar.

VERITY: She obviously has good taste.

GILES: Quite.

[Verity positions herself but sees Giles struggling somehow.]
VERITY: Everything, all right?
GILES: Erm. Slight hitch.
VERITY: Whatever's wrong?
GILES: Think it was all that chat about my mother.
VERITY: Oh dear. Another drink maybe?
GILES: Jolly good.

Have you ever heard them swear? They pronounce the entire word, as well as the end consonants, which gives no power to the curse word when delivered. Have you ever heard them say "mate" when they are being jovial? It doesn't sound right. They took that from us. Go back to chap and fellow, you entitled cunts. They are so awkward I'm amazed any breeding occurs at all. They are socially inept, yet money and alcohol helps, to some extent, to their survival.

After that inner monologue rant, I was definitely in character. I placed my empty glass on the bar and my friendly barman pours me another of the same. Good man. I raise my glass to him once again.

I look out into the crowd and I spy Schumacher talking with a well-dressed slim chap with tiny glasses and a white Panama hat. He points to me and double takes and then talks back to Schumacher. Schumacher gives a slow nod and Panama guy looks slowly back to me. I think it's working. I give a working-class sniff and scratch my nose to add more character. Scratching my balls would have been too obvious. Fuck, now thinking about it, my balls do need a scratch. I'll wait till he turns away first. Waiting. Waiting. Still waiting. C'mon you fuck. Fuck my balls need a scratch. C'mon.

"Turn, you fuck."

"I'm sorry sir," the barman says.

"Not you."

Panama guy turns and Schumacher continues to work the room. I turn to the bar and furiously scratch my bollocks.

"Everything okay, sir?"

"Magic. Fucking magic." I turn and resume my lean against the bar.

As I scan the crowd, I see Asami staring at me with her mouth open. We stare at each other for a moment, then I raise my bollock scratching hand and wave at her and smile. I sip my whisky and when I look up, she is gone.

I'm not surprised Asami was shocked, as she is that type of woman. Amelie would have laughed. I actually can't wait to tell her about this after I confront her about the Securus. I'm sure there is a perfect explanation.

Twenty years ago, a place like this would have intimidated me but now at my age I don't care. I don't let people or situations bother me anymore. I have a right to be here as much as anyone else, despite my class. I can walk amongst these people and share the same space. They are not superior to me. I'm just as smart and intelligent and savvy. The only difference between us is the wealth, and that makes money the thing that bothers me most. I don't have any and that bothers me. Thankfully the bar is free tonight but that's due to Asami and Schumacher's connection to the event. Money gives you freedom and happiness. I don't have either and that bothers me even more. I raise my empty glass, then place it on the bar and realise my friendly barman has already poured me another. I like this guy.

As I take a large gulp my eyesight is drawn to the upper balconies. More upper-class twats with flutes mutter and splutter. My eyes scan along the left row of people stretching to the front of the room and, like a Mexican wave, their heads turn. My eyes follow them all the way to the back as they swivel one by one looking back at me. The last person that looks down and smiles at me is Schumacher.

Asami taps my shoulder.

"Ready?"

"Nearly. How did it go?" I say distracted.

"Good."

"Good. I'm glad." I look back up and Schumacher is gone. So are the strange looks.

"You okay, Jack."

"Yes, I'm fine." I take a large gulp of my whisky.

"You drunk Jack."

"No. I'm just getting warmed up." I lean into Asami's ear. "It's my character."

"Right," she whispers back.

I neck the last of my whisky and the barman starts to pour another.

"No. We go now," she says to the friendly barman.

"Of course, madam."

Schumacher arrives at the bar and grabs both of our shoulders.

"Asami. How was it?"

"Amazing."

"Super. Me too. Jack you were great. They loved you."

"I'm very happy," I look and smile at Asami.

"Super babies. Let's move on because it's time to groove on."

"Hear the drummer, get wicked."

"What?"

"He little drunk. I think."

"Really, it's only been half hour. Did you have some drinky poos, Jack?"

"Just a couple of drinky poos, Schu."

"You are funny Jack. And I am not a Shoe. Shoe goes on your foot," she laughs out loud.

I laugh out loud too.

"You like that one, baby. C'mon, let's get you out of here. The night awaits."

Back in the car, Schumacher stays on the water and drives further down the Thames. We pass the RAF memorial and the Thames River boat pier, then past the Statue of Boudicca and then under Westminster Bridge. Within two minutes we are at The Houses of Parliament. Riverside obviously. Schumacher parks up and the roof transports us close to Black Rod's Garden. Within seconds armed security stops us.

"Passes and identification please."

Schumacher stares at them, "They are with me."

"I still need your passes."

Schumacher sighs. She raises her palms and gestures them in a passing motion. "You may go through, it's fine."

"You may go through, it's fine," the security guard echoes and gestures with his gun for us to pass.

"Thank you," Schumacher nods and walks by. We quickly follow behind and pass the guards.

"Thank, you," the security guard emphasises the last word to really show his thanks personally.

We walk through a courtyard which is a closed section, hidden form the rest of Parliament. The Gothic structure and the fact that it's dark make it eery and spooky.

"That was amazing."

"Sometimes Jack, things happen quickly when you do things

calm and slowly."

I laughed out loud, considering she nearly killed us with her driving on the way here.

"You okay, baby?"

"Yes." I quickly compose myself. "It was very effective."

"Genau."

"Are you a Jedi?"

"What's a Jedi baby?"

"Never mind," I realised I was a little drunk because I was getting a little bit cheeky.

We enter a building crammed in the right corner of the courtyard. We walk through a narrow corridor and arrive at the main reception.

Schumacher takes advantage of the absent receptionist and quickly lifts three identity cards and hangs them around our necks.

"Same rules as before babies. Jack make yourself look pretty at the bar. Maybe just a small drinky poos. Okay baby?"

"Okay baby," I smile back, trying to keep it together.

"One more thing. When someone comes to talk to you, say 'Is there a problem?'. It gives it more character baby."

"Sure."

"Say it, baby."

"Is there a problem?"

"No, baby. With feeling. Like a gangster."

I cough to clear my throat and find my inner Ray Winstone.

"Is there a problem?"

"Super. Let's go, Asami."

"We not allowed here," she looks at her identity card.

"Sometimes Asami, you have to fuck them all and go for it, baby."

While Asami and Schumacher merge into the crowd I walk through to a conservatory where it looks like it's set up for a wedding reception. My nose tingles so this must be the way. The way the tables snake around the room leads me straight to the bar. Good old nose, it never fails me.

I raise my hand to get the barman's attention. He cleans a glass and looks me right in the eye.

"Double gin, one slice of lime, ice and slim tonic?"

"I'm sorry."

"Your drink sir?"

"Absolutely not. It's a…"

"Very large Johnny Walker. Three large cubes of ice."

"Yes," I'm shocked.

I take a look at him closely and see that he looks exactly like the barman from the banqueting house.

"Aren't you the guy from earlier?"

"From earlier sir?"

"Yes, you served me earlier."

"I'm sorry sir. I serve many people."

"How did you know my order?"

"Well, on the second try I got it. Apologies sir, it's the face and name. They didn't match up. I'm sorry, Mr. Ahmed."

"Mr. Ahmed?"

The barman points to my identity card around my neck. I look at it and rip it off and discard it.

"A mix-up with the cards."

"Right, sir. Apologies once again. Your drink," he places the drink in front of me.

I raise my glass to him and take a sip, "Still, how did you know my drink?"

"Ah, we are all connected. We are like one big network, sir.

We recognise, record, pass on the data and deliver."

"Mmmm. Interesting." I was impressed but at the same time a little violated.

I take my drink and end up outside. I lean against the stone wall looking at the river and Westminster Bridge. Clouds of steam rise from the water and I can see my own breath. I drink a large mouthful of whisky to warm me up. It does the trick momentarily. Standing here you can't help but think how many important decisions have been made here. Also, how many bad decisions have been made here. I guess the obvious one is Brexit.

INT. HOUSE OF COMMONS - DAY

[A fly sits on the wall of The House of Commons. This is RONNIE. Another fly lands neatly beside him. This is REGGIE.]

RONNIE: Allo, Reg. What are you doin 'ere?

REGGIE: Fly-by Tony said there were mountains of shit in 'ere. Plenty of it, he said.

RON: He weren't wrong.

REG: Whatdoya mean? All I can see are bloody politicians. Oh, wait a minute. Is this a windup?

RON: Technically yes, but you got to listen to this shit. It's incredible.

REG: Go on then. What's 'appning?

RON: Well, it's the post-Brexit debate.

REG: Oh, Ron I don't know if I want to 'ere about this. I'm trying to forget it.

RON: You gotta listen to this. So, matey over there pledged the money we would save, leaving the EU. They could pump that into the NHS.

REG: Right. How much?

RON: 350 million a week.

REG: Seems fair.

RON: They didn't though. They only gave 100 million in 2019 and 170 million for 2020 and 2021. Only because of COVID, they decided to increase funding.

REG: Bloody crooks.

RON: I know. Also, that other fella over there. He said London banks would have to decamp to Frankfurt, Germany. Which is ludicrous, Reg. We know the European Union didn't create existing financial relationships. Britain's financial role goes back two centuries. Europeans need a financial centre in London. Europe doesn't want a trade war.

REG: Makes me sick, Ron. So much so, I want to eat it all up again and be sick again.

RON: Then that smug bloke over there.

REG: Oh yeah, that prat.

RON: He started the immigration row. Saying immigrants arriving in the UK weren't controlled properly by the European Union. And that made the media present it in a way that turned overly patriotic and racist.

REG: What they fail to acknowledge Ron, is that these immigrants looking for work were actually taking jobs Britons didn't want to do.

RON: Exactly, Reg.

REG: Sad state of affairs.

RON: Certainly was, Reg. The campaign was a technique politicians have used over and over and will continue to do many times over.

REG: You mean lying, Ron?

RON: Well, of course that, Reg. What I mean is, Fearmongering.

REG: Oh yeah, without question.

RON: Reg. I'm sick to my stomach.

REG: Don't waste it, Ron.

RON: Figure of speech, Reg. It's just all so disappointing.

REG: They've let you down. They've let me down. But more importantly, they've let the country down.

RON: Yes, they 'ave, Reg. They really 'ave.

REG: I can't handle this shit. I'm off.

RON: Where you going?

REG: To the hospital. Fly-by said there was shit there too.

RON: Sounds like a plan. Wait for me.

It just got so nationalistic and ugly. No one wanted to belong anymore, they wanted to be on their own. What happened to "...and the world can be as one?" John Lennon would be turning in his grave. Especially as I misquoted him.

Thankfully sixty percent of London voted for remain, but if I'm honest it should have been more. This melting pot of culture opens a Londoner's eyes to so much diversity and love for one another it should have been one hundred percent. The rest of the country were out of touch and they don't see what we see. The media didn't help and they had their own agendas. You can blame The Sun, The Mail and The Daily Telegraph, they riled the public into a frenzy. I think, generally speaking, most felt duped. Since talking to many "out of towners" after the result, many feel they were tricked. Maybe in London we are used to being tricked, so we become more cunning and curious for ourselves.

I look up at the Gothic spires and how their dark shadows loom down on me, the angry common man. I wonder, maybe one day a Prime Minister will arrive and tell things honestly and actually give hope and prosperity to our country. Will it happen in my lifetime? I thought I would see flying cars by now too. I hope I do soon.

I return to the bar to fetch another drink. Schumacher stands with a slim gentleman, with outrageously large black bifocal glasses. He also wears what can only be described as a zebra suit. To heighten this display of ostentation he wears a dark purple shirt with huge frilly cuffs that he must sway whenever he talks.

"Ah, there he is. Jack, let me introduce you to Hay Zee."

I stand for a moment and I look at the upright zebra and then I turn to Schumacher. Schumacher does a secret wink. I turn to the zebra.

"Is there a problem, Hazy?" I said in my best Ray Winstone. Hay Zee nearly chokes on his Champagne.

"Er, no. Not one bit." He turns to Schumacher. "Oh, he's such a darling. Isn't he wonderful? Who knew? I can see the headlines now. What shall we call him? How about Mr. London?"

I liked the sound of that and raised my eyebrows. He links arms with Schumacher and leads her away. My face turns to confusion but Schumacher turns and winks back to me and I am reassured again.

This continues for the next hour. Winks and Ray Winstone work in unison to get the desired reaction. I got so confident I mixed it up a little.

"Is this bloke bothering you?"

"No. It's fine. Honestly," Asami replies.

"If he is, I can sort it. You know the London way," I nod in the direction of the Thames.

Asami took the gentleman away as he looked rattled. I, on the other hand, was elated that I got to say my line. That's when my phone rang. I try to make out the name but either the drink or my eyesight is worsening. I hold the phone further away to try and read it. I quickly gave up and answered it.

"Is there a problem?"

"I'm sorry. Is this Jack?" says a startled Amelie.

"Oh hey. Sorry I was in Ray Winstone mode."

"Why are you in Ray Winstone mode?"

"Just a thing."

"Are you playing hard to get? Because you're doing a great job."

"No. No way. Sorry, I've just been a little busy."

"Well, you've found time to drink."

"Well, you can find time if you really want to."

"So, you still want to meet up?"

"Yes, of course."

"Well, I've got a few loose ends at The Savoy. How about you meet me there?"

"Er, yeah. Just…"

"What? What's wrong?"

"I'm just not sure what time I can get there."

"I'm here a while. Text me when you're on route."

"Okay, that sounds great."

"And Jack. Don't drink too much. I want you in good condition. I'll be the one who puts you in a bad condition, okay?"

"I'll be there." That last statement quickened my reply.

"You fucking better." She ends the call.

I walk with Asami back to the car.

"What you always wanted to do Jack?" Asami walks closer

with me.

"I don't know." I look out towards the river.

"Look to me. You know Jack."

"I…"

"Say Jack."

"To write. I want to write."

Asami squeezes my hands and smiles.

"But I don't know if I'm good enough."

"Wise friend say. You must have faith."

"Oh God, no."

"No, not God."

"Faith. It's just a magical word. It's make-believe."

"Okay. Wait. Wise friend say." I rolled my eyes.

"Wise friend say, 'Fuck them all. Go for it, baby.'"

I smiled at her and Asami smiled back. I started laughing and she laughed with me. She then pulled me into her and kissed me with purpose. Her lips were like soft small pillows of yumminess. It was hard not to reciprocate. They tasted sweet like marshmallows and when she slipped me her tongue it was like a serpent dressed in honey, slow dancing inside my mouth. I had to grab onto her in case I fell backwards but then she broke away. I opened my eyes and stood there in a daze.

"We go to Savoy. Schumacher waiting."

"Er. Yes. We go." I snap out of it.

She upped her pace along the river and I followed like a school boy with a crush. What the fuck, Asami? What are you doing to me? I don't need this now. But I didn't say what was going through my head. I was worried about The Savoy and my part.

"Wait. I still need to know what's happening and what I have to do?"

"You fine Jack. Do not worry."

154

"Asami. I am worried. I'm fucking worried." Asami stops and walks back to me.

"Your talent is strong. Securus says this. It's bright. So very bright. You are the bright Jack."

"I am the bright? It doesn't make sense."

"Talent. Bright. You. Talent." She grabs the back of my head with her hands, "Beautiful." She outlines my eyebrows with her left hand, "Talent." Her hands caress the top of my head. "Sunshine." She then rests them over my heart. My breathing slowed down and the stress slipped off me. I stood there relaxed like I was in a warm bath. I could feel the heat inside me pulsate through every bone. I felt super human. I felt awesome.

"I can do this."

"Hai."

"What happens at The Savoy?"

"Big dinner. Then," she closes her fist and opens it again.

This all makes sense now. I was the one being protected after all. Asami wasn't in some crisis. It was me. Do I have it written all over my face? Am I in a crisis? I mean I haven't been right for a while, but would I call it a crisis? I mean, the writing has plagued me for a while but only because no one is reading it. A writer not read or heard is a dustman of words. He just collects it and throws it away. You can't blame me for feeling down about that. I guess what keeps me going is the love I have for it. I love the idea I can pull something out of thin air and create something. I love how it makes me feel and I guess that has kept me alive. I start to feel dizzy.

"Jack. You, okay?"

The world around me starts to shake and my eyes roll into the back of my head. I try to roll them back to the front. I hear Asami's voice but it sounds like it's coming from a long narrow tunnel.

"Jack. Stay with me."

I feel myself falling so I stretch out my hands for help. I see Asami grab them and she yanks me hard and pulls me back into reality. She looks me dead in the eyes.

"You back Jack."

"I'm back." I pull her into me and hug her tight. She hugs me tight back.

I needed that hug. It's only when you don't have one for so long that you really miss it. It may have only been twenty seconds but it was long enough. It felt great.

As we got closer to Schumacher's vehicle, I couldn't help but wonder if there was a chance that my writing had purpose. Not only that, Asami was going to help me. If she can get someone to represent me and get my work read, all my dreams will come true. My dreams weren't extravagant either but for a while they seemed far away. Unreachable.

A girlfriend gave me Syd Field's book on screenwriting and on the inside she inscribed 'Because there's more to life than wage slavery'. Only now does it ring true. To be happy doing something you love is the sole purpose of life. This was my chance and I can't fuck it up. I had purpose again.

"Shit."

"Jack? You okay?"

I wasn't okay. Amelie popped into my head and now we were going to The Savoy, where she will be.

"Tell me Jack."

I like Amelie a lot but Asami put a spanner in the works with that kiss.

"Why did you kiss me?"

"I took the moment."

"Why?"

"You are bright Jack. I mean, your talent. You are sunshine, Jack," she smiles.

No "I like you", I guess this was the language barrier again? I wasn't satisfied. If anything, now she made me feel like a piece of meat. Like it was all for her job.

"So, it was for the job? So, I won't go with anyone else? You're trying to seduce me for your own gains?"

I walk off and Schumacher opens the front passenger door for me.

"Jack!"

I return a dirty look, get in the vehicle, and shut the door. Asami tries to open the back passenger door but it's locked so she looks at Schumacher.

"I got this, baby. See you at The Savoy. I'll talk to him." Schumacher drives across the river and swiftly takes to the air, just missing Westminster Bridge. I strap in safely post-haste. Asami is left standing on the embankment, stunned and disappointed.

"You know, baby, she can help you," she says, still driving the vehicle forty-five degrees into the air.

"I'm not sure," I struggle to say over the four Gs pushing against me.

Schumacher levels the vehicle up and eventually comes to an abrupt stop. We once again hover over the city as I hover over my thoughts.

"What have you got to lose? Why are you so sensitive? Where has it got you, baby?"

"I just…"

"Just what? You need to step it up. You need to go for it. Do it. Time isn't on your side. You like your current situation?"

My eyes stare off into the distance. Schumacher sighs and pushes a button. My door slides open and my set starts to edge out.

"You like your situation now, baby?"

"What the fuck? What are you doing?"

"You need to stop fucking around and be serious, baby."

"You're crazy."

The seat stops but then Schumacher pushes another button and the seat tips over the edge.

"You know it's all about perspective, baby. How is yours?"

I look down at the city below me and feel my balls and feet tingle. Nausea and anxiety levels increase by a thousand percent. Schumacher pulls a lever and my seat belt straps are released. I slide off the chair and my hand grabs the air and just when I think I'm going to fall to my death, the chair reacts by extending a robotic arm and clasps my wrist. I dangle in the air with one arm flapping around like a one-armed swimmer.

"You have to commit, baby. Do we have your commitment? The company likes commitment, baby," she screams.

"Pull me back in. Please Schumacher," I shout back.

"Are you with us?"

My arm was still flapping but now it was in a downward motion to try and get purchase. Obviously, it couldn't get purchase on thin air but my mind was telling the body to try anything. I thought it was working so I tried faster but then something strange happened.

Somehow, I had ripped the sky. I repeated the action with my arm and the rip got bigger. I did it again and then the rip extended into the city below. I even ripped it wider to reveal a black void lying behind it. I was compelled to jump through it but I was still attached to the chair. Like a moth to a flame, I couldn't resist the mysterious darkness so I tried swinging my body into it. Schumacher was still screaming but I couldn't make out the words. I continued to swing like a juvenile monkey but this time I did it with purpose and yanked away from my shackle. As I fell, my arms quickly scrambled for the rip in the scenery. I slid down and tore it some more and then ungracefully fell into the blackness.

Silence. Darkness. Music.

Simon & Garfunkel are singing again but they fade away on the next line. I'm back in the bar.

"Bonjour Jack."

I stumble as I get to my feet. I stroke my head as I have a headache. I sit on a stool at the bar. The French not-a-witch hands me a pint of water.

"Bois?"

I knock the water back and immediately I feel better. She pours me a large Lagavulin.

"Ca va?" she hands me the whisky.

I take a large gulp and let out a big sigh.

"What the fuck is happening?"

The not-a-witch taps her wrist, circles her finger and then taps her wrist again. She leans over the bar toward me.

"You're back in your happy place."

"Why?"

"Because you needed to be."

"How is this possible?"

"Because you wanted to."

"I'm not getting this."

"You're here because of you."

"But I need to get back."

"Back where?"

"Where I belong."

"Where you belong? You think you belong there?" she smiles at me curiously and then frowns sarcastically.

"What's so funny? Seriously, this whole day has been a mind fuck."

"And why do you think that is, Jack?"

"I don't fucking know."

"You do know. Drink," she shouts.

I do as am told and knock it back. She laughs but there is a tinge of anger behind it. She pours me another and stares deep into my eyes. I try and read her but she gives me nothing.

"Help me."

"Of course. You just have to think."

"About what? There is so much to think about."

"Think back, Jack."

"To when?"

"Think back."

"Stop saying that. Just tell me."

"Think," she slams her hand on the bar.

I drink some more whisky. I slowly put the glass down and watch her watch me. I take a deep breath and close my eyes. This is the part of the movie where the events of the day rewind slowly and then speed up like I'm flicking through a Rolodex of memories. It's to illustrate the inner workings of my mind. It's a stylistic device but you have to be original as it's been done many times before.

I would probably involve the imbibing of the whisky as it flows through my body, then appearing in the memory shuffle. Like the whisky was searching for answers. You got to mix things up.

The Rolodex stops at the part where Kukan corners me in the alley. The memory plays like a film reel that's stuck, so it plays forward, then back on a loop. The whisky lingers in the film like a floating stream of liquid, making parts of the film look sepia. After a moment it evaporates and then I open my eyes.

"I've been here before?"

"Yes," she says calmly.

"I've been here many times?"

"Yes."

"We've had these same conversations before?"

"Yes," she says with encouragement.

"This is about my writing."

"Yes."

"It's about self-doubt."

"Yes."

"It's about me."

"It's all about you." She leans back off the bar.

I drink some whisky and contemplate what I have said and heard.

"If I have been here many times before, then the reason I'm back here is because something has happened again? But something feels different this time. Other elements are at work here and it has changed the feeling."

"Are you asking or being rhetorical?"

"Well you're not going to tell me, are you? You're like those expensive therapists who charge a fortune just to listen."

"Fuck you, you self-loathing cunt. I'm here for support and guidance. You have to figure it out by yourself. It's for your own good. Sometimes Jack, you got to find your own way. Waiting for help and assistance has got you nowhere."

"What kind of therapy is this?

"I'm not a therapist?"

"Then, who are you?"

"Only you can know that."

"Great, we are back to that now."

"How do I know I'm good enough? Why won't anyone read me? Why can't they see it's a good idea? Why can't my stuff get made when that piece of shit does? I'm as good as them. Why didn't they choose me? Why did they pick them? Why can't I get that opportunity? When will they realise that my stuff is great? How long will it take? How long do I have to wait? What's wrong with me? Boo fucking hoo."

"Fuck, that's brutal."

"Sound familiar? This is what I hear from you every fucking time you come here. Normally I'm much nicer. I'm like your mummy putting a plaster on your little ouchy and I send you on your way inebriated with a smile. But you're right, things are different this time."

"I'm just trying…"

"You think you're the only struggling writer? A little birdy told me you are writing a novel too."

"Well yeah, I'm broadening my scope. Why stick with just screenplays?"

"Agreed. It's productive. How is it going?"

"Okay. I think it's going well."

"Keats, Poe and Kafka never got success till after they died."

"Well, I don't want that. I want recognition while I'm alive and some money to live on."

"J K Rowling was a struggling single mother on benefits."

"I'm on benefits. Universal credit. Raising a child would just about kill me. Worse, my predicament would probably kill the child. That's the thing. I need to succeed to give myself a life. I want to own a house. I want to settle and maybe start a family. To achieve all of this I need my writing to make me someone. I want to be something. I don't think I'm anything. I'm still a young man trapped in a middle-aged body trying to sort my life out. I got left behind."

"Who left you behind? You expected to be carried by the wind of success? All you did was just hold onto the dream because that is ultimately what you want to do. You just haven't executed it yet. You keep looking back to see where it went wrong. That's easy, I can tell you that."

"Go on then. I'm waiting."

She laughs, "You're always waiting, that's the problem."

"That's it?"

"You didn't try enough."

"I didn't try enough? Really?"

"Then why are you here Jack? Why aren't you in a luxury flat by the river? Why aren't people reading or talking about your work? Why aren't you happy?"

"Because I'm writing and nothing's happening," I shout.

My words cause the bar to vibrate and shake. The not-a-witch falls away, piece by piece, like a puzzle in the wind. Everything goes dark again.

My eyes struggle to open as the bright light invades them. My head feels heavy and clouded. I'm a deadweight. I hear music. *I Wanna Be Adored* by *The Stone Roses* plays but it sounds like it's inside a box. I then experience tinnitus in my left ear. I smell whisky which isn't unusual but what is unusual, is the amount. My nose feels like it's saturated in whisky and it's burning all the hairs inside.

My eyes try to adjust and I see I'm at floor level. I see two empty bottles of whisky on the floor and a DVD case which I can't focus on. I pull myself up by using a coffee table to get to my knees but I lose purchase as my hand slides on magazines and loose papers.

My eyes roll back into my head which has become super heavy and I fall once again. "Jack! Jack!"

I'm back in the bar and I'm sitting in front of not-a-witch.

"Why does that keep happening?"

"Because you want answers."

"Well, I got no answers there. Just a pounding headache. I've been there twice now and it feels awful."

"What did you see?"

"It's a room but it's all very blurry. This time I managed to make out, empty bottles of whisky and what looks like a DVD case."

"That's it?"

"A coffee table. Then I passed out again. What does it mean?"

"What does it mean to you?"

"Nothing. Oh, I did hear The Stone Roses playing."

"What song?"

"I Wanna Be Adored."

"Well, it doesn't take a genius to see why that was playing."

"I've always liked that song. Oh, I see what you mean."

"So?"

"So. I don't want to go back to that place. It gives me a bad feeling."

"So, what's your plan?"

"I'm not sure. I can't connect the dots."

"Clearly."

"I'm just not getting it."

"Sadly. You're not. I guess there is only one thing for it."

She steps back and holds her arms out and spreads her fingers like she is casting a spell.

"Just remember Jack. This time when you do it. Give it your all."

She flicks her hands and she throws me through the bar wall. My body tears through it like paper and I'm now falling against the night sky. Not just any night sky, but *Van Gogh's Starry Night Over the Rhône*. As I look down preparing for my landing, my surroundings become the painting and it rolls itself up, taking me along with it. I am then rolled out and discarded onto a star-covered floor.

A handsome black man dressed in a long blueish-white faux fur coat stands to the side. He has an identical one folded over his arms.

"Here, put this on."

I get to my feet and comply. The coat is very out there but very warm all the same. The interior is the same as the exterior and it's like I'm getting a warm hug from a cuddly polar bear.

"Follow me."

"Where are we going?" I say staying close behind him.

"To a party."

I check my surroundings and realise we are somewhere resembling the Arctic. Although, why would anyone have a party out here is beyond me.

"What party?"

"Your coming out party."

"Good one."

He was trying to hide his smile but I saw it. This annoyed me.

"You know that comment could be seen as offensive?" I added.

"Are you offended?"

165

"No. Not at all. But others might be."

"There are no others. It's just me and you."

"Well, I'm just saying, in case you say it in the presence of others next time."

"How do you mean? Who are we going to meet, then?"

"How am I supposed to know?"

"That's funny."

"Was it? Because I'm kind of not getting it."

"I'm gay. How is that offensive? I was just being jovial."

"So, being gay making a joke about being gay is fine then?"

"Look, it was just a joke. You can take a joke, right? No offense intended. Does being gay offend you?"

"No. I'm just conscious now of the woke generation."

"Are you trying to get me cancelled?"

"Fuck no."

"I don't think you fully understand it."

"Kind of."

"Well, that doesn't sound confident."

"Well you have to be careful, you can't offend anyone anymore."

"So why is it bothering you? It doesn't normally bother you."

"Well, I'm just saying."

"What? You're not normally like this."

"I'm sorry. Do I know you?"

"You could say that." He turns to look at me.

"To be fair, you mince like a good'un."

"Fuck sake. Another one. I think I'm offended at how bad the jokes are."

"Honestly, Jack. Do you know how many people you have offended in your lifetime? If you can't take it, don't give it out."

"I'm just tired. Your sly smile pissed me off a bit. It's been a hell of a day. My head hurts."

"Oh, we know."

"Okay, who are you?"

"The question is, Jack. Who are you? We are, after all, inside your creation."

"You what?"

"All this. This is all you. You said you didn't get it. Well, we are here to make you get it."

"We. Who are we?"

"Your subconscious kicked you out, into here. To make you get it."

"The not-a-witch?"

"We call her Adele because you couldn't think of a name, so we gave her something current from your subconscious. We used an earworm that has been bombarding your thoughts a lot."

"So, you used Adele? I mean she's good and I like some of her stuff but I'm a bigger fan of other artists."

"That doesn't matter. Your subconscious has been inundated with her songs. You know all the lyrics to at least a couple."

"Really?"

"We could have picked Ed but we didn't think it suited her."

"Hmm. I know a couple of his songs too."

"So anyway, she kicked you out, so that's serious."

"If Adele is my subconscious, then who are you? I mean, we? Who are you people?"

"You people? Now who's being offensive?"

"That's not what I meant."

"I'm kidding. Where did your sense of humour go? We are the people behind the subconscious."

"And who is that? Who are they?"

"We don't talk about it." He taps his nose twice and points at me. He then walks off.

"Are you fucking serious?"

"No one knows of us by name. But we do exist," he shouts back.

"So you hide behind the subconscious?"

"We don't hide. We are just there."

"So you lurk."

"Lurk? We do not lurk. We just are."

"So you're the 'imagination'?"

"What?" he laughs out loud and a bit too long for my liking.

"Fine. Okay, take a breath."

"You're funny. You see where we get it from? Sure, we're connected, but we are more intricately constructed. We are more secure. The imagination is a bit of a loose cannon. We are more organised. We are an organisation."

"So you're 'The Organisation' then?" I say it like I have solved the mystery.

"I like it. If we do need a name then that would be it. I'll bring this up at the next meeting." He takes out a pen and notepad and jots it down.

"Fucking hell. What the fuck? Why is everything a confused mess?"

"Don't worry, it's fine. Just put it to the back of your mind," he starts laughing again. "I'm on form today. You really bring out the best in me."

I wanted to punch his fucking lights out. His face was so annoying. You know some people just have that face where you take a dislike to them instantly for no reason? He had one of those faces. I was out of breath so I stopped and looked around at the vastness of nothingness. He looks at me.

"The most important thing is getting you to realise what's happening."

"Fine. So what's happening?"

"I don't have all that information just yet."

"Who are you then? What's your purpose?"

"Oh. I'm the guy who is taking you to Him."

"Oh. And who the fuck is Him?"

"That depends on you."

"For fucks sake. I need a drink."

"Well, we can join the party."

"What party?"

He points and there in a distance is a party, right in the middle of a large iceberg.

"Fine let's do that."

After boarding the iceberg, I stand on the edge looking at all the people. There must have been close to a thousand. Like most parties they are all divided in their own groups. Although they are all dressed identically in long black faux fur, I realise after careful inspection I know every single one of them.

"I love parties," says Annoying Face.

I carry on surveying the crowd.

"It's everyone I ever met."

"It certainly is."

"There's Steve, my first boss. He hasn't changed a bit. That over there is Anna, my first long-term girlfriend. Wow, she looks the same."

"They will look the same from the day you lost contact from them. You brain remembers them how you want to remember them."

"Bloody hell. There's Wilko. He looks great."

"You see?"

"But he's dead. He died twenty years ago."

"Yeah, well, you will always remember him like that. He won't be the only one."

"What is this? Is this some sort of Dickensian, Freud therapy? Are you the ghost of annoying therapists?

"Whoa, whoa, whoa, sweet child of mine. Dial the anger down a bit, would ya?"

"So what's the point of this?"

"Well, this party is you. All these people are part of you. You're everyone you ever met."

"And then some."

"What?"

"I'm everyone I ever met and then some."

"Yes. I suppose you are."

"We all are. You take things you like about someone and add it to yourself and then you become something extra. That's the 'some' part."

He smiles at me, "Shall we get a drink?"

"Yes, I think we should."

I carefully follow him as we squeeze through the crowd. I needed a drink before someone recognises me and stops me to chat. My faux fur didn't help matters.

"Jack!"

Pissed off, I turn and see standing before me Remarkable Les.

"All right Remarkable?"

"I told them you would remember me. They said you wouldn't." He throws his thumb to a group of guys behind him who now seem to be ignoring him.

To everyone at school, Remarkable was anything but and that's why he got the nickname. He was very intelligent and seemed to know everything and anything. Unfortunately, he had to share this knowledge with anyone that was in the vicinity or cared to listen. When you're kids, much of what he said was unremarkable. This was only because, as a young teenager, you weren't interested in stuff like that. Remarkable was ahead of his time and I'm sure he preferred being in adult company. One time I did see him hanging with the teachers at lunchtime and he seemed to be in his element. They were hanging off his every word. But I'm not sure he felt he fitted in either group, as sometimes I would see him wondering alone just talking to himself. It wasn't often I'd talk to him as to be honest most of us would avoid him. But when we did chat, he would give advice that was gold. These moments stayed with me as they helped me through rough times more than he can ever know. I think that's why I never forgot him and that's why he is here today. To me Remarkable was a fitting name. He never rolled his eyes at me when I called him that.

"How are you, Jack?"

"Not so bad. Not bad. You?"

"Same ol', same ol'."

"You're looking well."

"Thanks. I see the…" He points to my head.

"Yeah. Thought. Might as well take it all off."

"Suits you. Some people it doesn't but it suits you."

"Thanks, Remar…Les. You know I never said this to you. But you helped me through…"

"Oh, stop it Jack. We're mates."

"Yeah, but I just want to say thanks. That's all."

"Well, it was nothing really."

"Well, maybe for you but it meant everything to me. So thanks. Mate."

"Cheers." He raises his glass to clink with mine.

I look down and then back up at him with arms facing out, drinkless.

"Go get yourself a drink."

"Yeah, I need one."

"I'll see you around. I'm sure there are plenty more to catch up with."

I wink, smile and give him a thumbs up. I haven't done that since school. Remarkable disappears into the crowd and I go to the bar and join my annoying therapist.

I felt like a fake saying "mate" to Remarkable, but I needed to say it to him. While at school he wasn't, he was more of a punchline and I'm gutted I never spent more time with him. I never knew what happened to him or if he is still alive. I knew there was something sad hidden in him but I didn't want to pry or have to deal with it. When you're young you are selfish and you don't think about others too much. When you do think about others, sometimes it's too late. It's better if you act immediately. You have nothing to lose and everything to gain. I will never forget him.

My eyes are filling up and the therapist hands me a much-needed whisky.

"Remarkable's great, isn't he?" he says with a sympathetic smile.

"You know him?"

"If you know him, we know him."

"Of course."

"I wonder if he's de…"

"We don't know that information. If you don't know."

"You don't know."

"Who would you like to meet next?"

"I'm not sure I want to meet anyone after that."

"That's fine. We can just look and chill."

"You know I tried to organise a reunion once?"

The therapist gives me a look. I roll my eyes and continue anyway.

"So many people replied. It went viral. Then when I organised the date, my girlfriend pointed out that we were on holiday at that time. I changed the date so I could go. After all, I was organising it. In the end, only a handful turned up. It was a disaster."

"Was it?"

I roll my eyes at him again.

"Even my fortieth was a disaster. I decide to go out of my comfort zone and invite people from my different social groups. I wasn't comfortable mixing them but I thought fuck it, let's see what happens. The whole night they stayed in their groups and as a host, I was flitting from one group to another like a hummingbird gathering pollen. I was constantly on my feet saying my hellos and goodbyes."

"Nightmare," he says unsympathetically.

"You know you could at least act better. I did go to drama school."

"That was sarcasm."

"I know. I want sympathy."

"You're very hard to read of late. I guess that's why you're here."

"This is a nightmare."

"Me?"

"This," I say gesturing with my drink hand.

"Why?"

"Because everyone is here. It's going to be worse than ever."

"C'mon. These people made you. You made them. Everyone

affects everyone. It's nice to see them. No?"

I peruse the crowd to see who I can discover next.

There's Woolly Nelson. His name was actually Nelson Woolly but it's not so funny.

He wasn't musical or talented, just a bully and a twat. I'll skip him. Tara FitzMichael. The school whore or the town bike. Everyone has had a ride. I often think a lot about her and how much she was slut-shamed only because she was sexually active and curious at an early age. As teenage boys, all we could think about was sex, we just couldn't get any. At least Tara was experiencing it and discovering herself. Sadly, she got shamed and guys who did the same got glorified. I had a secret fantasy of her teaching me and showing me the ways of sex but shy friend-zoned Jack had no chance. Sadly, her reputation made her a pariah and she was short on friends as most girls hated her. I guess it was just jealousy. I'm sure she went through a hard time but she stuck it out and I always have an image of her now being a strong independent woman who doesn't take shit.

I give her a smile and a wave. She smiles and waves back. Anna, my first long-term girlfriend sees this, so I smile and wave at her too. No point talking to her. That's ancient history, I'm such a different person now. Nothing to be gained from that.

Billy Bunsen. Tried to blow up the school by leaving the gas on from the Bunsen burners. Yes that really was his name. I guess he felt he had to live up to it. Crazy fool. Pass on that one.

And then there's Miss Copper. She was a tall, dark and sexy English teacher who I had a massive crush on. She was only eight years older than me and she was a great teacher too. You never forget your favourite teachers. She taught me and shared her love for English Literature. I didn't realise at the time that I liked it but I responded well to it. I would always do different, funny voices whenever we would read text in class for the different characters in the book. I don't know where I found the confidence, or voices for that matter, but it was fun. I remember one day she asked me to audition for a play she wanted to put on but I immediately refused. No way was I going to perform in front of my peers and get laughed at. She must have made another three attempts but fear coursed through my veins and I never performed for her. She must have known I secretly wanted to do it because seven years later I went to drama school. I guess the fear slowly went away. Another thing that I remember about Miss Copper was her telling me to write shorter sentences. As a teenager, I thought adults wrote in long sentences with long interesting words. That may be true to a point. Only if they were coherent. It took me a while to realise shorter was better, coherent and more powerful. It has now become my style.

"I'll think I'll go and speak to Miss Copper."

"Ah, Miss Copper. Yeah, that will be nice."

We squeeze through people, like adventurers through a jungle. A goal and destination in site but thwarted by the elements. In this case people from my past and present. I hope there isn't going to be a future section to all of this.

"Thank goodness there isn't a future section to this," Annoying Face says as he pushes through the crowd.

I see Miss Copper in my sights. I also see members of 'the perm firm' close to her. They were the popular girls of the year. Blonde, with identical permed hair. Total bitches and waste of spaces. Even before the selfie generation they were obsessed with their looks and appearance. They were always photo-ready. I remember sitting next to one in history class and her watch had a mirror on it so she could constantly check her face.

"Tudo bem, Jack?"

I turn and see Benedito, a Portuguese guy I used to work with in room service.

"Hey, padre," I say with a large smile.

We always called him padre because he was a strict Catholic and always gave us youngsters advice. Actually, I heard he became a priest. I look at his neck and low and behold he has a collar on.

"It's so good to see you."

Despite being in England for thirty years, his accent was still strong but I loved that about Benedito. We used to laugh so much at work. Sometimes I would take him to the dark side and we would swear or talk about sex and he would say "I have to ask forgiveness. Go away, I have to say a prayer". His laugh was infectious. You couldn't help but smile in his presence. I always said to him, "Laughter makes you younger". He would say "I'm always a little boy with you". Then we would laugh some more. Those moments helped you forget the shit work we were doing. Good times. I grab his shoulders and he grabs mine. We hug. Already he starts to laugh, which begins like a car starting, then turns over into a cackle, then finally ends in a high pitched "Oh boy". Who needs drugs or alcohol when you have Benedito?

"Hey. You're a padre." I break away from him.

"I know. Crazy huh?"

"It was always meant to be Benedito. Padre Benedito."

"Where has your hair gone? Too much sex?"

"That's what happens."

"I wouldn't know."

We both laugh. Just like old times.

"Oh my god. Oh, sorry. Forgive me."

"I'm not sure I have enough time."

We grab each other again and laugh some more.

"Probably not, you're looking nearly dead."

"I'm actually dying, Jack."

"Oh fuck."

I look at him and my face drops. Life's not fair.

"Dying to kill you, you bandido."

"You mother fucker."

"Hey, that's two Our Fathers and one Hail Mary, you sinner."

"Oh my God, Benedito."

"Hey, enough with God already."

"It's so good to see you. You make me happy, padre."

"Have you not been happy lately Jack?"

The laughter dissipates and my eyes become pensive.

"I guess I haven't."

"Por que?"

"It's just been a bit tough, that's all."

"What is it? A woman? Your career? Your health?"

"Well, all of the above I guess."

"I see."

"Hey. You remember those stories you used to tell me at work?"

"Right."

"I tell them to my son."

"What, the sex stories?"

"No. You bandido. Those little short stories you used to tell me. The one with the morals?"

"Benedito, you were the one telling me the moral tales. In fact, they were biblical tales."

"Ah yes, but sometimes you came up with these crazy stories. With the animals."

"Oh yes, I forgot about those."

Sometimes when we were collecting tables from rooms, we would get alone time while we would wait by the lift. The time it took to transport the tables in the lift back to the basement and then to room service was a great opportunity to chat rubbish and make up some stories. Benedito was a great listener and furthermore a great audience as I would always get a great reception. Making him laugh was always a joy, but making him think and get misty was heartfelt joy. I guess I was always a storyteller but I never recognised myself as one. I was just messing around.

"I tell my son about the fox, the cat, the rat and the elephant."

"No way."

"Yes way. It's true. He loves them. I mean he loved them. He's a man now."

'The fox, the rat, the cat and the elephant' was a short tale. The baby elephant was lost in the city of London after the circus moved on. He wanted to get back to his mother but was faced with dangerous challenges whereby he meets the fox, the rat and the cat. The cat was the villain of the story trying to exploit the elephant, and the fox and rat turned out to be the elephant's friends as they knew about loyalty and survival. In the end they return him back to his mother, and the rat and the fox are happy eating a decent meal for once. It was something that came to me quickly. I mean, you had to before the lift arrived.

I knew Benedito would love it because it had these themes. The whole "don't judge a book by its cover" is a classic theme that never gets old.

"Really. That's so nice to hear. What does he do? Your son."

"He's a bandido. But I love him. So you still do the stories?"

"Actually it's all I ever do, Benedito. I just wish people would like them like you. I just wish they read them."

"If they read them, I'm sure they would love them."

"Obrigado Benedito. You should be my marketing manager."

"Too late. I'm God's marketing manager." We both laugh again.

"God's a lucky bastard."

"Jack. Just don't give up, okay. It will happen. I always wanted to be a padre. Look, it happened."

"I know. It's great. You look great, Benedito."

"Don't be sad. Life is too short. If things happened too easy, life would be boring. The longer it takes you, the better you will be."

"I'm just worried I'm coming to it too late. Maybe there won't be enough time."

"There is no time. It's an illusion. You just have to keep doing it."

"Or?"

"There is no or. If you do nothing. You have nothing. If you do something. You have something."

"Who said that?"

"Padre Benedito."

"I miss our chats."

"I love you, man."

"No. I love you."

Before he disappears into the work section of the crowd, he shouts some parting words.

"Jack... just do it."

"Who said that? Padre Benedito?" I shout back.

"No. That was Nike."

Good ol' Benedito. Still funny. I'm glad I bumped into him. He always makes me feel good.

Annoying Face turns to smile at me. He is feeling good too. Benedito is contagious. He has this effect on people. He continues to lead the way to the school section where Miss Copper is standing. As we get twenty-feet away, I stop. Annoying Face looks to me.

"What's wrong?"

"I think I'm going to skip Miss Copper."

"Because?"

"It's just going to bring me down. I'm feeling good right now. I like right now. I want to stay there."

"I thought you wanted to thank her."

"I do. But not yet. I haven't achieved anything yet. It's not the right time."

"Well, you can just talk to her."

"No. Let's skip."

"Okay. What next?"

"Maybe we should leave."

"Really? Okay. Shall we get another drink before we go?"

"You read my mind."

"Well, it's not hard."

"Right. Of course."

"There's another bar over there."

"Lead the way, handsome."

Annoying Face turns and smiles. He orders from the bartender.

"Can we have two large…"

"Whiskies?" the bartender swiftly replies.

"Yes, please. Can we have…"

Before Annoying Face can finish she picks a bottle from the

vast array of whiskies behind her and starts pouring the liquid into glasses.

"Wow, how many whiskies do you have?"

"Five-hundred or so," she says nonchalantly.

She had shoulder-length streaky blonde hair with the ends cut at different lengths. Messy, yet stylish. Her complexion was sun-kissed and her eyes were smoky. Her black uniform could be mistaken for combat gear if it wasn't for the long apron she wore finishing at her knees. She looked cool and she looked like she knew her stuff. This was a whisky ambassador. I was a bit nervous about her recommendation as I'm very particular about my whisky. She confidently slides them to Annoying Face and me.

We both sniff the whisky in unison. It smelt smoky. This was a good sign. One more sniff for luck and we got burnt barbeque aromas. Annoying Face smiles at me. We both take a sip and let it slowly slide over the palette and then down the throat. It was fucking gorgeous. The smoke and barbeque flavours added to the meat feast. Your mouth was tricked into wanting to chew that medium-rare steak that just passed your lips. It lingered there for a moment and Annoying Face and I looked at each other speechless.

"Wow."

"You like."

"I like." I took a larger sip.

This whisky was addictive. I couldn't leave it alone. No words passed our mouths while we repeated the experience. It was religious and ceremonious. I would have no qualms subscribing to this church.

"And this god-like nectar is?"

"Balcones." She pours us two more large ones and turns the

bottle for us to see.

It was from Waco, Texas. A single malt made from blue corn grown in New Mexico. The only thing I knew about Waco, Texas was some crazy cult that set themselves on fire. Now they made whisky that tasted of fire. I loved it.

"How did you know we'd like this?"

"I'm good at my job," she says wiping the counter down.

"Must be nice doing something you love."

"I said I'm good at my job. Who says I love it?"

"Is this not what you want to do?"

"No. This is a stop-off job."

"Right," I nod my head.

"What? You don't believe me?"

"No. I once said exactly the same thing."

I look to Annoying Face. He nods his head in confusion.

"Okay, I'll bite." I turn back to her. "So what do you really want to do?"

"I want to act."

"Right," I say with a hint of a smile.

"Why are you smiling?"

"Sorry. I wasn't being rude."

"I'm really starting to dislike you."

"No, really. It's just, once upon a time I tried to be an actor."

"And?"

"Well, it didn't work out."

"Maybe you weren't good enough."

"Maybe. Maybe I didn't try enough."

"Why didn't you try enough? You mustn't have liked it that much."

"I loved it."

"Really. If you were loving it, you would have tried harder."

182

I stop for a moment and stare right at her. Then I stare through her as her comment makes me flashback to twenty years ago, when I was just out of drama school.

I was back at my crappy job working in room service in a hotel, no agent, no auditions and no acting. Years passed in a blink of an eye and living arrangements seemed to take priority every year. I hated moving, so I kept my belongings to a bare minimum of ten bin bags to save the stress. The only upside was my accommodation got slightly better each time. Acting then became a distant dream and a memory.

"Sorry. I'm just passionate about the craft that's all. Nothing personal," she says.

I snap back out of it, "Maybe. Maybe you're right. It's tough, fucking tough."

"Believe me, I know. It's a fucking nightmare. I'm tired all the time with work, learning scripts and going to auditions."

"Well, make sure you save a bit of money. You know, for backup. Security."

"You're joking, right?"

"Well, maybe one day down the line you want to own your own place. Just putting away little by little helps big for the future."

"My own place? Me or my generation are not going to own our own place."

"Well, put some away for a rainy day."

"Put what away? I'm all in. I work so I can survive. I act so I can be alive."

I snorted and nodded reassuringly. I admired what she said. She was young and full of beans. I remember I used to be like that. Why does age hinder people? Was it hindering me? In my head I still feel young. I don't think I lost my mojo but age seems to have worn some of it away.

"The worst thing I can do is give up. I don't want to look back with regret and think I should have done it. I must give it my all. That's all I can do."

"What if it doesn't happen though? Sorry, I don't mean to be negative but it could not happen, through no fault of your own. Sometimes it's luck and right place, right time."

"I totally agree. But here's the thing. If I stop what I'm doing and give up, I'll be miserable. Furthermore, I'll be depressed not doing what I love and just working to live. Paying rent, food, working to fill someone else's pockets. If I carry on with my craft, my passion, just living hand to mouth, I still gain the best thing of all. Joie de vivre."

I couldn't disagree with her. It was a strong valid point. It was nice to hear again. It was almost like talking to my younger self. I couldn't help but smile and she was changing my perception. Her positive vibes were attacking my cynical drones. They were almost depleted.

"If it's good for my mental health, then it's all good. If I'm doing what I love during my pursuit, then nothing else matters."

Booooom. Cynical drones completely destroyed by a mega blast, killer of a quote. Extra bonus explosion for a Metallica reference.

"Do you have an agent?"

"Of course. I'm not shy of auditions. Just shy of getting parts."

"Well, it only takes one good part and then you're away." Her eyes light up.

"That's what I tell myself every day. I've just got to keep punching."

"Knock 'em out, kid."

It felt right to say it but at the same time a little weird. Yes, I was twenty years older than her but I felt the same age as her inside. I was behind her a thousand per cent and it invigorated my own ambitions once again. I felt good. I finished my drink.

"Okay, I think we're done here. Where to now?"

"I think it's time to meet Him."

"Him?"

"Yes. Him."

We leave the iceberg and Annoying Face leads me to the foot of a glacier. He knocks two times at the base and a secret door appears and swings slowly open. We enter the cold dark tunnel and our vision quickly becomes blind. All I hear are Annoying Face's footsteps.

"Hey, slow down, I can't see a thing. Can we get some light?" I whisper.

"I don't know, can we?" he whispers back.

"What kind of answer is that?"

"Actually, it was a question."

"I know. Why are you answering my question with a question?"

"Does it bother you?"

"Yes, it does actually."

"If you want light, you can have light."

"That would be great."

"So do it."

"Now you're getting on my nerves. You're really living up to your name."

"My name. I never told you my name."

"Whatever. Where is the light?"

"If you want light. You can make light. Also, why are you whispering."

"I'm whispering because it's dark."

"That's a strange reason to whisper."

"Why is that strange? Lots of people whisper in the dark. You're even whispering."

"Only because you are whispering."

"Well, maybe there is something in these tunnels, I can't see because there is no light."

"Like what? What do you mean? What could be in these tunnels?"

"Polar bears for one."

"Are there polar bears here?"

"How do I know, it's fucking dark," I shout.

"Maybe keep the voice down to a whisper. We don't want to wake them up if they are polar bears."

"You fucking kidding me?"

"You could always put the light on."

"Sure, I'll just feel for the light switch on the wall here."

"Okay."

"You really are annoying." There is a pause.

"Maybe try the other wall?"

"You know I was joking right?" I say, feeling exasperated.

"You say there is a light switch, there will be a light switch."

"For fuck's sake," I shout and hit the side of the wall and suddenly the tunnel is completely lit up by interior wall lights that look like candles.

"Nice. Well done. We got there in the end."

"How the fuck."

I look at the ice tunnel and see it curves down and to the right, the lights showing us the way.

"There we go. Not far now. Won't be long." Annoying Face turns to me.

I feel a stirring behind me and a large presence. "Oh bollocks."

I don't turn or move. "It's a polar bear isn't it," I whisper.

"Yes," he whispers back.

"What shall I do?"

"Only one thing for it."

"What's that?"

"Run," he shouts.

The polar bear lets out a mighty roar and I run, propelled by a flurry of farts which I'm sure gave me a head start or at least a big distraction for the bear.

Annoying Face annoyingly runs fucking fast, which makes me run faster. I was hoping to have a better chance if he was behind me. The tunnel is too narrow now to turn back. The only way out is forward and fast. As I hit the downward part of the tunnel my legs go faster than I can control them and they don't seem to be mine for the moment. I don't care as long as I'm still moving. The tunnel starts to bear right. No pun intended. I catch up with Annoying Face, who I'm happy to drag down to the floor if it saves my life but, annoyingly, he keeps ahead.

"Just a little more," he screams.

I turn and see the polar bear emerge around the corner. Annoying Face bursts through the end of the tunnel into a burning bright light. The bear gallops and leaps at me with his long deadly claws. He misses me by millimetres. As the bear climbs the walls he then transforms into a robobear. Now I got a scary polar bear terminator hunting me. I see the end of the tunnel and I leap into the big bright light. The bear leaps too but it's too late. I'm safe.

Again it's completely dark.

"Hey, Where are you?" I whisper.

Nothing. Annoying Face was annoying me once again. Here

I was stuck in fuck knows where and now I was on my own. He can't have gone too far.

"Hey," I whisper a little louder.

Again nothing. Not even footsteps. Is he winding me up?

"Hey, Annoying Face. Where the fuck are you?" I shout.

"Hey. Did you just call me Annoying Face? Is that the name you have given me? How rude."

"Yeah well, if the shoe fits. Why didn't you answer me?"

"I thought you were right behind me. I just came back to get you."

"Came back? Where have you been? Never mind. Where are you?"

"I'm over here."

"Where's that? I can't see a fucking thing."

"Just follow my voice."

"Seriously?"

"You know Jack, you can't have someone hold your hand all the time."

"Just asking for a little help. I'm not ashamed of that."

"You shouldn't be. But you know sometimes you got to do things on your own. It builds character."

The more he was talking the more irate I was getting. The only positive of hearing his annoying judgemental voice was working out his whereabouts.

"Is this you acting normal or do you practice being annoying?"

"Do you always get offensive when you're stressed?"

I manage to get to him as I feel his breath on the word stressed.

"I'm not stressed," I say, stressed, and put emphasis on the D so it hits him in the face.

"You sound it to me. Any closer and we would be kissing."

"I'm here now. Get on with it."

He pulls a curtain and white light shines through. He walks through it and I follow.

We are in a cinema lobby with bespoke mod cons. There is a popcorn maker, a bar that stocks all my favourite whiskies and a nacho machine. An action film poster with my face on it and a large LG screen showing film trailers also starring yours truly. There is a gentleman with his back to us dressed in a sharp suit watching it.

We walk up to him and stand behind him. The screen playing the trailers now shows us walking up behind the gentleman. Words across the screen read: HE'S BACK.

The gentleman turns around and smiles at us.

"Hello, Jack. Good to see you again."

"Jack. This is Him," Annoying Face proudly says.

"Er. Hi."

My response was one of confusion because on closer inspection, Him looked like me. Except he was a much better version of me. For one he had hair. And it was dark. He looked like a younger version of me but his eyes looked older. There were no wrinkles around the sides like mine but his eyes were wiser, like they had seen more things. Gained more experience. He looked like a version I always wanted to be.

"So you're Him?"

"I am Him."

"You're the one who can explain everything to me?"

"Of course. It's Him," Annoying Face chimes in.

"Shut it, Annoying Face. I've had just about enough of you today."

"Annoying Face?" Him says.

"Yeah that's his name for me. Can you believe it?"

"Actually, I can't."

"What do you mean, you can't? You must know what he's like?"

"Well yeah. But have you looked at him?"

"Of course I have."

"I don't think you have. Take a closer look," he says amusingly.

"What? Why?"

"Just look at him. Closely."

Annoying Face stands still and smiles at me. I walk over to him and examine him carefully. I take in his ears, his eyes and fuck, that nose. The realisation hits me and I jump back.

"Fuck."

"You see," Him says.

He looks exactly like me other than the fact that he is black. How did I not see this before?

"You see why I found it amusing?" I was annoyed by my own face.

"Why is he black?"

"You tell us. This is all your construct," Him smiles proudly.

"This is so bizarre. Well, he's not annoying because he's black, let me make that clear."

"Oh, we know that. He's annoying because he looks like you. It's not the first time when you wanted to be black, Jack. When White Men Can't Jump came out, you wanted to be Wesley Snipes."

That was true. His character was far cooler than Woody Harrelson's. However, not sure that a film like that could get away with a title like that today. Did I subconsciously make him black because I wanted him to be cooler?

Was it because he wasn't enough? I mean, was it because I wasn't enough? Is my image of Him how I want to be? Was I jealous and that's why I gave him that name? Isn't it natural to

190

not like parts of yourself? We are all insecure, right?

"You know I'm not that annoying. I'm actually a nice, fun guy," Annoying Face protests.

"I guess Jack, you got to love yourself a bit more," Him adds.

"I guess I do. So what's happening?"

"Right, let's get down to brass tacks. You're here because basically it's all gone tits up. Your mind is not well so we have intervened."

"So this is an intervention?"

"In a word, yes. And the Organisation…" Him winks to Annoying face here, "Is here to fix you."

"Fix me? I'm not a broken radio."

"Apologies. We are here to solve the current problem, situation. We would never treat you like a radio. An odd retro reference considering you only listen to podcasts now but we would never alter your radio dials or fixed radio stations, they will be intact. We are just merely here to help you to alter your perception relating to said problem, situation."

"Fine. So why am I here?"

"You're here because things have become difficult to handle, so your mind and brain have created these scenarios as a way of coping."

"Okay."

"Okay then."

"So?"

"Ah, so for some reason. This time it's different."

"How so?"

"Well, usually the subconscious sends you back post-haste. It's not often you get sent here. And we are having a bit of trouble collating everything so we can send you back."

"Why?"

"You have managed to miraculously create a chasm of infinite possibility which we are afraid to tamper with as it may be detrimental to your health, or worse, even your existence."

"What the hell are you talking about?"

"I'm talking about the risk of living your life or a life living inside your mind forever."

"You mean the possibility of being in a vegetative state?"

"Exactly. There is a high risk that this might happen."

"So what do we do?"

"That's why we're here. It's no accident that this cinema is playing the star's favourite movies."

"Yeah, I've noticed. What's all that about?"

"Each screen shows a different part of your life that we have labelled integral to the person you are today, Jack."

"Okay."

"They are more like turning points in your life that changed or defined you."

"You want me to go and watch all these movies?"

"In a word. Yes."

"That's going to take me ages... do we have time for this?"

"There is no time here. You can take as long as you want."

"As long as it takes," Annoying Face adds.

I should really stop calling him this but the name has stuck in my head now. This is weird because I'm actually in my head as I speak. Is that a paradox?

"And this will help how?"

"It will help us find out what went wrong and what caused the situation."

"The situation? You keep mentioning the situation."

"If we mention the situation, it could be catastrophic. We will not do that. Then your paradox would be imprisoned in a paradox and you would be lost forever."

"And now you're reading my mind."

"We are your mind, Jack."

"Right. Of course. So what about the mission? What about the Securus?"

"The fact that you just said Securus is both intriguing and confusing. We are still at a loss of what's real about this mission."

"Well, the talking crow for one can't be real."

"Or the talking rat, squirrel and demon foxes," Annoying Face smugly adds.

"Is any of it real? Is any of this real?"

"The fact that you are still immersed in this, when clearly you're standing here."

"You mean standing here inside my mind talking to the id and the superego."

"See, it's very tricky," Him shakes his head.

"If I'm the id, then who's the ego?" Annoying Face exclaims.

"For now, you're both, he called in sick," Him says.

"Interesting," I nod.

"To be fair they are just labels. We are The Organisation and we have a mission."

"You know I named you guys that."

"Of course, you are after all the CEO," Him laughs manically.

"I guess after all this is done and dusted, we should send you to the humour department."

"Very good Jack," Him laughs manically again.

"Seriously, how are you a part of me?"

"The mind is a very powerful and peculiar thing."

"That's probably from a book of quotes," I say to myself, not to Him.

"The mind can destroy and create. It can hurt and it can heal.

It can feel pain and it can feel pleasure. The mind is..."

"What about this room I keep ending up in? The little time I'm there I don't feel too good."

"Yes, we have recorded this. We are not one hundred per cent sure but it seems to be connected to the situation."

"I don't want you to send me back there."

"We won't. We don't know enough about it. It would be too risky."

"Fine. Shall we." I gesture to Cinema Screen One.

"Yes of course."

He walks to the door of Screen One, then stops and turns to me.

"Now, myself and Annoying Face."

"Really. That's who I am now?"

"We will both escort you and observe in order to make the necessary adjustments."

"So, all I got to do is watch?"

"Yes. But of course, your comments and own observations and what you surmise from it will affect the adjustments."

"These adjustments will help me get back."

"Of course," his tone unconvincing.

"I'm sorry, that wasn't convincing."

Him coughs. "Of course," he says with more vigour.

We enter Cinema Screen One. There are only two rows of seats. That bothered me as it told me not many came to see yours truly. I don't know what was more ridiculous, me being insecure or narcissistic. I sat in the middle of the front row. There were no trailers, the film just began as I relaxed into my seat.

The first image was the inside of another cinema, only this was bigger and had many rows of seats. It even had an upper circle and that's where I see my five-year-old self sitting down about to get his tiny mind blown by the silver screen. This was one of my earliest memories of being taken to the cinema. It was 1979 and I was watching a double feature. They used to have them in those days. You would get an interval after the first film and go and get snacks then return for the next feature.

I was mesmerised and so my love for cinema began. I've never forgotten that day. My tiny self is stuffing his mouth with popcorn and his eyes are smiling while fixed to the screen. I hold back a happy tear but then the scene changes to the inside of a church.

"I forgot about this."

Him looks over to me and then back to Annoying Face. They both take notes.

I'm seven, performing The Passion on Easter Sunday at my local church. Ever since moving to the area, the head mistress, Sister Delarosa, thought she would use the new kid (me) for main parts in plays at school or church. This could be down to the fact that I managed to remember my lines when she first chose me. She then continued to do so each year because I was an easy, reliable choice. To be honest it was quite a lot for a seven-year-old. At least two or three paragraphs. This occasion I was Pontius Pilate the man who would sentence Jesus to death and also the part with the most lines. I remember being nervous, I remember I didn't act much. I just said my lines, parrot-fashion, and when I was finished, I was relieved. I don't remember anything afterwards.

What's interesting is that I got on with it and just did it. It didn't appear to be a problem. Whether I liked it or not, I could do it. It wasn't cinema but I was part of a story, which I could tell.

The image on the screen then starts to skip forward, like it used to do on video tapes when you wanted to get to the good part again.

"What's happening?" I turn to the guys.

"It must be the subconscious," Him says.

"I thought they were next door. I mean, somewhere else."

"Technically, yes. But your subconscious is still connected. It's automatic. Your comments, feelings and observations are kind of editing your life by solving things on the way. This is great news."

"Actually, makes our work easier," Annoying Face smiles at me.

"What about the other screens? What's in the others?"

"Well, there are the erotic dramas, romantic comedies, comedy-dramas, thrillers, tragedies and the thought-provoking sad dramas," Annoying Face says in one fast breath.

"Can't I give those a miss. I mean, I've lived them once already. Some of them I don't want to relive."

"Honestly. I don't think we have to move from this screen. Your subconscious will pick the moments worth rehashing for us now," Him says.

The image on the screen slows down and plays a twenty-year-old me at film college. My friends are behind the camera filming a scene in our very own Tarantino-style short film. The film jumps ahead again. New York City, I'm twenty two. Work experience didn't pan out, so it is now a holiday for three months of drinking and discovering the city. A close up of some traffic lights, then everything turns blurry. Focus returns to normal, I'm twenty four standing in an aisle of a petrol station shop at midnight. I'm rehearsing a Shakespeare monologue. The staff on duty is a friend and former RADA graduate who is helping me perform it. Cut to drama school theatre. I'm performing Murder at the Vicarage by Agatha Christie. I'm the murderer. I take a bow and enjoy the applause. Celebratory drinks in our local bar meshes into graduation drinks. I'm twenty six. My excitement and smiles turn to dullness and frowns as I dissolve into my job as room service manager. The only joy of the job was working with certain colleagues and meeting superstars. The biggest stars were the best, like David Bowie. An absolute gentlemen. I had to bring him tea and honey to help his sore throat after his Glastonbury performance. Most of the A-list stars were actually nice people, except one who was a bit of a creep but I handled it. Actually it was the B, C and Z lists that were the worst. The ones who thought they were bigger than they were and far more important than the likes of you and me, were troublesome. The celebrity hotel lost its shine very quickly and I was becoming less star-struck. The job eventually wore me down. I didn't have an agent and I didn't get acting work and so life happened.

I sigh.

"Life is what happens when you're busy making other plans" is the quote. Except all I was doing was trying to survive living in London. When you have been living the student life for a while, all you can think of is living with less people and somehow have a better apartment. Well, that can only happen when you've got a good wage coming in. At the time, the hotel work was good money but the job had ground me down. Unemployment follows. The film skips.

Cue montage of me leaving the hospitality industry and entering the property industry. I thought I would try my hand at selling property and having a normal nine to five. This just showed me how colleagues would stab you in the back for a sale and that all salespeople were complete wankers. Also, I was shit at the job. I guess I wasn't a complete wanker. I can cross that off the CV. Unemployment follows yet again. The film skips.

Quick cut reveals I'm back in hospitality. This time in a bar as manager. I stay a year and a half before I whisk myself off to Antibes in the South of France, to use my hard-earned money to go work on the super-yachts. In six weeks, all my money is spent, I get no job and I come home with my tail between my legs. Massive failure. However, I did manage to fall in love with a town not so far away called Nice, which I have developed a special fondness for. Unemployed again. The film goes blank momentarily. I make a heavy sigh. It's horrible watching this again. It just reminds me of my failures. Thankfully it skips the unemployment parts. They weren't fun. I guess my subconscious is protecting me.

The film comes back to life. I'm at the whisky bar. I remember starting here, I was so happy. It was just what I needed after being unemployed for so long. I learn about whisky and get paid to drink and eventually get paid to do tastings and events. Good times. I'm thirty six. My path has changed and I need to live. Two years later, the company employs a part-timer who's a struggling actor. A young guy from Zimbabwe trying to make it in the West End. He reminds me of my dream and it reignites my passion. I start to write a screenplay I've always wanted to write.

I realise throughout my life there has been so many starts and stops. I realise emotionally that I wasn't ready to profess my love for acting. It took me a long time to accept it and follow it through. I miss it terribly and I think writing will help me reconnect with it.

I end up another ten years as a whisky ambassador. I write a movie script and two television pilots. My writing has improved a lot since the very first one and after writing many drafts, I'm starting to hone my skill. Acting is a distant memory now but I have fallen in love with writing. Storytelling was always a part of me and maybe this had always been the plan.

I entered my scripts into competitions and entered them into writing courses. Every year it was the same, 'Sorry, due to the high volume of scripts this year, the standard was very high. I hope this doesn't discourage you but please keep writing'. I keep writing and send the same script I sent in the year before. You are told not to do this but I do it to test a theory. I get a reply and I'm through to the next stage. Unfortunately, I do not go through to the last stage.

The screen shows a close-up of my dejected face.

Rejection is common and you're told about it frequently. However, it still fucking hurts. The big revelation about these writing courses for me is that they are bullshit. I failed because the next reader at the next stage just didn't like my script. Basically, it's all subjective. I was not judged on the quality or diversity. He just didn't like the story. It wasn't his thing. So this just told me it was down to luck. The luck of who reads it. It was a lottery. I watch myself click out of an email and open a bottle of whisky. I drink.

Then something extraordinary happens. COVID. Unemployed again. I'm angry and uncertain but I decide this can be a great opportunity. I had become sick of hospitality. I after all had served people for thirty years. I was sick of people and now COVID was too. I decided to retreat into myself. I decided to write again.

Him makes some notes and looks over to Annoying Face.

They both give each other a reassuring nod.

I write two comedy scripts, a television pilot and a movie feature. I have done more during COVID than I have in my ten years at the whisky bar. It was great that I could dedicate my full time to my passion. I had no money but I was happier. The major problem was that, no one was reading my work. The last image is of me on the floor surrounded by notes and scripts. I look tired. The film stops. The screen fades to black.

"That's it," I say.

"It seems so," Him says.

"But that was like a long trailer. Four minutes at most."

"Your subconscious really kicked in and did a lot of the work."

"It really fucking helped," Annoying Face adds.

"So are we done. Are we good?"

"Let's go through and talk about our options."

Annoying Face opens the door and Him and I walk through into a white room.

The room is completely bare except for a large oak table. Him sits at the top. Annoying Face and I sit opposite each other and either side of Him. There is also a roaring fire which warms the room and our faces.

"How are you feeling?"

"Exhausted. Better but not entirely. If you know what I mean?"

"I know exactly what you mean, and this is what we are going to discuss."

"I think I have an idea."

"Please go on. It's better for you to start."

"I think my desire to succeed has been scuppered by trying to survive. Trying to live, especially in London, has killed my dreams."

"Yes, this is true, but it's not the complete truth. Of course this has played a part, without question."

"Then what else?" I ask dumbfounded.

"Your age definitely has played a part."

"Yes."

"You have failed to network to help you succeed."

"Okay?"

"You reduced your social media."

"Right?"

"You reduced your friends."

"Well, that happens with age."

"Exactly, but whether you like it or not it will not help with your goal of achieving. You're blaming London. You said it has hindered your success."

"Well, to an extent. It has. It's bloody tough to get a decent job to pay the rent and do your passion on the side."

"You know why you moved to London?"

"To find success."

"Why?"

"Because everything happens in London."

"Do you like living here?"

"Of course. I love it. Because you can be anonymous and be someone here," I say, then do some naval gazing.

Annoying Face pumps his thumb up over to Him. I pretend not to see it.

"Good. Let's move on. Now did you notice any patterns form in the film?"

"Er. Unemployment?" I volunteer, thinking it's the wrong answer.

"Yes, that's true," Him replies, making me feel it's not a wrong answer. "Anything else?"

"Er. Not sure, it was quite harrowing."

"Yes it was. Okay. How about the fact that confidence has played a huge part?"

"How do you mean?"

"Well, it took you a while to decide you wanted to get into film? After you completed the course, you decided you really wanted to have a go in front of the camera. Considering fifteen years before you were already performing on stage. You developed a love for cinema during your teens and then writing for cinema in your late thirties. The love and passion was always there but something was preventing you from going for it."

"Yeah. I guess you're right."

"Don't blame yourself just because it took you so long. You just weren't ready."

"But I did go for those things in the end. I was ready."

"Yes you did. And it did wonders. You're looking at it as a failure. The person you are now has far more experience and insight than the actor twenty years ago or the screenwriter ten years ago."

"Much more. Then what's my problem?"

"Your problem. Your situation. Is that… you're unhappy."

"I am unhappy." My eyes start to fill up.

The room turns blue and cold. The flames of the fire die down.

"You want to achieve success with your passion and it hasn't happened yet, but you got to hang in there."

"It's fucking bullshit though."

"We know. Those production houses that only receive solicited material. Those writing courses. Those competitions. They are not for you."

"Yeah, it was like pulling away the curtain and seeing the shitty wizard." I'm crying now. "They would never write a popular Netflix show." There is a pause and I become aware of it and look up.

"What's happening to me?" I look to Him.

"You've taken a beating. You've had enough and you can't take it any more. It's understandable after such a long period."

"You are having a nervous..." Annoying Face stops after reacting to Him nodding left to right.

"I'm what?" I look at them and wipe my eyes.

The room turns a darker blue. The flames of the fire reduce to a flicker.

"Look at me, Jack."

"What did I do? What stupid thing did I do for this to happen?" I plead.

"It's just a relapse, Jack. You just lost..."

"Don't say faith, you fuck."

"Okay. Listen to me otherwise this will all metastasize and you will be fucked forever and end up like a zombie." Him slaps me and holds my chin in his hand.

Annoying Face's eyes widen in shock. I am shocked too and the tears have stopped. Annoying Face hands Him his notepad. Him turns his head and reads it. He then looks back to me.

"This situation you created. This story. The Securus. Asami. Amelie."

I don't speak, I can only nod.

"Initially we thought it was escapism so you could cope, but now we see it could be much more than that."

I make a noise. He releases his hand from my chin.

"So, what is it?"

"We think you have created it, as a kind of backup solution."

"What? Why?"

"We think you created it to save you."

Annoying Face wipes his tears and smiles.

"Although you have felt that you can't go on, the subconscious has created this other world as a means of survival. You have created this narrative. This story."

"Why?"

"Why do you create comedy sketches in your head at particular times? You splice them all over the place."

"I do?"

"Also, you seem to be talking to someone all the time," Annoying Face adds. Him nods in agreement.

"What?"

"Yes. You are talking to someone or some people. It's like you are narrating to an audience."

"I am?"

"All the time," Annoying Face proudly states.

"It's fine. It's not a crime pretending someone is listening to you," Him smiles from ear to ear. "It means you haven't given up, Jack."

"You're a fighter, Jack," Annoying Face cries happy tears.

"But what's real about this story?"

"We are not sure. But the story is important. It's serving a purpose," Annoying Face says with serious intent.

"I have a theory," Him says and gets up from the table.

My eyes follow him looking for an answer.

"A theory?"

"While theories are not factual or by any means truth, they are a guide and give meaning to what we see. They help us understand what is needed for practical action." Annoying Face and I look to each other to see where this is going.

"Sometimes you have to lose yourself to find yourself. This

is exactly what has happened with you. You have gone into survival mode with this story because you have realised you will die if you don't. It's worse for you to carry on with your current unhappy life. Your subconscious is fighting for you to live but it's at a loss as to what to do next. It doesn't know how to solve it. It's stuck. So…"

Him stops and stares deeply into the fireplace. The flames barely flicker.

"So?" I finally say.

Him turns to me. "So it sent you here. It couldn't deal with the situation as it wasn't sure where it was going anymore. It's like it's lost. Sorry to say. Faith. And it needed help. But Jack, I think this may be the start of your Opus."

The fire roars back to life. The room glows and we feel warm. I stare at Him, speechless.

"I believe the only way out of this is to clear your obstacles. You have to confront them in order to move forward. Then you are free."

I stand up. "Okay. What do I have to do?"

"We will send you back, exactly at the point you left the story."

"Er. With Schumacher. I was holding on for dear life."

"Exactly. This traumatic event most probably scared the subconscious as it lost control, or worse, confused it."

"Yeah, but surely it would be better to skip this part?"

"Absolutely not. You are now aware of the situation and so is your subconscious. You must follow this through."

"But how do I know what parts are real?"

"For whatever reason it's unclear why this story is designed this way but we believe the answer is seeing it through to the end."

"Okay let's do this."

Him walks over to me and grabs my head between his hands. Annoying Face gets up and stands in the corner.

"Are you ready?"

"Yes."

Him squeezes my head a little.

"Wait," I shout out, "What if I get sent to the room again?"

"Don't worry, we are always here. Just think of us and we will come get you."

"Okay, good. I'm ready."

"Remember this, Jack. The mind is limitless. It can make you do anything."

I look him dead in the eyes. "Thanks. Both of you."

I feel him squeeze my head again and the pressure throws my entire body through the wall of the room. I hear his last parting words.

"Don't drink too much." Everything is a blur.

Annoying Face sits back down at the table, emotionally exhausted.

"I can't believe he said, thanks."

"He's changing. Which is for the greater good." Him goes to stand by the fire.

"You really think this could be the start of his Opus?"

"Maybe. That depends on Jack doesn't it?"

My eyes adjust and I'm back in the bar. Adele's bar. I'm a little disorientated but I feel more focused and confident than ever.

"Well. Did you see Him?" Adele says.

"Yes."

Adele smiles back, "Do you know what you have to do?"

"Yes, I got this."

"That's good to hear, Jack. You know we love you, don't you."

"I know," I grab her and kiss her. "Thanks." I turn and take in my surroundings. I turn back to her. "Was that weird?"

"Not at all. Don't worry about it. Go and do what you have to do," she says with a broken voice and smiles.

I run and launch myself at the wall like a tiger pouncing on its prey. The wall rips like wallpaper as I claw into it and I disappear into the void.

A crackle of electricity and I'm back hanging off Schumacher's vehicle, hanging on for dear life. London below me awaits.

"Well baby, what's it going to be? Are you committed?"

"Yes," I shout back.

"What's that baby, I can't hear you?"

"Yes, I'm committed. I'm super committed," I scream.

"Then get back in, baby."

Schumacher pushes a button and the chair hooks me back in and it recoils back into the vehicle. The door closes behind me. I'm safe again.

"Let's go to The Savoy, baby."

Schumacher puts her foot down and we speed off.

Even though I feel considerably better, I'm still having doubts. I mean it's understandable right? The crow and the squirrel and the rat are nothing more than glitches. The demon fox? I never actually saw it that clearly, anyhow. My mind was just playing tricks. Maybe it's peppering the mission with these animals as metaphors for my vulnerable position. Yes, that's it. So what about the flying vehicle? Maybe it's not flying. It's my mind exaggerating things. I'm a storyteller, after all. What did Him say again? The mind is a very powerful and peculiar thing. He also said it is limitless. Schumacher stops the vehicle. I look out and it is obvious we are on the road. I didn't feel a transition. We must have been on the road all along. Yes, things are beginning to make sense now.

"We're here, baby."

We exit the vehicle and Schumacher locks up.

"This doesn't look like The Savoy."

"Relax, baby. She's just up ahead. This is the closest I could park, my baby."

We come out of Savoy Hill and walk into Savoy Way. Schumacher is still in her robo get- up. She doesn't appear to get any looks from people we pass. Must be my imagination again. Remember what Him said, 'Follow it through'.

As we get near to the end of Savoy Way, we turn down an alley that goes down the side of the Savoy Theatre. On our right is an open door, where a guy in kitchen whites is smoking. He nods to Schumacher and I follow her through the door.

We walk through the kitchen but the staff are too busy to acknowledge us even though it's clear we don't belong there. Saucepans crash and dishes smash. Same shit, different day.

Schumacher navigates us to a lift that's used for staff only. We enter and Schumacher presses the fourth floor. We stand in silence.

The Savoy has always been a place I've wanted to go. The fact that it is one of the most renowned hotels in the world and epitomises wealth and luxury. Even though I have passed it many times, the idea of actually being here was like me going to the moon. Out of my league and impossible.

The name Savoy goes all the way back to the thirteenth century where Count Peter of Savoy built his palace on the site where the hotel now stands. It was also one of the earliest hotels to be technologically advanced. It was the first hotel to have electric light, ensuite bathrooms, electric lifts and room service was conducted by 'speaking tubes'. The biggest stars and artists also stayed here, Charlie Chaplin, Monet, Marilyn Monroe, Marlene Dietrich and the founder of Gucci started life here as a luggage porter.

One story that stays with me is the story of Kaspar the cat. A two-foot statue, which serves as a good luck charm for The Savoy. The story goes back to 1898 with Woolf Joel who was big in the diamond industry. He organised a dinner party for fourteen people. However, one guest couldn't make it, leaving thirteen guests for dinner. Superstition said that the first guest to leave the table will die. Woolf Joel didn't give much concern to this and left the table. A few weeks later he was shot dead. Ever since, The Savoy has used Kaspar the cat as the fourteenth guest whenever tables of thirteen happen again. I look down at the number 13 tattooed on my finger. It's like a badge of honour that says "fuck you superstition". I grin to myself.

Now I was here I was a little upset I was coming through the service entrance. I guess it seemed appropriate as I hadn't made it. Still, it was disappointing.

The lift opens on the third floor and two male staff enter. They roll in a table stacked with plates, cutlery and coffee pump-action air pots and box us in. They are too work involved to acknowledge us. The door closes and a voice comes from a radio attached to the guy on the left.

"Where are you guys? It's nearly time," says the female voice on the radio.

"Yes, we are here. Just coming out of the lift now," the guy says in an over-exaggerated polite tone.

"Well, hurry," she adds.

"No problem," he fires back.

"Mama mia. She is like a mosquito. Always in my hear. Even when I sleep I hear her."

The other guy laughs. "I can't wait for the weekend."

The lift door opens and they roll the table out with urgency. We also exit. Schumacher and I follow the two staff members who take us out of the service wing into the guest area. While they turn left, Schumacher leads us to the right.

I can't help but look at the carpet. It's blue and white with a swirly pattern that is quite hypnotising. I look at it too long and it makes me dizzy. Everything is so opulent, with chandeliers hanging down to create the right amount of light needed. Even the wall lights look like part chandelier. Schumacher peers in the first room nearby. Her eyes scan the room.

"No. Not this one."

Schumacher continues and walks with tenacity.

She peeks her head into another room without stopping.

"Nein."

I peek in too. It's a small room and no one is there. I pick up my speed to catch up with Schumacher but she turns a corner and I lose her. I do however hear voices, so I follow the noise and investigate.

Before I can enter the Abraham Lincoln room, I am stopped by security. As I try and look past these twin towers, Amelie spots me and waves. I wave back but security push me away.

"I'm with…"

"Hello darling," Amelie says, coming to my rescue holding a flute, of course.

She is wearing a long satin blue evening dress with a split. She looks gorgeous and sexy. She kisses me on both cheeks. She smells great and instantly I feel warm inside.

"Come with me, I need to get some air. It's too stuffy in there."

"Er. Sure. You look amazing, by the way."

"Thanks."

"Is that a Mecklestein?"

"Damn fucking right it is," she smiles at me.

She leads me down another corridor and past other event rooms.

"What's going on here?"

"It's the event of all events. London's finest. All in one place. This is where anybody can become somebody."

"All these rooms are hosting talent?"

"Yes. Absolutely."

She owns the dress as she walks. Every man that we pass can't help looking at her. Even security can't help but turn their heads. She sips her flute and turns to me and we catch each other's smile. A raucous room interrupts our exchange and causes us to stop.

"What about this room?" I say as I sneak a peek.

"This room. Absolutely not. Avoid this room at all costs. Actually, avoid these people at all costs."

This of course made me more curious so I scan the room even more. These guys were not wearing Mecklestein suits. They were wearing wannabe Mecklestein suits. They all seemed to be trying to outdo one another in the conversation stakes. Their gestures were grand and over the top. Their faces looked weathered and worn, including the few women that were there. They certainly had character.

My eyes fixed on a gentlemen sat in the middle. No one was talking to him and he sat in silence like he was plotting something. Unlike the others in the room, this man didn't need to command presence. You knew just by looking at him that he was the most powerful person in that room and you didn't want to fuck with him. He turns and fixes his eyes on me and smiles. The smile was devious and sly. It was familiar and unsettling all at once. It was hard to look away from his gaze. Luckily Amelie pulled me away.

"C'mon you. You need a whisky."

"Er, well. Alright, but we can't be long."

"Don't worry, you won't miss anything yet. I'm here for the same reason you are."

"You are?"

"Of course. First let's get that drink."

She takes me to the Beaufort bar and orders two large whiskies. This was The Savoy I wanted to see. I didn't feel out of place either. I didn't with Amelie, she made me feel great. There wasn't a better person to enjoy this place with.

We both take a sip and smile at each other. You know when people name a song and say 'that's on the soundtrack of our lives.' Well, this whisky was part of our taste track. Obviously, her kisses and her secret garden are way up there on a loop, but Johnny Walker Double Black will forever remind me of Amelie. I hope it reminds her of me too.

She leans in, pulls my head to her and kisses me. I taste her soft lips, whisky and her luscious tongue. I lose myself for a moment. She lets go of my head and smiles at me.

"That's better." She looks around and takes in the bar, then back to me. "Let's sit down."

We leave the bar, which was like leaving the stage of a theatre. We then navigated through the stalls to find a comfy secluded table where we could be alone.

"What do you think of this place?"

"Yeah, it's great. Good choice."

"I know right. The American Bar is too bright. I prefer it here. Nice and dark."

"Yeah, I love bars like this. I look great in this light."

"Yeah, me too. We look fucking sexy in this light."

"So sexy."

"So sexy, it hurts."

We both laugh and sip some more whisky. We stare at each other for a moment but it's not uncomfortable. It's nice being in her company.

"So."

"So," I smile back.

"So. You got the Securus back?" My smile disappears.

Fuck. She did take it. She had it all along. Asami was right. She is Kukan. Fuck. Fuck. Fuck. No fucking way.

"So. You took it."

"Erm. I wouldn't say took. I found it."

"Ah. You found it. Why didn't you give it back then?"

"I was. Remember, I asked the porter to get my bag. I was going to give it to you then."

"But you didn't."

"Because that fucking dog scared the shit out of me."

"And why was that?"

"Because I fucking hate dogs. Okay?"

"Okay."

"You don't believe me, do you?"

"I… I don't know."

"You don't know? Seriously? I've been honest with you from the start."

"Have you?"

"Well. Mostly."

There is an awkward pause.

"I've let you inside me for fucks sake," she raises her voice.

Some people in the bar turn their heads towards us.

I crunch my body. "Okay. Let's not cause a scene," I whisper.

"I had plenty of time to use your Securus but I didn't. I'm not like those thieves in that dodgy room."

"Is that what they are?"

"They are the worst kind. They are also hustlers, manipulators and liars. They will do anything to get an activated Securus. Why do you think there are so many security about?"

"I just thought that's how The Savoy rolls."

She sniffs and drinks her whisky.

"They can't refuse them and they know that. They have money to book event rooms but they are banned from the Starmaker's annual event. But they arrive every year to try and steal some talent."

"Is that why you're here?"

"Fuck off," she raises her voice again.

"I didn't mean that. I mean you're here to acquire some talent."

"Of course. It's my job. That's what I do. I told you. I've worked bloody hard to get here."

"I'm sorry. I wasn't totally clued up. My head is a bit cloudy. I'm here for the event but I'm not sure what I've got to do."

"So, you're invited?"

"I think so. I think Schumacher is making sure I am."

"You're here with Schumacher? Wow. Your Securus must be very worthy?"

"I guess."

"Why is it called a Securus?"

"It's Latin. It means many things. Fearless, confident, cheerful, untroubled, tranquil, composed, safe. These are also components to your talent. Most importantly it recognises truth and it protects everything. Keeps it secure. It's quite magical."

"Interesting."

"Well of course, I knew you had something. Securus or no Securus."

"Thank you. That's very kind."

I drink my whisky and stare at Amelie. She looks at me then looks down to sip her drink. I can see I have hurt her feelings. I'm about to say something but she speaks.

"So are you looking for representation?"

"Erm. Well I think I'm with…"

"The Company?" she interrupts.

"Yeah. Asami has been…"

"Asami?" she interrupts again.

"Yeah. You know her?"

"I know of her. But I don't really know her."

"Oh. How do you?"

"I used to work for the company," She interrupts for the third time.

We sit in silence. She stares into her drink and I stare at her.

"So, what happens at these things?"

"Basically, all the new talent gets cherry-picked and the Starmaker takes a large slice off all of them. But every year a special prize goes to the one for being the most special. The most promising. This all depends on the Securus. And this is all performed in an elaborate display at the Starmaker's dinner."

"Sounds a bit ostentatious."

"It is, but it's good for the talent and it's good for people like me," she says casually.

"Sounds like it's good for the Starmaker too."

"Yeah well, she has the monopoly. She's been doing it for years."

"There's no other way? I mean, can the talent go down another route and make just as much as the Starmaker?"

"Well. Yeah, but it's more certain this way and reliable. She's called the Starmaker for a reason."

"But I don't have to. I mean, I have a choice?"

"Of course you do. Risky. But yes, you have a choice."

I make a satisfying grunt. My eyes turn up to the ceiling.

"What are you thinking?"

"Just thinking."

Amelie sips her whisky. She puts the glass down on the table so that it makes a noise. My eyes look at her.

"Have you signed anything?"

"No," I say, unsure.

"You don't sound sure."

"I haven't signed anything but I feel as if I'm committed."

"If you haven't signed anything. You're not committed."

"Then. No, I haven't."

"Good."

"So when did you work at the Company?"

"About two years ago. Time flies." she stares into the distance.

"So, what happened?"

"Well. Don't get me wrong, I learned a lot, but after a while, it just got too corporate. It used to be about the talent then it was about the money. I lost the passion."

"Right."

"And I lost a big client."

"Ah, that will do it."

"She went on to have a very successful career on her own. We used to be so close. Go to yoga. Go out for drinks. One night I may have had too many and been very transparent about the company's tactics and motives and their financial cut."

"Oh shit."

"She left at the end of the week. I was fired. She never kept in touch and the Company made my name shit, until I fought back now."

"Wow."

"Yeah. It's been pretty exhausting. But I'm happier. I got the passion back."

"Maybe that's the way forward. Stop working for the man and start working for yourself."

"Absolutely. Stop working for them. So does that mean you're going to join me?"

"I'm not sure just yet."

"Well, you better decide soon."

"I have to see how this will pan out. Everything depends on it."

"What does? Is there something you're not telling me?"

I look away and see Asami standing in the corner of the room looking at me.

"Oh shit."

"What?" Amelie follows my eyes and they stop on Asami. "Shit. I guess it's time to go." We knock back our drinks. I gather myself and then we walk towards Asami.

"She looks pretty," Amelie says and looks at me to see my reaction.

"I guess," I said using my best poker face.

"Seriously, Jack. If that's your bluffing face then you would have just lost all of your money."

I knew she looked great but I didn't want Amelie to know I knew that, but Amelie knows me too well already. This scared me a bit but, at the same time, I liked that she did in such a short time. I cared for her feelings as I realised I had feelings for her. The closer we got to Asami my heart raced as I knew I was in trouble. Her face was still the shy demeanour but it was incongruous to her body. I knew that behind that face was a woman burning with anger.

"Asami," Amelie says very formally and smiles.

"Amelie," Asami replies and mirrors Amelie.

I look at them both for a moment. They are like two steely empresses at war, waiting for the other to weaken or crack in the stare-off. None of them were going to relent. I realise I hadn't spoken yet.

"Hey."

Asami breaks away from the stare and turns to me.

"Jack. We must go."

"How is the Company?" Amelie says, stirring things up.

"How is your Company? Lonely?" Asami says and leads me away.

It was a bitchy comment well delivered. I didn't think Asami could be so cutting and quick. She also seemed to be articulate when she was insulting. Amelie makes sure she has the last word.

"I'll see you later, Jack."

I turn and make an awkward smile. Asami quickens her pace.

"Schumacher, not happy. She's been trying to find you. She wants you to meet the Starmaker."

Asami marches me back to the room where I was refused entry. I notice the sly gentleman from the raucous room nod and smile to me as we pass him in the corridor. No matter how friendly he was trying to be, it made me feel uneasy. Security lets us through and she waves at Schumacher. Schumacher acknowledges us and points for us to stay put.

Asami takes her hands and brushes my shoulders, smartens my suit and even strokes my beard. A little bit invasive.

"They come, Jack. Be awesome. This is your chance now."

She places the Securus in my pocket. "When she asks. You show her Securus."

"Okay."

"Don't be nervous."

I wasn't nervous until she said that, plus she looked like a nervous wreck herself. This wasn't helping. I looked around for Schumacher but my attention was taken by this extremely tall woman that glided towards me in a long purple velvet gown. It looked like she was floating. She must have been at least six foot six and her feline eyes and slender frame made her look alien. She carried the longest vape that dangled from her fingers to finish the look. Obviously a homage to Audrey Hepburn. Her black skin glistened and seemed to shine as she moved and when she got close to you she smelt of coconut and chocolate. I didn't want to blink in case I missed anything. She stops and looks at Asami.

"Hello, darling," the Starmaker stoops and kisses the left and right sides of Asami's forehead. "Who is this intriguing specimen?" Asami bows and gestures to me.

"You are he?" the Starmaker looks to me.

"I am he."

"This is the Commuter," she says.

I'm surprised at this and not overly excited by the name. It sounds boring. Who wants to be a commuter. I know millions commute to London every day but it's exhausting and boring. I can think of only one advantage to commuting and that's reading. The Starmaker leans down and examines me carefully. I feel like an unfortunate whore before she is picked by an undesirable client. She sniffs and breathes me in. I feel my body sway towards her as she does this.

"Interesting name."

"He knows London very good, Starmaker."

"Nice to meet you," I say, giving myself more purpose than a display doll.

"I am not a you. You can call us they or them."

"Nice to meet them," I say sounding ungrammatical.

"Enchanted we are. You have your Securus?"

I remove it from my pocket and hand it to them. They lift it up to the light and like a giraffe, their neck and head arc to get a better look. I watch and stare as they take it in.

"I've never seen one like this in more than twenty years," they then look down at me. I can feel them looking at my skinhead and tattoos.

"Oh, my. This makes it even more delicious. You were right to interrupt me." They turn to Schumacher who is hiding behind them. "Have you ever seen such a creature?" Schumacher laughs. Asami laughs. I grimace.

The Starmaker hands me the Securus back with a smile.

"Set three more spaces for dinner. I want them close to us. I don't care what you have to do."

It wasn't clear who they were saying this to until three feral-looking people popped their heads from behind them. They looked like they were triplets, each with digital devices, earpieces, and microphones. All of their heads were shaven and their eyes were spookily massive behind the largest bifocals I have ever seen. As soon as the Starmaker made their request, they just quickly acquiesced in their own language. One typed into her device, one spoke into her microphone and the other whistled to staff out of earshot.

"Arigato, Starmaker," Asami bows.

"Dinner starts at…" The Starmaker looks down at their feral assistants. The assistants mumble back. "Eight o'clock. Do not be late." The Starmaker floats away and exits the room.

"Excellent, babies. I don't know about you but I need a drinky poos. And make sure this one doesn't run off again."

"Jack, we must talk."

As I sit in the American Bar, I realise that sitting down with Asami is a pole apart from Amelie. It's bright, cold and uninviting. I didn't want to be here but I needed to hear her out. I wanted to see where this was going.

"Jack, your chance is here. Tonight it will happen."

"Okay. What do I have to do?"

"You must do one thing."

"Okay?"

Asami pulls out a letter and lays it on the table in front of me.

"What's this?"

"You must sign contract, Jack. I will. We will. The Company will look after you now."

"Shouldn't we wait until after the dinner?"

"You will shine so bright, Jack. This is guarantee. This here is security. We will help your success."

I sip the whisky Asami got me. It didn't taste right. She sees me wince.

"What's wrong, Jack. You not trust me? Have I not been good to you?"

"Of course. I have just been thinking of other things."

"What things you been thinking Jack?   Thinking of her. Amelie?"

"How come you never said you knew her?"

"Everyone knows her. She is Kukan."

"Well, I like her."

"She can't help you like Company, Jack. The Company can do anything for you."

"Like what?"

"Everything that you want."

"Sure," I laugh.

"We can get you everywhere. People will hear you Jack. Finally, they will listen to what you say."

This was the first time I'd seen Asami like this. She was in sales mode. Totally out of character, but she was making me think. Her words were working their magic, carefully seducing my brain waves and injecting them with dopamine. I wanted more.

"No work for Jack anymore. You will do what you love and get more money than you ever had."

My eyes were dilating. My heart was racing. My head was tingling.

"You will be somebody, Jack. Finally. You will have that apartment by the river."

The last part echoed in my head. I saw that apartment by the river. I saw myself lounging on the balcony, drinking under the sun, sharing it with someone I love. Her face was blurred but it didn't matter, I had made it and I was happy.

"Would you like a pen?" Asami says in a whisper.

"Yes," I hear myself saying.

I'm in some sort of daze but I grab the pen and try and focus on the contract. I attempt to sign my signature but instead, I make strokes in the air.

"Closer, Jack," I hear Asami whisper again.

As I try and steady myself, I am brought out of my confusion as whisky is now running down my face. My eyes are stinging but I'm released from this seductive spell. I refocus and I look to see Amelie standing next to me.

"That's pretty low, Asami. The Company still stooping to

these tricks? I should report you."

"What happened?" I say rubbing my eyes.

"Wasabi here was trying to fuck you over with her contract by using mind tricks."

"How? Why?" I say gathering myself.

"Kuso shinu," Asami stands and screams at Amelie.

Amelie grabs me by the arm and leads me away. She takes me down the corridor once again. We shimmy past people and security.

"What did she say?" I enquire as I try to shake myself out of my stupor.

"She told me to fucking die."

"Kukan," Asami shouts. Everyone stops and turns to Asami. Security turns too.

"Oh no she didn't," Amelie turns around and faces Asami. "You really are a crazy bitch."

Security turns their heads to me and Amelie.

"You want to do this?" Amelie shouts.

I was wondering what this was and did I really have to see it. This wasn't going to end well and we haven't even got to the dinner part yet. This can't happen. What the hell was security doing? They seem frozen into confusion, or maybe wise like me and not getting involved. Other people emerge from other rooms and poke their heads out to see the fuss. I look behind me and see a bundle of people rolling towards us buzzing like bees. When they reach me, they stop and separate to allow their queen to enter and investigate. The Starmaker glides forward and leans down.

"Is there a problem ladies?"

"No problem here."

"Asami? Is there a problem?"

Asami seems embarrassed and stares for a moment. Every-body is looking at her. You can tell she's weighing up her options. The man with the devious and sly smile emerges and takes his position against the wall opposite me. He looks to me then to Asami.

"Gomen-nasai," Asami bows.

"Good. It's eight o'clock which means it's time to dine. You know who you are." Amelie turns to me but, before I can say anything, the Starmaker intercepts us.

"You're coming with me," the Starmaker links in with my arm and we glide away.

As I turn, I see Schumacher comfort Asami and Amelie gets lost in the bundle of people that roll after us.

The Chugu room is not listed as a room in The Savoy. Only the secret members that use it know of it, and the odd feral staff that works it. The room itself is styled in traditional Japanese from a Western perspective. In other words, cliché and stereotypical. The floor is wooden, there are frosted paper screen doors, and the giveaway that a Westerner designed this is the presence of a large thirty-seat table. Obviously, they didn't want to sit on the floor as it was very awkward and uncomfortable for them. My deductions, therefore, made me arrive at the conclusion that this was down to the Starmaker's request. Chugu also means "residence of an empress". The one that lives there is also called Chugu. Case closed.

Surprisingly, the Starmaker did not sit at the head of the table. Maybe this was an old patriarchal tradition. They stop at the centre of the table and everyone waits for them. I see Asami and Schumacher a couple of seats down. Opposite, across from The Starmaker and me, a seat is free.

Everyone looks to see where the mystery person can be. We

then hear the heels crossing the wooden floor and see Amelie arrive and take her place. The Starmaker checks their watch. They smile and then sit down. Everyone else sits after and the staff slides their chairs behind them. I am seated next to the Starmaker.

At least half of the guests remove their Securus and place them on the table. I follow suit. The table is illuminated by a blue glow. Mine seems to be brighter than others. The Starmaker smiles proudly and then everyone else starts to look, some with envy, some with surprise, and some with jealously.

I try to avoid their looks and glances by turning to the Starmaker but they are already talking to someone else.

"Hi," a gentle voice says.

I look to see a small gentleman sitting to my right. He must be the size of a seven-year-old boy in a tweed coat, but he looks sixty. His eyes look tired and lazy and, strangely, he reminds me of Droopy Dog.

"Hi," I say, uneasy.

"I'm Fiodor," he says in a slow and smooth tone.

"Get to fuck? Like Dostoevsky," I say in disbelief.

"Yes my parents named me after Dostoevsky but they changed the spelling. Instead of Y they used an I."

"I thought Fyodor was an F."

"Ha. Very good. I see your talent is humour."

"Some may say that."

"Why wouldn't they all say that?"

"I guess the world would be a boring place if everyone thought the same."

"True. So very true."

"I'm Jack."

"A pleasure to meet you. Fiodor."

"With an I," I smile at him.

"So, do you know what happens at these things?"

"Actually I do. I've been here before."

"Really. I thought they only brought new talent here."

"In the beginning, yes. It even used to be young talent. It even used to be white, young talent. It even used to be just men."

I look around the room and I see black, white, Asian, Indian, young, old, trans, non-binary and others I'm not sure my middle-aged self can get my head around, but they are here too. I realise this is definitely an inclusive table.

"It's all thanks to the Starmaker. It's been better since they took over."

"How long has she, I mean they, been the Starmaker?"

"Oh, quite long. Very long. Before my time."

"Really. Wow. How old must she, they, be?"

"You must never ask how old they are."

"Of course. I was only just... I mean they look good. I mean, what moisturiser do they use?"

"Ha." Fiodor lets out a loud laugh that makes the Starmaker turn to us. Fiodor just waves back and the Starmaker resumes their conversation.

"So, what happened the first time?"

"Well," he leans in, "I didn't get chosen," he whispers.

"I guessed that, but why?" I whisper back.

He laughs again but tries to hold it in. "Because," he pauses, turns away to check if anyone is listening and leans in to me once again, "Because."

"Yes," I say, grinning and stifling my laugh.

Fiodor is now stifling his laugh, "Because of my Hooy," he finally says.

To contain his laughter he grabs my arm and smothers his

face in my Mecklestein suit sleeve, so the Starmaker can't hear or see him. This display causes me to laugh more. I just met this guy and already I love him. His laugh is infectious but I have no idea what he said. I guess this is what it would feel like if I had dinner with Billy Connolly or Robin Williams. Some people just have this gift and you warm to them immediately.

Laughter truly is good for the soul.

"A what? What did you say?" I giggle as I look at him pulling my sleeve.

He reminds me of Dudley Moore now. Peter Cook, his comedy partner, would always make Dudley corpse. Laugh out of character. Dudley would always do his best to hold it in but he would always crack up in the end.

"My. Hoo," he says but laughter gets the better of him and he can't get the rest of the word out. He tries again, "My Hoo."

"Your what?"

"My Hooy," he finally says and lets go of my sleeve, and straightens himself up.

"What's a Hooy?"

"It's Russian for…" he then makes a head movement in the direction of under the table.

"Your foot?"

He bursts out laughing again. Other people at the table look over at us. Even Amelie starts to laugh.

"Hooo…y," he says with a thrust of his hips.

"Oh. Your Hooy."

"I think I broke my hip."

"Seriously?"

"No." He pulls my sleeve again. "But don't let me do it again."

"Okay," I snigger back. "What did you do with your hooy?"

"I did nothing, Jack," He says composing himself, "I just had

227

to take him for a walk."

"A walk?" My snigger starts to jump, "What do you mean, walk?"

"He had to go."

"Where? Not here?" I say, motioning to the room.

"Of course not. I'm not a fool."

Actually, he was and I loved him for it. He was a beautiful fool.

"I mean, I might as well have. All I did was get up and go to the toilet. Unfortunately, it was during the big ceremony. The Starmaker wasn't impressed and I was ignored for the rest of the dinner because of my rudeness. That was three years ago. I'm only back because I used the old card," he whispers.

"The old card. Do I need a card?"

He starts to laugh again, "No. The old card. The fact that I'm old and I have a weak bladder."

"Right. Right. Sorry, was being an idiot."

"Hey," he says sternly, "this table only has room for one idiot." We both laugh.

"Tell me about the ceremony, Fiodor."

"Usually after the first course, we activate our Securus and the Starmaker makes their choice. Seating is very important. Close to the Starmaker is good. They want the favourites next to them. The further away you are. Not so good."

I couldn't help but notice that Asami and Schumacher were further down the table.

"What about the agent's seating? Does that matter?"

"Erm. Not really. It mainly depends on who they represent but I guess if they are far away from the Starmaker it's also to do with respect. So yes, it does matter."

I glance over to Amelie sitting opposite.

"Then what happens?"

"Then agents bid or in some cases fight for their cut. The Starmaker always wins but what is important is the cut of the agent."

"And the talent?"

"Well, we're just happy to be here."

"Really?"

"Well, we don't have a choice, do we? It's the best we can do?"

"I'm not so sure, Fiodor."

"What do you mean? This is the only way."

"Is it? I'm not so sure."

"So? What's the other way?"

"How about doing it ourselves?"

"You're a crazy fool."

"Well, I'm in good company then."

"So, how are you going to do it?"

"I'm still working that out."

"When you do, be sure to tell me." He stands up. "I got to take the hooy for a walk. Best to go now. Don't you go anywhere."

"I'll be right here."

My smile lingers on him and then it falls on Amelie across the table. She returns it with a cheeky smirk. Before I can engage with her the staff arrive on ceremony with the first course. They all stand behind, waiting to serve us our dish. There is a long pause until the head of staff shouts the order, or rather, war cry.

"Banzai."

The staff place the dishes in front of us and then they march off in unison.

The first dish is Toro tuna. This was premium Otoro. Pink, fat belly meat renowned for its buttery flavour. I love raw fish. In fact, most of my diet is fish nowadays. I like the way it fills me up without feeling heavy. Plus, it's a good form of protein. There was a tiny ramekin with soy sauce on the side but you always have to taste the fish without it first. Why would you put salt on your dinner without tasting it first? It might be salty enough.

I pick up the first piece and bit off half of it. It really was buttery and it melted in my mouth. I tried to savour it but it just slid down my throat. The room fell silent and my eyes closed uncontrollably as I held on to the sensation. I look across to Amelie and her eyes roll into the back of her head. I saw the same look last night and she looks over to me like she knows what I'm thinking. I raise my eyebrows, she resumes eating. I too dive back in.

I have to say I never really enjoyed food like this before. My relationship with food has always been to fuel my energy, increase muscle and basically to stay alive. I suppose that's why I have always been a fast eater. Food just served me as a biological purpose. I seem to enjoy drink more, although that can be quick too but I still acknowledge and savour the taste. Eating this dish now has made me pause for thought. The only time I can think where I take my time eating is when I'm consuming dark chocolate. That's always worth it.

After I finish, I push my dish aside and pick up the sake on offer. I smell the aroma of rice cakes, vanilla and maybe some herbs.

"Herbs?" I say out loud.

"Wild herbs. Very good, sir."

I'm startled by the feral staff that has appeared just under my armpit.

"This is Hakkaisan Tokubetsu Junmai."

He speaks very eloquently considering his appearance. They

do say never judge a book.

He interrupts my thoughts, "It's a perfect pairing for such a buttery dish as this. It's a great palate cleanser and it's great warm or chilled. Very versatile."

He waits and smiles with his hands behind his back. I still have the drink half raised and millimetres from my lips. He nods at me like he is giving me the order to drink. I do as I'm told and sip.

It's fresh and it does indeed compliment the buttery tuna.

"Mmmm. Beautiful," I say but he still stands there. "Thank you so much," I add.

"You're very welcome, sir," he bows and leaves.

I never knew there were sake sommeliers. I mean thinking about it now, why wouldn't there be? He was very pleasant. This was turning out to be a nice evening. Shame I had to ruin it.

Like before, the staff all turned up at once and removed our dishes on the command of "Bansai". Like regimented soldiers they all strode out together.

Fiodor returns.

"Better?" I say.

"Much better."

"You missed the first course."

"Typical. When you have to go, you have to go. By the way, I've been thinking. I'm in."

"You are? Okay, but I still haven't worked out what I'm going to do."

"Well, I can get things started."

"How?"

"Just promise you will take me with you."

"Yes, of course. Are you sure about this? I mean you've waited this long. This is your second chance and now you're risking it all."

"Well, I might regret it if I don't."

"You might regret it if you do."

"I'm old enough and ugly enough to know that sometimes you just have to go for it." We smile at each other.

Fiodor leans over and grabs my Securus.

"What are you doing?"

"The ceremony is useless for us now. Let's get out of here."

I grab the Securus as well. "I haven't figured things out yet. Let's just play this out and see what happens?"

"There's no point. Let's go."

I try and wrestle the Securus off him but for an old man, Fiodor is pretty strong.

"What are you doing? Give it back."

"What are you doing?"

I glance over to Amelie who is giving me a strange look.

"Trust me. You asked me to trust you."

"I just need more time."

"You've had enough time."

"What?" I say confused.

My grip lessens and suddenly it flies from our hands and into the air. This would be the dramatic part of the film where we watch it flip in slow motion, until it finally lands across the table right in front of Amelie. There is an awkward silence which is then broken by powerful blue rays of light blasting from the Securus. It was activating again.

"What the…?" the Starmaker says in surprise.

Before I can make my excuses, I see Asami leap onto the table and launch herself in the air over the Securus. My eyes cannot believe what they are seeing as she transforms into a white fox with several tails flowing after her. She dives in the air, then swims out of it, finally hovering over the Securus looking majestic and proud.

"The Company makes bidding for this Securus," the fox says. I mean, Asami.

The Starmaker keeps their cool regarding the surprise interruption to their event and goes with it like it was planned.

"What say you?"

I'm still aghast at Asami's form, with her fur well-groomed and fluffy. Not like any fox I've ever seen. It's only when I look at her eyes that I really see her. Those eyes are so unique, it now starts to make sense. She was Katarina serving us drinks. At least towards the end anyway. Also, the creepy porter at the hotel. That was her too. All the time she was keeping an eye on me but hid the secret that she was this shape-shifting demon fox. Then, who was the demon fox chasing us and cornering me in the alley?

Before Asami can answer, Amelie speaks.

"Under the Absolute Securus Act of 1703, I challenge the bidding."

"Do you have proof to back this up?" She looks to Amelie. "Is this true?" She looks to Asami. She receives no answer and looks to me. "Have you signed a contract yet?" I look to Amelie and then to Asami. I look to the Starmaker.

"I have not," I reply.

"Then, the challenge is accepted. We haven't had a challenge in over one hundred years."

The Starmaker raises her arms and shouts, "Banzai."

Everyone around the table rallies around and thumps the table. Everyone starts chanting "Banzai", the word growing louder every second. Everyone looks to Amelie and I do too, not sure what to expect. I feel it's my fault I got her involved. She returns my look, with one of shame, then finally she stands up and leaps into the air.

"Fuck me," I say aloud.

The first time I was duped was finding out Father Christmas wasn't real. The second time was finding out a girlfriend didn't really love me. The final time was when Amelie turned into a demon fox.

Now there were two of them. Amelie gracefully takes her place opposite Asami. Her fur is immaculate and she has many tails too and she is almost completely black. What makes her stand out is her white fur that runs from her chin to her belly like a painted stripe. Is it wrong that I fancy a fox? Of course not. Have you forgotten she lied to you? Yeah, let's not forget that.

Before I can dwell on it and have a heated discussion with myself, both demon foxes take a combat pose. The Starmaker stands up with her hands raised.

"Kitsunes, stake your claim. Banzai." The Starmaker taps their temple and sunglasses appear over their eyes. They sit.

"BANZAI," the others in the room echo.

Amelie and Asami circle each other in the air and just as they come to a stop, Asami strikes at Amelie and the fight begins. The light of the Securus intensifies with the furiosity of the fight and it feels like I'm at a nineties rave party. The strobing is hurting my eyes but I can't stop looking as I'm concerned for both these women, foxes. Even though they both lied to me I don't want them to get hurt. Even though they are fighting for me, I feel it's futile as I have finally made my own decision. They just don't know it yet.

"Wow, you're really popular." Fiodor hands me some sunglasses to put on. He has his shades on already.

"What were you trying to do?" I say shouting and exasperated.

"Well, to ruin the ceremony. This has kind of changed things," he shouts back.

"You think?" I say sarcastically.

"Well yeah, they are kind of fighting for nothing. You should tell them."

"I think they are a little busy right now."

"You're going to have to let them finish."

"When will that be?"

"Who knows? I guess when we have a winner?"

This wasn't going well. I don't have an end game yet and now Asami and Amelie are ripping each other to shreds. Asami manages to grab Amelie by the neck and proceeds into a death roll, like alligators do to their prey. It looks like the end but in her daze, Amelie manages to flip Asami onto her back and she drags her like a helpless turtle and spins her very fast in circles. They fly around the room and bounce off the walls but furniture and fittings stay intact. They are graceful and respectful to their surroundings but to each other they haven't a care in the world. Was this business or personal? Either way, blood was being drawn and wounds were exposed and it looked like neither of them were going to give up. They were relentless.

I had to do something but I couldn't fly and also, I wasn't a demon fox. What could I do? I couldn't clap my hands at them like I do to foxes when they try to get into my rubbish. That would be ridiculous.

"That would be ridiculous," Fiodor says still looking at the fight.

"What?"

"What?" he says.

"What did you just say?"

"Isn't this ridiculous?" He shouts.

I look at Fiodor for a moment thinking, who is this guy? Then from the chaos comes a high-pitched howl. I turn and see Asami is hurt and she has retreated to a corner.

"Enough," the Starmaker stands and holds their hands up, "It is settled."

Amelie turns to the Starmaker and bows her head. Asami is upset however, and her anger causes her to claw at Amelie's eye. Amelie lets out a howl and a scream and she returns back to human form and falls out of the air into my arms.

"You call this honour?" the Starmaker berates Asami and gives her the coldest stare,

"How dare you disobey my command."

"She used Kukan move. She is a Kukan."

"These are serious accusations," the Starmaker stands firm.

"It's true," Asami insists.

Amelie uses me as support and stands up straight, looking at Asami and the Starmaker with her bloodied black hole where her left eye used to be.

"Fuck you," Amelie leaves the room in silence. The door slams behind her.

Pandemonium ensues. The staff rally around the Starmaker. The Starmaker starts pointing and delegating. Each leave with their missions and others arrive with their duties. It's a whirlwind of chaos, inside a vacuum of despair.

I'm standing, stunned.

"Now is a good time, I think," Fiodor nods towards the door.

I snap out of it, "Yeah. Right."

I walk with purpose. A little faster than London walking. Before I get to the door, I see a blue eyeball on the floor looking up at me. It was a lot prettier in Amelie's head. I pick it up and leave.

As I rush through the hectic corridor, I bump and crash through people like obstacles in a game. I glance through rooms hoping to find her but a lady's shriek soon alerts me to her whereabouts. As I arrive at the ladies' toilets another woman comes running out scared shitless. Yep, she looks like she has seen a one-eyed woman.

As I enter. I hear a stall slam its door.

"Hey, it's me."

"Hey," Amelie's voice comes from the middle stall.

"Well, I didn't expect that," I say, upbeat.

"Well, you know me. Full of surprises."

"Good news. I found your eye."

"Are you sure it's mine."

I let out a little laugh, "Pretty sure. It's a lovely blue one."

I hear her cry a little. I look down at her eye in my hand all bloody and disgusting.

"Yeah. Sounds like mine," she sniffs.

I try to pass it under the stall, "Here. Would you like it back?"

"No. You keep it. I can grow another one."

"Really?" I surreptitiously place it in my pocket and sit on the floor.

"We can do that. It will take a while though."

At that moment Fiodor slides in. I mime for him to go out. He exits on tiptoes.

"I'll just have to wear an eye patch in the meantime."

Fiodor tries to go out of the door stealth-like but the door makes a loud creak each time he tries to open it further.

"Is someone else there?" Amelie says startled. Fiodor disappears.

237

"No. There's no one." There's an awkward silence. "So, you're a Kukan."

"I am not a fucking Kukan. Fuck sake, you're just like that eye-gouging bitch."

"Asami's a Kukan too."

She makes a big sigh. "None of us are Kukans. We are Kitsunes."

"What's a Kitsune?"

"We are spiritual foxes with paranormal abilities..."

"Shapeshifting," I interrupt her.

"Being one. Yes. But most importantly we are guardians, friends," she sighs again, "Lovers."

"You and Asami are lovers?"

"No. Get your sexual male fantasies out of your head and listen for a second."

"Sorry. Still trying to get over the fact that you are a fox. I mean Kitsune."

"Yeah, sorry about that. I was trying to find the right time."

"Well, you certainly pick your moments."

"Well, a girl has to make an entrance."

"Your exit was pretty good. Considering you only have one eye." She lets out a huge laugh and I laugh with her.

"So, I did see a tail. Your tail. In the hotel?"

"Probably. Usually happens when I'm drunk or aroused."

"Good to know."

Silence falls again. "So, what is a Kukan?"

"A Kukan is a dark Kitsune. They feed on chaos, pain and negative emotions. They will use and manipulate you until they get what they want. They are selfish and very dangerous."

"What do they look like?"

"Usually, dark. Wolf-like. Completely black."

"I think I met one in an alley."

"You know that's why they call me Kukan. Because I'm mostly dark. I know I'm a half breed but I don't know who my parents were as I was an orphan. What makes a Kukan is how they are on the inside. It's not what you look like on the outside."

"Well, I like your inside and outside."

"Thank you," she sniffs. "I hope you didn't mind me fighting for your contract? I made a big assumption that you would go with me."

"Right. About that."

"So, you want to go with her? The Company?"

"No."

"I don't get it."

"Can you open the door?"

"I'm not sure I want to now."

"Fine. I'm not going with anyone. I'm going to do it myself."

"That's brave."

"I know. But I need to do this. I have to."

"If that's what you want?"

"It is. I've thought long and hard about it. I'm always waiting for others to help me but I have to do it myself."

"It's perfectly doable. It's not impossible."

"I mean the rewards are better, right?"

"Is it just about the rewards? Don't do it just because of that. Think about artistic freedom. You can do what you want. You're in control. You answer to no one."

"You're right. You're so right. I'm going to do this."

"If you get stuck, there is always a video out there to help you or someone giving helpful tips. People are not always bad you know, they can be helpful too. And you're right, the rewards are better. You get a bigger slice of the pie, as it were."

"Thanks, Amelie."

"You're very welcome. And if you really need help, I'm always here. I'm a guardian, after all."

"I definitely know that."

"Well, yeah. I lost an eye for you for fuck's sake."

"Just how am I…"

"What?"

"How am I going to get out of this? This Securus ceremony."

"You know there is an old story, a myth about one guy who disappeared from one of these ceremonies. It's a kind of legend."

"Go on."

"This was a few Starmakers ago. Like two, three hundred years. Some say he was a crazy man, others say smart and curious. The Company was going to represent him but on the day of the ceremony he disappeared."

"What happened to him?"

"No one knows for sure. One rumour is that he alone looked straight into the Securus during the second activation and he disappeared into it. The optimists and spiritualists say he went back to the place where his soul wanted to go. His happy place."

"What's the other rumour?"

"The Company had him killed? I guess he asked too many questions."

"I like the first rumour. Do you reckon it's true?"

"I want to believe it's true."

"So that's your plan? I have to look into the Securus so I can get to my happy place. It's a bit of a long shot."

"So, what plan do you have?"

"Good point. Well made."

"It's not that much of a long shot you know. The Securus follows the talent and belief of the owner. The second activation allows another party to announce itself to the Securus, so two parties are then bound together to it."

"I see. So, it's a big con. A scam."

"Well, it's just the Company and the Starmaker monopolising the business."

"A con."

"Well kind of, but they would argue that the success of the talent is down to the symbiosis of both parties."

"Right. I guess their reach and experience helps."

"I mean, this is a theory that many of us have talked about over the centuries."

"It's a very good theory."

"Jack. You have nothing to lose."

I look down at the floor tiles. Fuck, they are dirty. They need a wash. I've been sitting on this scummy floor all this time. I quickly get to my feet.

"You're right, I've got nothing to lose. I'm going to do it."

"You're going to need my help."

"I'm going to need your help."

She takes a big sigh but I imagine there's a smile behind it.

At that moment Fiodor sneaks in and hands me a makeshift black eye patch.

I give him an impressive smile and a thumbs up. As he leaves, I see the back leg of his trousers with an eye patch hole in it.

"Here. This is for you," I pass the eye patch under the stall to Amelie.

"Nice. You are resourceful. Love the colour."

She unlocks the door of the stall. I stand back as she opens the door. She looks badass.

"How do I look?"

"Like a sexy pirate."

She walks up to me, holds the back of my head and kisses me. She then breaks away and looks me dead in the eye. With her good eye.

"Where is this happy place of yours?"

"In my apartment, writing," I say quickly.

"Am I there?" she says.

I flash back to the beautiful woman on the terrace. Her face is not a blur anymore. It's Amelie. We clink glasses. I snap back out of it.

"Of course. Who else loves Hitchcock? Whisky? Spoof? Jokes?"

"I know, I know." She jumps up like a swot at school. "This gal," she points to herself with her thumb.

"Damn right." I pull her towards me and kiss her with passion and purpose.

"It's because of this foxy body as well, right?"

"Absofuckinglutely."

"Okay, this is what's going to happen. I'll resume the fight and go beast mode."

"Beast mode? Do you have to?"

"Is there something I should know? Is there something going on, with you and Asami?"

"No. No. Do you know what she called me? How she introduced me to the Starmaker?"

"Go on."

"The Commuter."

"That's a shit name."

"I know, right? I mean it's awful. Who wants to be a commuter? Even commuters don't want to be commuters. They commute to be somebody."

"So, who do you want to be?"

"A journalist gave me a better name earlier tonight. I like that one."

"Go on."

"Mr. London."

She whispers it to herself a couple of times, "I love it. Much grander. Who said that?"

"I think his name is Hazy?"

"Good journalist. He would know."

"I mean Mr. London sounds important, right? You want to know who he is?"

"Oh yeah. Mr. London is a somebody all right. I can tell you that from first-hand experience," she chuckles.

"Anyway, back to Asami. It was bad form what she did. It's just, do you have to fight her?"

"We need a distraction."

"Yeah, but just a little fight."

"What the fuck is a little fight? She took my eye out."

"Fine. Just don't go crazy."

"Whatever. Then you grab the Securus, look straight into it and bam. Happy days."

"Great. Sounds easy."

"You know it could be suicide, right?"

"How do you mean?"

"Well, what if you don't go to your happy place? What if it sends you somewhere else or worse it just ends you."

"It can't?"

"It could."

"It won't?"

"It might."

The word suicide started to ring inside my head. It was swirling around, spinning like a cyclone getting faster and faster until my mind conjured up another comedy sketch.

EXT. LONDON BRIDGE - DAY

A man in a suit with the head of a crow stands at one end of the bridge with a clipboard and pen. This is the CROWMAN. There are about twenty men lining up behind him. In the middle of the bridge a man is carrying a heavy stone and jumps off the bridge. We hear a big plop.

CROWMAN: Pity.

The Crowman turns to the next MAN in line.

CROWMAN: Suicide?

MAN: Yes.

CROWMAN: Good. Middle of the bridge. Grab a stone. Off you plop.

The man walks off. ANOTHER MAN moves up in the line.

CROWMAN: Suicide?

ANOTHER MAN: No. Living.

CROWMAN: Living?

ANOTHER MAN: Yep. Changed my mind. Decided it's selfish and I'll have another go at it.

CROWMAN: Oh. Jolly good. Well done you.

ANOTHER MAN: Only joking. I've really had enough. Can't take it anymore. Thought I'd have one last laugh. You know, before I go.

CROWMAN: Oh, good show. You really had me there. Always good for the soul to have a laugh.

ANOTHER MAN: Yep. Why not?

CROWMAN: Good. Middle of the bridge…

ANOTHER MAN: Yep. Grab a stone. Off I plop.

We see the man jump. We hear a big plop.

CROWMAN: Pity.

I snap back. I haven't thought like this in a while. Him said comedy was a coping mechanism. Is it because I'm anxious again? Is it because this story is nearly played out? Am I worried about losing Amelie? What was it the not-a-witch, I mean, Adele, said again? "The answer sometimes is right in front of you."

"Hey," Amelie shouts at me. "Where you been?"

"Sorry, I was just thinking."

"You having second thoughts?"

"No. Just wondering when I look into the Securus, what about you?"

Amelie's eye gets watery but she holds it back enough for the tears not to run.

"Then you better take me with you."

"Deal. I'll give you the signal then you get clear and get your ass over to me."

"What's the signal?"

"I'm going to go with… NOW."

"That's a good signal."

"Okay. Let's do this," Amelie laughs.

"What's so funny?"

"I was expecting a bigger, cooler line."

"Okay. Let's kick some foxy ass."

"Says the person who fucked a fox. Nice. You love them and you hate them. Sounds like you have issues."

"Okay. You try."

Amelie clears her throat and adjusts her eye patch.

"Let's waste this Asami army."

"There's only one of her. That's ridiculous."

"Let's just go," Amelie opens the door and takes the lead.

Back in the Chugu room, it seems less chaotic. The Starmaker is talking to their feral staff but all their heads turn to pirate Amelie. The room goes silent. The Starmaker slides over to her with their staff cowering behind.

"You know I'm not Kukan."

"Under The Securus Act, I have to investigate the matter if challenged. It's the rules."

"And how will you do that?"

The Starmaker turns to the door and shouts.

"Let him through."

Two large security guards march the sly, devious guy from the dodgy room to the Starmaker. He seems a lot bigger now he is upright and walking. Four other guards appear and surround him.

"You've got to be kidding me," Amelie protests.

"To find a Kukan, you must use a Kukan."

"This is crazy. You know how unsafe this is?"

"You are perfectly safe." The Starmaker motions for more guards to surround him.

"I need to get closer," the Kukan says.

The guards give him some room.

The Kukan walks up to Amelie and starts sniffing her. She rolls her eyes at me so I move. I slowly edge away to where Fiodor is standing. The Kukan sniffs Amelie's face, behind her ears, her torso and then as he gets further down Amelie stops him.

"You can fuck right off."

The Kukan retreats and addresses the Starmaker.

"I need her to transform."

"This is ridiculous and humiliating," Amelie stresses.

"Transform," the Starmaker says wearily.

Amelie transforms and hovers in the air with a look of

penetrating disdain. The Kukan's eyes widen as does his smile as he studies her.

"Where are the Securus'?" I whisper to Fiodor.

"The staff hid them under the table in the corner," Fiodor whispers back.

"Why?"

"Because they brought the Kukan in."

"I need my Securus."

"I know."

"Do you think you can get it for me?"

"I can try."

"That would be great."

"You want it now?"

"Of course, I want it now," I raise my whisper.

"Okay. I'll just slowly creep away."

"Okay."

"Which one was is it again?"

"It's the really bright one. The fucking bright one."

"Oh yeah. Back in a jiffy."

The Kukan's eyes examine Amelie thoroughly and even to watch it feels uncomfortable and intrusive.

"Well?" the Starmaker says impatiently.

The Kukan narrows his eyes and takes a deep breath. Before he says anything, Amelie shouts, "Enough."

She dives down and scoops the Kukan up and throws him against the wall. In an instant the security guards collapse and other Kukans appear from their bodies in attack stance. The door flings open and other Kukans flood in and start attacking the guests.

The Starmaker transforms and leaps into defence. Kitsunes appear and join the fight. It's a mad battle for survival.

Fiodor is still fumbling in a pile of Securus'. He picks one and holds it up.

"I think I got it," he shouts.

"Great. Throw it over."

Fiodor throws it but unfortunately, it's intercepted by the leader of the pack. The whack against the wall obviously wasn't hard enough. He transforms.

"Hello," he smiles at me, "We meet again."

I recognise him and his smile now. It's Nogitsune from the alley.

Amelie swoops down to my rescue but Nogitsune in his Kukan form is stronger and swats her away like a fly.

"This is mine now." He scoops the Securus into his mouth.

Without thinking I pounce on him. He tries to shake me off but my grip is relentless. I wasn't doing much more than being a nuisance but at least it was something. I was however getting dizzy and I was losing my grip. Just when I thought all was lost, Amelie swoops back in and sends Nogitsune flying across the floor. I roll off and so does the Securus.

As the Securus slides across the floor, I slide after it. I'm oblivious to the battle above me, everything slows down, I reach extending my hand, my fingers just touch it, then finally I grab it. Everything speeds up again.

Nogitsune jumps and lands in front of me. Amelie blocks his path and guards me and they wrestle. Nogitsune is too strong and Amelie yelps and screams but she doesn't give up. He pins Amelie to the floor. She turns to me breathless.

"Now. Now would be good."

I activate the Securus, beams of blue light emanate and as it starts to vibrate, I struggle to hold on to it. Nogitsune leaps off Amelie into my direction but is thrown back by another

Kitsune. It's Asami. She swoops around him and gets him in a chokehold. Amelie leaps on to him and both of them restrain him. I look into the Securus, I can feel myself being drawn into it but I'm distracted by three other Kukans who appear to the side of me.

"It's okay, I got this," Fiodor raises his hand.

He unzips his fly and proceeds to urinate in front of them. He turns to me.

"Got to take the Hooy for a walk," he shouts, then laughs manically. The Kukans look disgusted and run away like misbehaved dogs.

I concentrate all my efforts and look right into the Securus. The power grows more intense and draws me in further. I see my face staring back at me. At least that's what it looks like. On closer inspection, I'm on the floor and I look dazed. I shout the loudest I can.

"Now. Now Amelie."

The blue beams of light swirl and take over the room, it starts to burn and melt the whole environment, putting it out of existence. I see Fiodor's face melt away, revealing Annoying Face.

"See, I told you I'm a nice, fun guy," he says before he disintegrates.

I turn to Amelie and hold my hand out for her to grasp. I see her jump off Nogitsune, reaching out for me, and that's when the Securus explodes and I am sucked into the blue void.

I open my eyes and I can smell carpet and whisky. I can also smell sick. I get to my feet and look at my surroundings. I'm in that room again. My head still feels a bit off. I look at the floor and there are two empty bottles of Johnny Walker. I see the sick and around it are ripped-up pieces of paper. I pick them up.

They are pages from a script. I start reading it. It's my script. This is my room. I take a step back and I nearly lose my footing on a couple of DVDs. I pick them up, squint and examine them. *The Life of Brian* and *Amélie*. Two of my favourite comfort films. Always get played when I'm drunk and down.

I walk to my kitchen and pour myself a pint of water. It never tasted so good. The coldness rejuvenates me and already I feel better. I grab a cloth and bin bag and return to the mess in the living room. I throw away the Japanese takeaway boxes and whisky bottles. I move my Science fiction magazines away so I can attack the wretched sick stain. I sit on the couch and take a breath. I'm exhausted. Only now do I realise *I Wanna Be Adored* by *The Stone Roses* is playing. I switch it off and go to the bathroom and take a shower.

As I leave my apartment and dump the rubbish bag out, a fox stares at me from across the street. We look at each other for a moment then it lowers its head, turns and moves on. I'm not sure if it winks at me. I move on too and walk myself to the river.

As I sit on the bench, taking in the view, I take in a deep breath and realise how good it is to be alive.

As I gently nap with the sound of bird song, I hear a loud, heavy laugh. I open my eyes and see my neighbour Mrs. Johnson in the distance. She is Jamaican and you could recognise her laugh a mile away. It's so infectious, you can't help but smile. She has her church clothes on so it must be Sunday. Her coat is large, black and feathery and matches her large personality. She joins me on the bench.

"Peace be with you, Jack."

"And also with you, Mrs. Johnson."

"Still writing?"

"Trying."

"Tryin' is doin," she lets out a big laugh.

"Whatcha writing now?"

"I think, maybe a novel."

"A novel? Any romance in it?"

"A little. Maybe a little sex too," I say with a cheeky smile.

"Oh Lord help me. I'm too old for that business," she lets out another huge laugh. "I must be going to church now. I'll say a prayer for you."

"Take care."

"God loves you, Jack."

"He loves you too."

I look back out to the river and smile. I watch the current get stronger as the tide comes in. It's getting ready to change.

Acknowledgments

This book wouldn't have been possible without the support of my family and friends. Thanks to Mum and Dad. Just because. Thanks to my partner Anja who always has faith in me and gives me the encouragement I need. Thanks to Emily Vousden who is a great sounding board and an awesome editor. Lastly, I'd like to thank COVID. Without you, this never would have happened. So, fuck you, fuck you very much.

References

Amelie - 2001. UGC Fox Distribution. Directed by Jean-Pierre Jeunet.

Monty Python's Life of Brian - 1979. Handmade Films. Directed by Terry Jones.

Stage Fright - 1950. Warner Bros. Directed by Alfred Hitchcock.

Cinema Paradiso - 1988. Cristaldi films. Les Films Ariane.

Rai.3. TF1 Films. Forum Pictures. Directed by Giuseppe Tornatore.

The Long Good Friday - 1980. Paramount Pictures. ITC Entertainment.

Embassy Pictures. Directed by John Mackenzie.

Break on Through (To the Other Side) The Doors. The Doors. 1967.

I wanna be adored. The Stone Roses. The Stone Roses. 1989.

Sounds of Silence. Simon & Garfunkel. Sounds of Silence. 1966.

Carl Orff. O Fortuna. Carmina Burana. 1935-36.

Mistletoe and Wine. Private Collection: 1979-1988. Cliff Richard. 1988.

The Weeknd. Blinding lights. After Hours. 2020.

About the Author

This is Ris Dabrowa's debut novel. He has been writing mostly screenplays for the past ten years. He still hangs on to his dream. He lives in South West London.

You can connect with me on:

🔗 https://www.instagram.com/RisDabrowa

Lightning Source UK Ltd.
Milton Keynes UK
UKHW011242190622
404637UK00002B/80